Killer Country Club

by

Suzanne Rossi

The Snoop Group, Book 4

This is a work of fiction. Names, characters, places, and incidents are either the product of the author's imagination or are used fictitiously, and any resemblance to actual persons living or dead, business establishments, events, or locales, is entirely coincidental.

Killer Country Club

Contact Information: info@thewildrosepress.com

Cover Art by *Kim Mendoza*

The Wild Rose Press, Inc.
PO Box 708
Adams Basin, NY 14410-0708
Visit us at www.thewildrosepress.com

Publishing History
First Mainstream Mystery Rose Edition, 2020
Print ISBN 978-1-5092-2941-3
Digital ISBN 978-1-5092-2942-0

The Snoop Group, Book 4
Published in the United States of America

Marian's eyes narrowed. "Life can be dangerous. People need to pay attention to what they're doing. Why just the other day, I read where a guy was jaywalking and got nailed by a crosstown bus."

Anne looked at Gil who shrugged. She had no idea what to add to this conversation and wasn't about to admit she was with Jen when they found the body.

The waiter set Marian's drink in front of her and left.

"Here's to a good evening," she said in a booming voice and hefted the glass in a toast.

After taking a generous swallow, she set her gaze around the room.

"I see Bertie and Wes are here. Must have let him out of his cage for a while. They normally don't show up after dark. Especially in the bar. Of course, with that Lassiter woman biting the big one, I guess she figures it's safe to let him off the chain again."

The Canfields clearly heard. Wes coughed and looked into his glass, while Bertie glared.

"I take it Mr. Canfield was friends with the woman," Gil said in a smooth tone.

Marian laughed. "According to my sources, she flirted like crazy with him, but he was too chicken to do anything about it except boast about how he still had the power to attract younger women. Bet old Bertie was ready to kill him—or her."

Anne lowered her wine glass. Suppose he wasn't too chicken. Suppose he'd succumbed to Barbara's charms.

Would Bertie be pissed enough to do something about it? Like murder?

Other Titles by Suzanne Rossi

A NOVEL DEATH
A TANGLED WEB
A TASTE OF DEATH
ALL IN THE FAMILY
ALONG CAME QUINN
DEADLY INHERITANCE
DEATH IS THE PITS
JUDGE NOT
KILLER CONFERENCE
KILLER COUNTRY CLUB
NEARLY DEPARTED
POINT OF VIEW
RENDEZVOUS WITH DEATH
THE ASSASSIN
THE GOOD TWIN
THE MURDER OF GRACE BRYANT
THE REUNION
THROUGH MY EYES

Dedication

The idea for *Killer Country Club* came after a hard workout at my gym. I stared at a five-pound weight in my hand and thought, "What if…"

A country club is like a small city, complete with strong personalities, opinions, likes, dislikes, and all that comes with people who congregate at a specific place for social purposes.

I mentioned the San Sebastian Country Club in other books of the series and thought it would make a fun read. Murder amongst the golf course, tennis courts, fitness center, and fine dining intrigued me.

I had planned to wrap up the series with this book, but by the time I got to the end, well…who knows? Book #5 may be in the works.

So, I dedicate *Killer Country Club* to the readers who enjoy this wonderful bunch of enterprising women.

Chapter One

Anne Jamieson set a plate of donuts on the sideboard in her dining room where they joined other assorted pastries. A quick inspection of the coffee urn showed it was doing its job. Maybe she could get another page or two of her latest book written before her critique partners arrived for their meeting.

She was at the foot of the stairs when the doorbell rang. The clock in the foyer read nine-thirty. Way too early for anybody to arrive.

*If this is some kind of salesman, I swear I'll…*She jerked the front door open and stared in shock.

"Candace!"

"Hello, Anne. I hope I'm not intruding."

For a moment, she didn't know what to say, then her mind thawed and she stepped back.

"Of course, you're not intruding. Come in. Uh, when did you get out?"

Candace, a former member of the critique group, had spent the last two years in a minimum-security prison for killing Isadora Powell, another group member.

Anne led her surprising guest into the living room. Candace perched on the edge of a chair and smiled.

"It still looks the same. I'm so glad. Memories like this kept me going while I was away."

Candace looked good. Her hair, which had grown

out to her natural light brown color during her prison stay, had been styled and highlighted with blonde streaks. With little exercise and a high carb prison diet, she had also gained weight, but her figure, while still slim, had lost the emaciated look of her heavy drinking days. The lines were deeper around her eyes and mouth, yet she didn't seem all that different from two years ago.

"When did you get out?" Anne asked again taking a seat on the sofa.

"Three weeks ago. Good behavior. Once I got sober, I realized everything I'd done had been self-destructive, so I tried to make myself a better person. It paid off."

A dart of guilt stabbed Anne. "Candace, I'm sorry it's been so long since I've seen you, but I just got so busy with the chapter and the new direction my writing has taken that somehow…"

"That's all right. Don't apologize. I understand."

"Did any of the rest of the group come to visit?"

"Jen did once or twice, but I understand why the others didn't. Everybody has their own lives to lead. The world moves on."

The tap-tap-tap of tiny toenails on the foyer floor signaled the approach of a dog. Anne's heart plummeted.

Bruno. Of course, she's here to get her dog back. For the past two years, she and her kids had been looking after the little shih-tzu. He was now a family member.

Bruno trotted into the room with curiosity in his eyes and a wagging tail. He delicately sniffed the newcomer, and then came over to Anne who scratched behind his ears. With a satisfied shake of his head, he left the way he'd come. Candace neither looked nor spoke to him.

"Don't worry, Anne. I'm not here to take Bruno away. As much as I'd love to cuddle him, it wouldn't be fair. You've given him a home for almost two years. You have kids who play with him. I can't rip him away from that."

"Candace, are you sure?"

"Yes, I'm sure."

Relieved, Anne remembered her manners. "Would you like a cup of coffee? Perhaps a donut? I've got them all set up in the dining room."

"I'd love both. Oh, this is Thursday—critique day. I forgot. Maybe I should leave and come back later."

"Don't be silly," she said rising. "Nobody's due for another half-hour. Have a little something and stick around. I'm sure they'll be happy to see you again."

Anne wondered if she'd stretched the truth about her last statement. Would they be glad to see their former critique partner?

Candace followed her into the dining room where they filled cups and selected pastries, then took seats at the table.

"So, now that you're out, what are your plans?" Anne asked as she nibbled on cherry Danish.

"Well, I think it's best if I move on. My lawyers and I had a long talk with the parole board plus whatever other authorities were involved, and I've been given permission to move to another city. I have a sister in the Tampa area, so I sold my house and bought a two-bedroom, two bath condo overlooking St. Petersburg Beach. I may even get another dog or a cat.

But I think from a shelter this time. Maybe give a deserving animal a second chance. I can relate to that." She crumbled a piece of donut onto her plate.

"What a great idea. You've been busy. When do you leave?"

"In a week or so. As of now, I'm staying at the San Sebastian Inn until I close on the property on the Gulf Coast." She sipped from her cup, and flashed a grin. "You'll get a kick out of this. I sold the house to Eric and the bimbo."

Anne laughed. "Your ex-husband and his new wife?"

"Missy coveted that house from day one. So I finally decided to let her have it. My attorney contacted Eric two weeks ago and we set it all up. I officially moved out last Monday, and they moved in on Tuesday."

"You've been living there?"

"Since my release. It made sense until I decided what I wanted to do. At any rate, my furniture is in storage until I relocate to St. Pete."

"Well, I hope you gouged them good on price."

"Got top dollar for it. Non-negotiable. Eric wanted to dicker, but Missy must have put the pressure on him. He finally caved and gave me what I asked."

"Talk about irony."

Eric Warren and his mistress had been the catalyst for Candace's unraveling. Divorce at age fifty had left her friend shattered. She had taken solace in vodka, which had also led, in a roundabout way, to her killing Isadora Powell.

"Candace, what ever happened to the book Dorie stole? The last I heard that nasty sister of hers was trying to get it published."

"The whole mess went to court. In the end, the judge decided that it was my book. The hard drives on my and Dorie's computers proved that from the dates. However, it was Dorie's rewrite that the publishing house had contracted. They agreed to terminate the contract since the book was submitted under fraudulent circumstances, and I agreed not to publish it as written by Dorie, which is part of why I'm here today."

"How so?"

"I want to ask you a favor," Candace said finishing her donut and coffee.

"Ask away."

"The edits and revisions Dorie did will never see the light of day, but my original manuscript is still on my computer. I was wondering if you would do the rewrite."

Surprise washed over Anne. "Me?"

"Well, you seem to have a natural propensity for finding bodies and sniffing out killers, including me."

Anne choked on her Danish and stared at her guest.

"No, no, don't take that the wrong way. What I did was terrible, but you solved the murders of those two agents at the conference last year, and you found the real killer of Fran Harrison last fall. With your switch in genres to romantic suspense, I thought you'd be the best person to tell my story. We both know I don't have the talent to do it. My story was rough and if Dorie had played by the rules and helped me, none of what happened would have happened, if you get my drift. Not that that's any excuse. I did kill her," she hastened to say.

Anne got the drift and was intrigued by Candace's

proposal. She'd often thought about rewriting the story herself, but had no access to the original book. *Unlike Dorie. Candace is right. If the greedy bitch* had *played by the rules she'd be alive today.*

"I'll agree on one condition, that your name is on the cover with mine. We'll share any advance and royalties fifty-fifty."

Candace's eyes filled with tears. "Anne, you don't have to do that."

"But I want to. Are you going to continue writing?"

"No. We all know I'm no good at it."

"If I can do a decent job of rewriting, then you *will* finally get published. Those are my terms. You're sure you still have the original manuscript?"

Candace dabbed at her eyes with a napkin. "Oh, yes, and thank you, Anne. From the bottom of my heart, thank you. In spite of all I did, you remained a good friend. I'll never forget that."

Anne patted the woman on the arm and blinked tears from her eyes, too. She always liked Candace and had long ago forgiven the woman for trying to brain her with a champagne bottle. It was the booze, not Candace.

"How about another cup of coffee?"

Candace rose. "No, no, I should be going before everyone gets here. It might be awkward and I don't—"

The doorbell interrupted the sentence. Anne glanced at her watch—nine fifty-five.

"Too late. At least one of them is here already. Stay and say hello."

Without giving Candace a chance to reply, she stood and headed for the front door. Rose Bennett and

Jennifer Swanson stood on the porch.

"Come on in, ladies."

"Hi, Anne," Rose said. "Boy, I had to work like a fiend to get this chapter straight last night. I'm looking forward to some good feedback today."

"Is Ellie already here?" Jen asked naming their newest critique partner. "Doesn't look like her car."

"No, it's not Ellie. Why don't you go into the dining room and see? I think you're in for a surprise."

The newcomers looked at each other, shrugged, walked through the archway, and then stopped in their tracks.

Rose stared before emitting a gasp. Jen squealed and ran forward.

"Candace! Oh my God! When did you get out?" She gave her friend a huge hug.

Rose followed. "Candace, it's so good to see you!"

Candace hugged them back, tears streaming down her cheeks.

"Oh, I'm so glad to see you, too. I wasn't sure how you'd react to seeing a jailbird. I was ready to run out the back door."

"Don't be silly," Jen gushed with a grin. "And I'd never think of you in that term."

"Me, neither," Rose added. "So, how long have you been a free woman?"

"About three weeks."

"I'm so sorry I never got around to visiting," Rose said. "But with the kids, the house, and writing, there never seemed like enough time."

"I know," Jen replied with a slightly shamed expression. "I came a couple of times, and then just didn't again."

She echoed her words spoken to Anne when she first arrived. “That’s all right. I understand. And there’s no need to apologize.”

Her look of earnest sincerity put the other two women at ease. They relaxed and smiled.

“So, are you going to be rejoining us?” Jen asked.

Anne looked on from the doorway, a warm sensation coursing through her veins. It was almost like old times. She entered and poured everyone a cup of coffee and arranged selected pastries on a plate while Candace brought the others up to date, then served her friends before taking a seat.

“You sold the house to Eric and Miss Fake-Titties?” Jen crowed. “I love it. I saw them at the country club last Saturday and wondered why she had such a smug look on her Botoxed face.”

“Jen, you’re terrific,” Rose claimed with a laugh. “You managed to insult what’s-her-name twice in one sentence. And St. Pete sounds like a good idea. While we’ll miss you, a fresh start is probably for the best.”

Candace nodded. “That’s what I thought, too.”

“And here’s something else.” Anne told them about Candace’s proposal for a book.

“What a fabulous idea!” Jen exclaimed. “It’s your story, but Anne will be like the editor or something. I can’t wait to see Eric’s face when it’s published.”

“He’ll probably never know. The only things he reads are investment journals and Missy is barely literate.” She paused and gazed around the room. “Where’s Nancy?”

The last member of the original critique group, Nancy Carlyle, was a no-show today.

“Nancy is on some island in, I don’t know, Samoa

or Fiji—somewhere in the South Pacific," Anne told her.

Candace's jaw dropped and she stared. "The South Pacific! What the hell is she doing there?"

Anne laughed. "Last fall she met Gil's younger brother, Brad. They hit it off, and I mean really hit it off. Anyway, Brad is a volcanologist, so when some volcano started acting up, he asked her to go with him to investigate it—or whatever it is volcanologists do."

"What floored all of us was that she agreed," Rose said.

"Within a week she was on her way to the island of New Britain. That was five or six months ago," Jen added between bites of a donut.

"Have you heard from her since?" Candace asked.

"Oh, she keeps in touch once a week with emails," Anne assured her. "They've left New Britain and are now on some other island where there have been volcano rumblings. Officially, she is listed as Brad's assistant. Gil was as astonished as the rest of us. He couldn't believe his no-commitment brother has found love."

Candace's eyebrows rose. "Is it love?"

"It must be or Nancy wouldn't have gone schlepping off through the jungles of wherever," Jen said.

"And Brad wouldn't have asked her along for the ride," Rose concurred.

Candace sat back and chuckled. "I can't believe it. Nancy! The most down to earth person in the world, off on an adventure. Has she given up writing?"

"Oh, no," Anne said. "She's still at it."

"She sends things to us for critique electronically,"

Rose replied. "This latest is all about a woman who follows her missionary brother to the South Seas and finds true love with the captain of a merchant ship. He's a drunk and a bit of a beast, but she tames and reforms him."

"And speaking of true love," Candace turned to Anne. "Have you and Gil set a date yet?"

After solving Fran Harrison's murder five months ago, Anne's boyfriend, Gil Collins, a detective with the San Sebastian Police Department, had finally popped the question.

"Not yet. We're waiting for his house to sell. We didn't want to uproot my kids from the only home they've ever known, so he'll move in here. We wanted to get married right away, but maintaining two mortgages would put us in a financial bind. As soon as I say, 'I do,' my ex is off the house payment and alimony hooks."

The doorbell rang again. Anne hurried to answer and found their newest critique partner, Ellie Campion, on the front porch.

"Hi, Anne. I'm so sorry I'm late, but first I got caught by a slow-moving train, and then a drawbridge. It never rains, it pours. Oops, that's a cliché, isn't it? I have to get out of the habit of using them. Thank God you guys catch them in my writing."

Anne led Ellie toward the dining room. "Don't worry. We haven't started yet. In fact, we may not even get around to critiquing today. Ellie, I'd like you to meet Candace Warren, one of our former critique partners. Candace, this is Ellie Campion."

Anne held her breath. How would Ellie react? Would she even recognize Candace's name?

Ellie stepped forward, her hand out-stretched. "How do you do? Candace Warren, it seems I've heard that name before. Are you a member of the chapter?"

"Uh, I used to be," Candace said with an uncomfortable expression. "I don't write any more."

Anne glanced at Jen and Rose. They eyed Ellie, but said nothing.

"I just moved here last year, so I'm glad to have found such good authors willing to help me," Ellie said.

Anne relaxed as did Jen and Rose. Apparently, the name meant little or nothing to their new critique partner. "Have a seat, Ellie, and I'll get you a cup of coffee and a pastry. Any preferences?"

"What? Oh, no. Whatever is close at hand." Ellie frowned in puzzlement at Candace, as if still trying to place the name.

Anne served her quickly and resumed her seat.

"You know, you guys have work to do, so I think I'll be on my way." Candace finished her coffee and rose. "Anne, is your cell number the same?"

"Yes, and you're still listed in my contacts, too. Don't move to St. Pete without telling us."

"We'll all go out to dinner and have a bang up of a sendoff," Jen exclaimed. "Lots of margaritas!"

Candace smiled. "Sounds like a great idea, but I'll skip the margaritas. Almost two years on the wagon has broken me of the habit."

Anne also rose to escort her to the front door.

"See you soon, Candace," Rose said.

"Nice to have met you." Ellie's forehead was still furrowed with thought.

Before she could leave the room, Candace's phone rang.

"Hello… Oh, hi Eric… What are you talking about? What smell… Well, nothing smelled when I left… Eric, it's not my problem and I'm not about to pay for your hotel expenses… Noon? Impossible, I have a meeting with my parole officer at one and with my attorney at two plus I need to run a few errands. Four is the soonest I can make it… Do I have to meet with her? Why don't you come… Oh, for crissakes, all right. I'll be there at four." She hung up and made a face.

"Something wrong?" Anne asked.

"Oh, it seems there's some kind of smell permeating the house. It's so bad that they had to leave this morning. And get this, they think it's all my fault and want *me* to foot their hotel bill."

"You're joking!" Rose stated.

"What gall," Jen sniffed.

Ellie stared with a growing look of horror as if the nickel had just dropped regarding Candace's identity.

"And Missy is demanding I meet her at the house to smell it myself. Like I give a rat's ass. The bitch probably wants me to pay for any de-stinking that has to be done."

"Don't go by yourself," Anne said with a worried look. "Why don't I come with you? That way there's a third party around if things get nasty."

"Good idea. I'll pick you up a little before four. Is that all right?" She moved to the front door.

"It's fine."

Anne waved as Candace left, and then hurried back to the dining room.

Ellie looked at the group with wide eyes. "Oh my God, Candace Warren! She's the one who killed…"

"Isadora Powell," Rose finished for her.

"She just got out of prison and dropped by to say hello," Anne explained.

"And she was drunk at the time, so didn't really understand that she'd killed Dorie, but Dorie had it coming. She stole Candace's book and tried to pass it off as her own, the thieving bitch—Dorie, not Candace. At any rate, she did her time and is about to move to St. Pete for a fresh start," Jen said in her typical rambling fashion.

"But she seemed so normal," Ellie said.

Not wanting to explain the past to Ellie, Anne took charge. "She is normal—now. Why don't we get busy and critique? I know I need some feedback on my latest chapter."

****

"And they'd better not be staying at the San Sebastian Inn, either," Candace ranted as she weaved in and out of slower moving traffic.

Anne held her breath when her chauffeur made another move. She should have volunteered to drive. Obviously, her friend needed some time behind the wheel before regaining her driving skills.

"I mean, can you imagine seeing them every day for the next two weeks?"

"No, I can't and please, slow down. We aren't in a race to get there."

Candace complied. "Oops, sorry. I guess I'm a little out of practice. Tell me about the critique group. Is Ellie a good fit? And whatever happened to that awful woman who took my place?"

"Ellie's a good fit. She's new, but willing to learn and takes our suggestions in stride. She reminds me a bit of you."

"Only with more talent, I hope."

"She's got good instincts. As for Susan Lynch, well, the last I heard she was petitioning the Writers Association of America to get another chapter started in San Sebastian, claiming that our chapter was poorly run with no leadership. To the best of my knowledge, she hasn't had any success. I heard through the grapevine that several chapter members wrote the WAA telling them she was a troublemaker and that I, and the board, showed good leadership."

"What a bitch. Is her writing any good?"

"Not really, although her plots were interesting, but she can't take criticism and isn't a fan of following the writing rules. She thinks clichés and adverbs are exciting."

"Even I outgrew those. I'll bet she also thinks her writing is the best ever. You know, I had an idea earlier. You can rewrite the story Dorie stole, but if you want to write about her stealing it and the aftermath, I think that's a terrific idea. You'll get two books out of the whole mess."

"You wouldn't mind? I have to admit, I tossed that idea around a few months ago."

"Have at it." Candace braked for a stoplight and glanced at the dashboard clock. "I guess we're going to be late. It's already four."

"And of course, you got caught up in traffic."

Her former critique partner grinned. "Traffic, hell. Let her wait for me."

Ten minutes later they pulled into the driveway next to a black Lexus. Candace shut off the engine and sighed.

"I can see Eric is sparing no expense on wife number two." The words held a slightly bitter tone.

"Are you sorry for selling them the house? Would you rather live here than in St. Pete?"

"Yes, but it's the right thing to do. My neighbors are uncomfortable with me around. In the weeks I lived here, not a one of them came to say hello, and I'm sure they were locking their doors and loading their guns at night. I can't blame them."

Tears pricked behind her eyes. She felt bad for the woman. "I'm sorry."

Candace shrugged. "It's my own fault. St. Pete will be fine. I'll see my sister—she's divorced, too, and her kids are also grown. And my kids will come visit. Thank goodness, my grandchildren are too young to understand that Granny was in the slammer. Plus, I'll make new friends who live in my condo complex. No one will know about my past. You'll see; it'll all work out." She heaved another sigh. "Well, shall we go in and beard the lioness in my den?"

Anne laughed and exited the car. Candace had a plan. She just hoped it worked out.

They walked onto the front porch where Candace rang the doorbell. When no one answered, she repeated the action.

"Come on, you hussy," Candace muttered. "Or are you taking pleasure in making me ring my own doorbell?"

Finally, she tried the doorknob. The door swung open and they entered the foyer.

A shiver raced down Anne's spine. This was so similar to when she, Nancy, and Candace had entered Dorie's house two years ago.

"Missy? It's Candace. Where are you and what's all this bullshit about a smell?"

No one replied.

Anne sniffed. "You know there is kind of an odd odor."

Candace didn't answer, but walked into the den. "Missy?"

"Good God, it's much stronger back here," Anne said holding a hand over her nose.

"It's probably a dead rat. You know what a problem roof rats are in South Florida. Where is she?" She retraced her footsteps to the foyer and paused at the foot of the stairs. "Missy?"

"Try calling her phone," Anne suggested. "She may be out back."

"I don't have the number." Candace climbed with Anne behind her. "If she's luxuriating in my Jacuzzi just to rub it in, I swear I'll kill her."

Anne winced at the choice of words.

They entered the master bedroom. Here, the smell was overwhelming.

"Oh my God," Anne gasped.

"It is pretty foul," Candace agreed. "Matches Missy's personality to a 'T.'"

"Well, she's certainly not up here. Let's check out back."

They descended the stairs and opened the French doors in the den leading to the patio and pool. The back yard was large and the pool located just off the patio. Anne remembered spending more than one pleasant evening being entertained by Candace and her husband on the huge terrace.

"Missy?" Candace called. Her tone had changed

from aggravated to puzzled. "Do you suppose she got pissed because I was late and went for a walk?"

"Leaving us here to cool our heels? Possible, even though from what you've told me about her, I'd have to say walking isn't her thing. Maybe she's teaching you a lesson in punctuality," Anne replied taking a deep breath of much needed fresh air.

"Well, screw her. Okay, there's an odor in the house, but it has nothing to do with me. Not my problem. Let's get out of here."

For reasons she couldn't identify, Anne walked across the patio toward the pool. It was deathly quiet. Not even birds chirped or insects hummed. She was five feet from the side of the pool when she stopped and cried out.

"Oh my God!"

"What's wrong?" Candace hurried to join her. "Oh, shit!"

A woman's naked body floated a couple of feet below the surface in the middle of the pool. Blood had turned the water around her a deep red.

Chapter Two

Oh, damn not again!

That was Anne's only thought as she grabbed Candace's arm and pulled her back to the covered section of the patio. Her friend sat with a thump in a chair at the table. A striped beach towel was draped over one of the chairs. A crumpled T-shirt lay on the table.

"It's Missy, isn't it? I don't believe this," Candace muttered.

Anne took a deep breath, fished her cell from her purse, and speed dialed Gil.

"Hello, beautiful." His cheerful voice sounded in her ear. "I was just getting ready to call you."

"Gil?" she asked in a wobbly tone.

"What's wrong, honey?"

"I've…I've done it again."

"Done what again… No, don't tell me you've found a body?"

"I'm afraid so."

"Where are you?"

"Seven…seventeen-twelve Bedlington Avenue." She swallowed and blinked tears from her eyes.

"If you're in the house now, get out. Meet me in front and don't touch anything. I'll be there in ten minutes."

He hung up before she could say anything else.

"Gil's on his way."

Candace looked at her with a frightened expression. "He's gonna think I did it, isn't he?"

"I have no idea, but it wouldn't surprise me. Come on, let's get out of here. Gil said he'd meet me out front." She had no clue what he'd think about seeing Candace again.

In a scene horribly reminiscent of their actions when they'd found Isadora Powell's body, Candace sat on the porch steps. Anne followed her and put her arm around the woman's shaking shoulders.

Within minutes, Gil pulled up along with four patrol cars, the paramedics, and a forensics unit. Policemen erupted from all of them and ran into the house. Anne met him halfway down the walkway.

"Are you all right?" Gil asked, giving her a quick hug and kiss.

"Yes."

His gaze slid past her to the woman still seated on the steps.

"Mrs. Warren!" His eyes narrowed and he gave Anne a questioning look. "I thought this address sounded familiar."

Candace rose to join them and answered in a trembling voice. "I swear to God, I didn't do it."

"When did you get out?"

"Three…three weeks ago."

"Where's the body and who is it? Do you know?"

Candace stood silent, quivering. Anne gestured toward the house. "In the pool, and it's Candace's ex-husband's new wife, Missy."

Gil took a deep breath and motioned to one of the officers still outside. "Mrs. Warren, this is Officer

Dunlap. Officer, take Mrs. Warren to your car and get a preliminary statement. Anne, stay here. I'll talk to you in a minute."

Candace followed the officer and sat in the back seat while the policeman wrote in a notebook as Gil and the other men entered the house. Anne wanted to comfort her friend, but knew enough about police procedures now to understand that she and Candace needed to be questioned separately. Their versions of the events had to match.

The minutes ticked by. Finally, the officer finished with Candace just as Gil returned from what was now a crime scene. It was hard to imagine the house she'd visited so often in the past in those terms. He handed Gil his notes. Candace remained in the car with the door closed. Not a good sign.

"Gil, Candace didn't do it. She was with me from four o'clock until now."

"Seems to me she was with you when you found Ms. Powell's body, too," he said in a crisp, no-nonsense tone.

"All she wants is to start a new life. She's planning to move to St. Pete."

"Tell me what happened."

Anne related the details of the day, from Candace's surprise visit at her house to them finding the body.

"How did she die? Seemed like there was a lot of blood in the water," she said in a low tone.

"Looks like she was shot."

"Shot! Surely someone must have heard *that*."

"We'll interview the neighbors."

"Are you arresting Candace?"

Gil glanced at the woman sitting in the patrol car

and sighed. “Not at the moment.”

Anne rushed to the car and opened the door. “Come on out. He’s not going to make an arrest.”

Candace slid from the back seat and walked toward Gil who flipped open the officer’s notebook to read what Candace had told him.

“So, you were supposed to meet the victim here?”

Candace explained again about having sold the house and the strange smell.

“It does smell of something, that’s for sure,” he said when she finished. Gil paused before asking, “Do you own a gun, Mrs. Warren?”

“That would be a violation of my parole, Detective Collins.”

“Yes, it would, but that doesn’t answer my question.”

She inhaled a deep breath. “I owned one a couple of years ago, but have no clue where it is now. Certainly not in my possession. I just assumed the police confiscated it after my arrest. Or maybe one of my kids took it.”

Gil stared hard at her. “I’ll check.”

“I guess someone should call Eric, my ex,” she said.

“I’ll do it,” Gil told her. Candace gave him the number. He dialed. “Mr. Warren, this is Detective Gil Collins of the San Sebastian Police Department. I’m currently at your house at seventeen-twelve Bedlington. I need you to come home. There’s been an accident…” He listened for a moment before cutting a swift glance at Candace. He hung up. “Mr. Warren is a couple of blocks away. Seems he was on his way here.”

A minute later, tires squealed around the corner

and screeched to a halt at the foot of the driveway. Eric ran from the car and halted in front of them.

"What's the problem? What kind of accident? Where's Missy?"

"Mr. Warren, I'm sorry, but Ms. Jamieson and your ex-wife found a body floating in the pool."

Eric's face drained of color. "Missy?"

Anne nodded. "I'm so sorry, Eric."

He immediately whirled to confront his former wife. "Candace, what the hell did you do?"

"Eric, I swear I didn't do it."

His ashen face twisted in rage. "Of course, you did, you bitch! You hated Missy and killed her at the first opportunity."

He stepped forward and raised his hand as if to strike Candace. She stumbled back and fell to the ground. Gil quickly stepped in front of Eric as Anne ran to comfort the stunned woman, helping her to her feet.

"Mr. Warren, that's enough. Don't do it or I'll be forced to arrest you for domestic violence. Mrs. Warren and Ms. Jamieson arrived for a meeting with your current wife and found her in the pool."

"She did it! I know she did!" He broke down in sobs.

Gil led him to the front porch as Anne, a protective arm around Candace's shoulders, followed. They all stood at opposite ends of the wide veranda. Her friend shivered as her ex glared at them.

"Are you all right?" Gil asked.

Candace nodded. "He's upset and in shock. I'll be fine."

Several minutes passed as additional law enforcement arrived. A car with the word "coroner" also pulled up. A man with a medical bag rushed inside.

More time passed. A forensics team soon completed the scene. Neighbors gathered on the sidewalks and in front yards staring and whispering. Finally, a gurney bearing a body bag was pushed through the wide front door.

"Mr. Warren, I'm sorry to have to ask this, but we need you to identify the body," Gil said in a sympathetic tone.

Anne backed away to the furthest corner. She didn't want to see this. Candace, however, wasn't so reluctant. She moved forward to stand across from Eric and stare at the encased body. Anne closed her eyes when Gil unzipped the bag.

"What the hell is going on? That isn't my wife," Eric exclaimed.

Anne's eyes snapped open.

"What the fuck is going on here?" another voice demanded from the foot of the porch steps.

They all whirled. Candace gasped as Eric cried out, "Missy!"

He rushed down the steps to embrace a shapely blonde.

This was the first time Anne had ever seen Eric Warren's new wife and the cause of so much grief for Candace. Everything about her was impossible from her young age, to her long, perfectly curled blonde hair, her skin-tight clothes, her impeccable make-up, and above all, her enormous chest.

Gil hurried down the steps. "Are you Mrs. Warren?"

"Of course, I'm Melissa Warren. Who the hell are you and what's going on?" She fisted her hands on her hips and stared, then blinked at the sight of the gurney on her porch.

"How did you get through the crime scene tape?"

"Ducked under it, of course. Now, what the hell is going on."

"Candace and Anne found a body in the pool. We all thought it was you," Eric said, giving Missy a hug.

She broke away from the embrace and ran up the steps to gaze at the face of the dead woman.

"Oh, my God! It's Barbara!" Then she saw Candace. "You! You killed her, didn't you? Once a killer, always a killer!"

"No, no," Anne hastily said. "We found her."

"Fuck off! Who are you anyway?"

"My name is Anne Jamieson and I came with Candace. You were supposed to meet at four to discuss some kind of smell in the house."

"Not some kind of smell—a stench, and that's your fault, too."

"I have no idea what the smell is and don't really care. You bought the house without an inspection, so it's your problem, not mine. And where the hell were *you*?" Candace demanded.

Anne noted that her friend's stunned disbelief had faded. She was in full attack mode and not about to take any crap from Missy. The words surprised her. Candace had never been assertive—well, not usually.

"None of your business."

"But it is my business," Gil stated in a firm voice. "And first of all, I want to know the identity of the woman in the pool."

"She's Barbara—Barbara Lassiter, a good friend of mine, and the ex-Mrs. Warren probably killed her by mistake."

"I wondered about the strange car in the drive," Eric said more to himself than anyone else.

"What was Ms. Lassiter doing in your pool if you weren't here?"

"I asked her to meet me here at four so I wouldn't be alone with *her*," Missy said giving Candace a glare. "She hates me and I didn't feel safe."

Candace sniffed. "Safe from what? With those inflatables on your chest you could float to England or rent yourself out as a raft to Cuban refugees."

"Jealous bitch. No wonder Eric strayed. You're old and what little boobs you have probably hang to your knees. Not my fault if he prefers a younger, prettier woman."

"Ladies!" Gil had to shout to make himself heard. "Knock it off. I haven't got time for this. Now, Mrs. Warren—the current one—if you had a meeting at four, why weren't you here?"

"I forgot I had a hair appointment at two followed by a massage, so I told Barbara I'd meet her here, but that I might be a little late," Missy explained with a pout.

"A little late? It's after five-thirty," Candace snapped. "Did you expect us to still be waiting?"

Missy shrugged. "Of course, I did."

Anne sighed. It was so South Florida. No one had a sense of time and never thought to call with a time change or an apology for being over an hour late.

Gil waved his hand. "Can we get back to this? And how did Ms. Lassiter get in? Did she have a key?"

"No. I told her there was an extra key under the flowerpot, that one over there," she said pointing to a large potted dracaena beside the front door. Its twin stood on the other side. "I warned her about the stench. She said she'd sunbathe by the pool until I got here. I advised her not to answer the door."

"Is there a Mr. Lassiter?" Gil asked.

"Yeah, but they're divorced. He split town several months ago. I think he's living somewhere in California."

"Any next of kin we can notify?"

Missy shrugged. "I have no idea. Barbara didn't talk much about her past."

"I thought you said she was a good friend. Seems to me she would have talked about her family."

The newest Mrs. Warren rolled her eyes. "Well, she didn't. For all I know her childhood sucked and she didn't want to talk about it."

"We'll check for any relatives when we search her house. I assume you have the address."

Missy glared at them all before telling him.

An officer appeared with a cell phone in a plastic baggie. "Scooped this out of the bottom of the pool, Detective."

"Thanks. I hope we can recover something useful from it."

"If she was talking to someone, you'd think they'd have called the police immediately," Anne said. "I mean I would if I heard what sounded like a gunshot and the conversation suddenly ended. Plus, wouldn't the victim have made some kind of noise before hitting the water?"

"If she was talking to someone," Gil replied. "She may have just ended the conversation. We'll check. Exactly, when did you call her, Mrs. Warren?"

"Around two or so when I remembered my hair appointment. I didn't talk to her again." Missy swept an errant lock of hair over her shoulder and shot another angry glare at Candace. "I still say she's good for it. She hates me and has always wanted me dead."

The man with the medical bag appeared in the doorway.

"Hi, doc. Any preliminaries?" Gil asked.

"She was shot in the back, but not up close and personal. No stippling from powder burns on her skin. My guess is at least ten feet separated the victim from her killer. Blood spatter shows she was standing about two feet from the edge of the pool."

"So she's standing there, perhaps on her cell phone, when the killer shoots her from the patio area. She falls into the water, and the shooter walks out of the house." He turned to Candace. "Any other way into the back yard?"

She nodded. "There's a gate around the garage side of the house."

"Go check and see if it's been opened recently," he ordered another officer.

"If someone came in by way of the gate, they'd be taking a chance that anyone in the back yard or by the pool would have seen them."

"Unless their back was turned and they were on the phone," Anne added. "Could have masked any noise the killer made."

"True. There's not a whole lot of cover. When I was in prison, the yard maintenance was hit or miss. Several bushes died. I had them taken out a couple of weeks ago," Candace informed him.

"You probably know a dozen ways into the back

yard," Missy said with a pout.

"Eric, she's your wife now. Shut her up before I smack her," Candace said with a glare.

Anne put an arm around the woman's shoulders. "Ignore her. She's not worth the effort."

"You're one of those writer friends of hers, aren't you? Well, shut the fuck up! Why she has any friends is beyond me. Eric, I'm scared. Barbara is dead and as far as I'm concerned the killer is your ex-wife."

Anne noticed Eric had been quiet during most of the past few minutes. He watched Candace closely with a worried look on his face. He slipped his arm around his wife's waist.

"Have you found the gun?" he asked.

Gil shook his head. "Not yet. If the killer was smart, they took it with them and chucked it into the nearest canal."

"I assume you'll be searching *her* place," Missy demanded thrusting her chin toward Candace.

"We'll do our job, Mrs. Warren."

"And while you're at it, search her buddy's house, too. Maybe they're in it together. One stood lookout while the other killed Barbara."

"God, Candace is right, you are a moron," Anne replied.

"Moron! Why you used up old hag! I oughta…"

"Missy," Eric interrupted. "I don't believe either Candace or Anne killed Barbara Lassiter thinking it was you."

Missy jerked away from her husband's comforting arm and turned toward him with an outraged expression her hands fisted on her hips. "What! You're taking her side?"

"I'm not taking sides, honey. Barbara played around with a lot of men and made a lot of enemies. For all we know she was meeting some guy here. You yourself said she had the time. Detective, can we leave? I need a drink."

"I think we all need to let forensics finish doing its job," Gil said in a calm tone. "If you don't mind, I'd like to get a preliminary statement from both you and your wife, Mr. Warren. You can't stay here. Do you know where you'll be?"

"The San Sebastian Inn for now. We checked in this morning due to the smell in the house," Eric told him.

Candace emitted a strangled groan while Anne sucked in a deep breath. *Swell, Missy and Candace staying in the same hotel. Not good.*

"Why do you need to talk to us? We weren't here," Missy demanded.

"Because that's *my* job," Gil replied. "It won't take long. Mr. Warren, please go with Officer Burns. Mrs. Warren, if you'll come with me."

The Warrens were led to different locations as Anne and Candace stood behind Candace's car in the driveway. Anne watched as Gil worked. Twenty minutes later, Eric and Missy walked to their cars, but not before Eric detoured to talk to Candace.

"I'm…I'm sorry for almost hitting you. I've never even thought about doing something like that before. My only excuse is I was so upset, I wasn't thinking straight."

"Whatever, Eric. Go take your wife home." Candace's expression was curiously blank.

Eric nodded and walked toward his car. The new

Mrs. Warren had already left.

"I'll want to talk to both of you further about Ms. Lassiter," Gil called out. "Don't leave town. Candace, Anne, I want you down at the station immediately to give a formal statement."

"Right," Anne said relieved this ordeal was almost over.

Well, here I am smack in the middle of a murder again. Maybe I should change careers and become a detective—or join a nunnery.

Chapter Three

Anne slipped her arm around her friend's waist. Candace shook and her breaths came in rasping gulps. Her earlier bravado with Missy had evaporated.

"Come on, I'll drive. Okay?"

A nod was the only answer. She led her to the car, and then slid behind the wheel.

As she drove away from the curb, she noticed neighbors still gawked at the activity around Candace's house. Some had their hands to their mouths in horror, while others, after glimpsing her passenger, grabbed their children close or stepped back as far as they could. The rumor mill was likely already in high gear.

Candace groaned. "My poor neighbors. I'm sure Missy will let them know long and loud how I probably did it again."

"Oh, who cares about Missy? How are you feeling? I can't believe your jerk of an ex-husband was going to hit you. What an asshole!"

Candace sighed. "I'm all right. Eric lost control."

In spite of what Eric had said, Anne wondered if it was the first time. "Did he ever lose control while you were married?"

"No, he'd get mad and holler, but he never hit me. Oh, God, I just know I'm going to be arrested."

"If Gil thought you'd done it you wouldn't be in this car, but in a patrol car," Anne replied.

"Not necessarily. He just might not have probable cause for an arrest yet. He'd also have to wait for forensic evidence to come in. And the murder weapon is nowhere in sight as far as we know. With my luck, the damned gun will probably be mine."

Anne stopped at a red light and turned to Candace. "You sound like a cop."

"Yeah, well, two years in the slammer can give you a whole different perspective on the world. You learn things."

"Did you have anybody to talk to?"

"Sure. There were a couple of women who kind of looked out for me at first. I was scared and lonely, so they saw to it I wasn't harassed."

"Harassed? You mean like…like…"

"Sexually? No, nothing like that. This was a minimum-security place. Sometimes inmates were transferred there from other more secure facilities and to show how tough they were, tried to push us around."

A horn honked from behind. Anne glanced at the now green light and stepped on the gas.

"I have to admit, I was surprised at how you answered Missy back today. I don't recall you ever being confrontational."

"I was plenty confrontational whenever vodka was involved, but one of the first things I learned from those women was how to be assertive while sober. In a way, prison is kind of like high school. Cliques were formed and your status depended on your crime. I was in for manslaughter, but on a reduced sentence from murder two. That gave me status, so I wasn't hassled too much. Both of the women who helped me were in for the same thing. One killed her abusive husband with a baseball bat while he slept. She pleaded battered wife syndrome and plea bargained down to man two. The other was a prostitute who shot and killed her pimp when he threatened to beat her up. A witness said she just pulled out the gun and shot. If she'd waited until he hit her, she'd have gotten off with self-defense."

"Good Lord, I guess I never stopped to think of what it was really like inside a prison, even a minimum-security one."

"Don't envision private rooms, tennis courts, and workout equipment. We all had jobs to do and regular therapy sessions, especially those of us with addictions. Guards were present during any free time we had, even in the library and TV rooms. At night, the cell doors are closed and locked." Candace leaned her head back and sighed again. "Thank God you were with me today. Can you imagine if I'd gone there alone?"

"I'm just glad I came along. Which reminds me, I've got to call the kids and let them know I'll be late."

At the next red light, she called her daughter, Lisa.

"Lisa, I'm going to be late tonight, so if you and Ken want to eat leftovers, go ahead. I think there's some pot roast in the fridge."

"No problem, Mom. What are you doing?"

Anne hesitated. She didn't want to tell her daughter she'd found another body.

"Oh, nothing important. Something just came up, that's all."

"Mom, did you find another body?" Lisa asked in a teasing tone.

Surprised, she could only stammer, "Uh…Um…"

"Oh, God, you did, didn't you? Did you know this one, too?"

Anne sighed. Lisa knew her so well. “Yes and no. Yes, I found another body, and no, I didn’t know her. I’m on my way down to the police station with Candace to give our statements.”

“Candace? As in Mrs. Warren? Is she out of jail? When did this happen?”

Too late, she realized what she’d said. *Damn and blast.*

The light turned green and she moved on. “Yes, and I’ll tell you all about it when I get home—whenever that will be.”

“Are you all right? I mean, how fresh was the body?”

“Lisa!”

“I’m sorry, but sometimes you worry me. *Are* you okay?”

Anne marveled at how both her fiancé and her daughter often used the same terminology.

“Yes, I’m fine and I was never in danger. The killer was long gone from the house before we showed up.”

“House? Mrs. Warren’s house?”

“Yes, and we’re almost at the police station. We have to give statements, so have a good dinner and I’ll be home as soon as possible.”

“I hope Lisa isn’t too upset,” Candace said when Anne hung up.

“Lisa can handle herself pretty well.” She explained to Candace how Lisa had saved the day when George Harrison had held her at gunpoint.

“It doesn’t sound like your daughter will need any kind of assertiveness training,” Candace drawled.

Anne laughed as she turned left into the San

Sebastian Police Headquarters. No, Lisa would definitely not need assertiveness training.

****

Candace joined Anne in the waiting area of the police station. “Thank God, that’s over.”

“You were in there a long time. I was beginning to worry,” Anne told her.

“They wanted to know my every movement since I was released three weeks ago. I have the feeling if they discover I turned left instead of right, they’ll slap me back behind bars.”

“If you were going to kill Missy, you’d have done it two years ago while under the influence.”

“Anne, I can’t thank you enough for being here for me. The food at the San Sebastian Inn isn’t too bad. Let me buy you dinner. It’s after eight and I’m sure your kids have polished off that pot roast by now.”

“You have a deal. I’m famished. Can you drive?”

“Yes, the shock of it all is wearing off. I just kind of lost it there for a moment. “

“Okay. In that case, drop me off at my place so I can get my car.”

“Have you heard from Gil?” Candace asked as they walked through the parking lot.

“No, but that’s not unusual in a murder case like this. He’s out interviewing neighbors and friends of the victim. I called and left a message in his voice mail when I was done with my statement. He’ll call back eventually.”

At her house, she poked her head in to let the kids know what had taken place, where she’d be, all the while managing to stave off their eager questions, and then headed for the San Sebastian Inn.

The drive to the hotel took less than fifteen minutes. Traffic was manageable. It was May. The tourists and snowbirds had already migrated back north. Candace awaited her in the lobby.

As soon as Anne walked through the entrance, memories crowded her mind. She saw the hustle and bustle of a busy conference—writers, editors, and agents talking and laughing. She visualized finding Carmella Radcliff dead in the ladies' room, and later Alan Grayson's body in his hotel room. But most of all, she remembered Jackie Simmons and the letter opener the agent had tried to use to kill her. She shivered at all the images.

By a curious stroke of fate, the same desk clerk was on duty tonight as when she'd informed the hotel of Carmella's death. The woman looked up from her hotel duties, took notice of the newcomers, smiled, and then did a double take, her eyes widening, obviously recognizing Anne from over a year ago. Avoiding eye contact, she and Candace made their way to the dining room.

"What was that all about?" Candace asked. "She looked like she was ready to stroke out."

Anne explained the circumstances of what happened when she'd reported Carmella's death.

"The poor woman stared at me as if I was crazy or something. I don't blame her. I was a bit upset." *Upset? I was terrified.*

The hostess seated them at a table. Within a few seconds, the waitress stopped to take drink orders. Candace ordered iced tea. Without thinking, Anne ordered white wine, and then hesitated.

"Maybe you'd better make mine iced tea, too," she

told the server.

"That's all right. Other people's drinking doesn't bother me. Go ahead. Goodness knows you need one." She paused as the waitress left. "Can you believe Eric, Missy, and I are staying in the same hotel? Talk about a set-up for murder."

"Avoid them when you can and ignore them if you can't," Anne advised.

"Easier said than done." Candace fiddled with her napkin and lowered her eyes. "I know I've said this before, but I can't tell you how sorry I am that I tried to kill you. I was so drunk and so scared that to this day, I'm not sure if I could have brought that champagne bottle down on your head."

"Desperate people do desperate things," Anne replied thinking of Jackie. "I don't believe you would have done it either. Now, let's talk about something else."

Candace smiled. "So tell me all about these murders you and the rest of the group have solved. Do you really call yourselves the Snoop Group?"

Anne laughed. "That's Jen's doing. She decided we needed a name to go along with our actions. Only Jen would come up with something that silly, but it stuck."

Their drinks arrived and they ordered dinner, after which she told Candace about the last two cases they'd helped solve. Her phone rang as the narrative wound down. Caller ID showed it was Jen, not Gil.

"My God, you found another body? Are you guys all right?" Jen asked in a breathless tone.

"We're fine. I guess you've heard about what happened at the house this afternoon."

"Carl and I were having dinner at the country club

when Eric and Missy showed up. The bitch let everyone in the room know what happened, including her opinion that the two of you killed Barbara by mistake. Plus it's all over the TV. What happened?"

Anne gave her the basics, and then asked, "Do you know this Barbara person?"

"Yeah, she's—or was—a member here. Joined about a year and a half ago. She's just like Missy, young, blonde, big tits she loves—loved—to flaunt, and a royal pain. The staff here hates—hated—her. Always giving orders, complaining about things, and demanding as hell. I sure won't miss her. Missy said something about her being shot."

Anne had to pick through the verb tense changes to keep up with Jen's narrative.

"Missy told everyone the victim was shot? Oh Lord, if the police haven't released that information yet, Gil's going to be pissed, but, yes, it's true," she confirmed. "When we left Candace's the police still hadn't found the gun."

"Probably ditched somewhere."

She remembered a comment Eric had made at the house. "Jen, I heard Barbara Lassiter fooled around. How about it? Have you heard anything?" She figured that if anybody would know, it would be Jen.

Jen's derisive snort came through loud and clear. "I'll say. Rumor has it she balled half the male population of the club and then some. Probably offed by a jealous wife or girlfriend. Hey, maybe that's it! Barbara was doing Eric and Missy blew her brains out! Sounds like another job for the Snoop Group."

Anne had to laugh at Jen's enthusiasm. "I think you're probably right—about us investigating, not necessarily Missy being a killer."

"How's Candace holding up through all of this?"

"She's upset, but hanging in there. At least, she hasn't been arrested. We're having dinner at the San Sebastian Inn."

"Ooo, that brings back some nasty memories. Look, I've gotta go. Carl's going out of town and can't seem to pack an overnight bag on his own. I'll call Rose and email Nancy with all the news. Let us know if you discover anything new, okay?"

"I will." She hung up and told Candace about Jen's information. "She thinks the Snoop Group should be on the prowl again. How about it? Would you like to help?"

"I'd love to, but have no idea how to go about it."

"We find out who knew Barbara—her friends, her lovers, her almost lovers—things like that, then we ask questions. People tend to clam up when the police are involved, but they'll talk a mile a minute if a civilian wants to know something. Why is it people are only too eager to diss someone they didn't like?"

"Basic human instinct? Who knows?"

"So do you want to help?" Anne asked.

"But I didn't know this Barbara. How can I help?"

"Listen to what people say, try to jog your memory from two years ago concerning Eric and Missy. Anything."

Candace sighed. "Missy was a secretary at Eric's work. I know that the word 'secretary' is now considered demeaning, but we're talking about Missy here. At any rate, she wasn't Eric's secretary, but one of the higher-ups. The man was older and why Missy didn't go after him is a mystery."

"Probably too old even for Missy, or he already had a trophy wife."

"Maybe. At any rate, we were at some company party when they were introduced. She liked what she saw. Never mind that I was also at the party. She flirted and can you believe I was amused? Sheesh. Talk about dumb. I should have seen it coming from a mile away, but didn't.

"You weren't expecting it," Anne said.

"No, but Eric was susceptible. He was fifty and didn't want to be. He worked out religiously to keep in shape, and wasn't above touching up the gray in his hair. I was his wife, also fifty. Missy was young, pretty in a common sort of way, and appealed to his sense of stopping the aging process. He was flattered. It didn't take long."

"I know she showed up at the country club not long after they were married. Jen told me."

"Oh, yeah, they were there a lot. She coveted the membership and hobnobbing with people she considered socially upward. But I can tell you this much, Missy flirted with other men at the club. She'd bat those eyes and thrust those boobs out to any man who'd notice."

"I'm assuming from your tone, men noticed," Anne said not surprised at the bitterness in her friend's voice.

"Of course they did. They were men."

"Was Eric aware of his new wife's activities?"

Candace shrugged. "If he was, he ignored it. She went home with him and undoubtedly made him forget anything he might have seen. I'm sure there's more than one wife at the club who's wishing it *was* Missy in the pool."

Their food arrived and as they ate, Anne wondered if Candace understood that she was still a suspect.

"Don't take whatever the police may ask as anything personal. They have to do that."

"Given two years ago, I understand I'm a suspect, probably the best suspect so far. However, if Jen's information is right, then the list is about to get a lot longer. And surely *somewhere* on that list is a person with a better motive than I."

"Like Eric?"

Candace rolled her eyes. "No way. He's besotted with Missy. No way he'd mistake anyone else with her. Besides, I don't think he'd have the guts."

"I'm sure you're right. Now, let's talk about something else."

They discussed writing for the rest of the meal with Candace promising to email her original stolen manuscript in the next few days. Anne was looking forward to doing the rewrite.

"And if you have time, jot down your emotions and memories of what happened after Dorie died."

"You mean after I killed her. There's no need to be discreet. I have to admit that those first few days were a blur of vodka and fear. I might not remember everything, but I'm sure you can fill in the blanks." She smiled. "You're a writer. Use your imagination."

The waitress brought the check, and after Candace had signed it with her name and room number, they rose and left the restaurant walking down the glass enclosed hallway from the dining room toward the lobby.

"So what are you going to do to keep busy in St. Pete?" Anne asked.

"I'm not sure. Maybe get a part time job at a souvenir shop or a clothing store. Something retail sounds like it will work best. Being single again, I can work weekends."

"Good idea. It'll bring in a little extra cash if you should ever need it."

Their attention was diverted by a commotion in the lobby.

"What's all that shouting?" Candace asked as they approached.

Anne glanced outside. Several TV remote vans dotted the parking lot, a couple with full klieg lights blazing.

Oh, crap! Reporters!

Chapter Four

Anne grabbed Candace's arm to halt her steps, and then shoved her toward a restroom door. "Quick, get inside. Don't come out until I tell you."

"What? Why?"

"Reporters. They must have tracked you down. Do you really want to have them in your face?"

Her friend took one look at the milling crowd in the lobby now some thirty feet away. Her expression changed to one of total horror as she bolted for the door.

Anne stood for a moment and thought. There was no guarantee they were here to harass Candace. For all she knew another murder had taken place at the hotel. But why take a chance?

I have to get rid of them or Candace will be hounded like a fox on the run.

An idea formed. She grabbed her phone and slapped it against her ear, then walked briskly into the lobby pretending to listen.

"Yes, I know," she said with a loud voice in her fake conversation. "I talked to Candace a while ago. She said she left it at the desk for me. Poor Candace, she's really upset at what happened."

She paused as though listening again. As soon as she uttered the name "Candace" conversations ceased. Like vultures, the reporters heard every word she said and descended.

"Candace? Are you referring to Candace Warren, the convicted killer?" one of them shouted.

"Is she here? We want to talk to her," another demanded.

"Do you know her? Did she kill again?" a third added.

Anne slipped her phone back in her purse. "Excuse me?"

"Do you know Candace Warren? Did she kill again this afternoon?" persistent asshole number three repeated.

"Are you here to meet her? What's her room number? We'd like to get her side of the story," the second guy stated.

"Candace didn't kill anyone," she said in a firm tone.

"Then why was she at her former home now owned by her ex-husband and his wife this afternoon?" reporter number one asked.

"Oh, she was there to give them a key she'd forgotten about, I think."

"Who are you and why are you here?" the third reported inquired.

"Me?" Anne stared as if in surprise while she thought. "My name is Susan Lynch. I saw Candace earlier and she'd been so appalled by what happened that she clean forgot to give her ex the key. She asked me to leave it at the front desk before she left."

"Left? Where's she gone?" the first lady insisted.

"Then she isn't under arrest?" the second guy asked.

"No, of course not, and she went to visit a friend in

Miami for a few days."

"Where in Miami?" a fourth voice chimed in.

"Oh, I really couldn't say, but I think it may have been down Homestead way," Anne replied thinking of the furthest place away she could.

"Excuse me," the desk clerk shouted above the noise. "But I'm going to have to ask you all to leave the premises. Mrs. Warren apparently isn't here. You are disrupting the operation of this hotel and disturbing our other guests."

The woman shot a suspicious glance toward Anne, then scanned the area as though seeking the person who'd arrived with her earlier. Her gaze shifted back and her eyes narrowed.

Anne shrugged as if to say, at least they aren't bugging you anymore.

The ploy worked. The desk clerk made a waving motion with her hands. "Ladies, gentlemen, please, we have other guests. As you heard, the person you are looking for isn't here. I'd appreciate it if you left."

Slowly, the herd of reporters dissipated.

"You going to Homestead?" one of them asked another.

"Hell no. But I think I *will* track down the ex and his wife. Might be something there."

Anne almost laughed at the plight Eric and Missy could soon experience.

"You might try the San Sebastian Country Club," she suggested. "I understand they're members and dine there quite often."

"Good idea," one of the reporters replied. "It's not too far away. Let's see what they have to say."

Anne chuckled as they moved en masse for the

doorway like lemmings heading for a cliff.

It took another fifteen minutes for all the vans, lights, cameras, and other assorted action to leave. Only then did she return to the ladies room, ignoring the stare of the desk clerk as she ran past.

“Candace?” she called out as she entered.

A stall door opened. “Are they gone?”

“For the moment. What are you going to do?”

Candace staggered to the wash basins and gripped the counter. “God, I don’t know. Change hotels? Wear sunglasses? Buy a wig? I didn’t envision this.”

She whirled, clasped her arms over her chest, and sniffed, making no attempt to hide the tears rolling down her cheeks.

Her last words caused Anne to pause. Envision? As in not take into account? As in not taking into consideration the consequences of killing someone?

She swallowed. “You didn’t envision what?”

Her friend shot her a look and unfolded her arms to wipe the wetness from her face.

“This. Reporters. The police station. Another murder. I didn’t kill this Barbara person.”

Guilt at doubting the woman made Anne squirm inwardly. “Of course, you didn’t. I have an idea. Why not stay with me?”

Candace shook her head. “No, you have kids and I won’t subject them to any of this.”

“All right, let me make a reservation at another hotel under my name.”

“But I’ll have to show ID to check in.”

“I’ll check in, and then you can stay there. They won’t know the difference. Park your car in the rear of the lot, and back into the space so the license plate can’t be seen."

"That might work for a while, but reporters are relentless. They'll find me eventually."

"Not unless the police find the killer first."

Anne helped Candace pack and stood guard over the lobby doors as she checked out, all the while making a reservation at a large hotel on the beach from her cell. She hoped reporters wouldn't think to look in someplace so well-populated with tourists, although the tourist season was basically over.

"Are you sure this is gonna work?" Candace asked as she slid into her car.

"No, but it's the best we can do at the moment. Now when we get there, you park while I check in. I'll meet you around the back of the hotel and give you the key."

Anne walked into the lobby of the Bonanza Beach Resort with Candace's suitcases. Her gaze darted around the area as she showed her driver's license and signed the registration card. No one lurked with a microphone or recording device.

"How long will you be staying?" the desk clerk asked.

"Uh, I'm not sure. I'm having the interior of my house painted. I guess it sort of depends on how long they take." She inhaled a deep breath. Did that sound plausible?

The desk clerk handed her the key card with a smile. "Here you go. Room four-fifteen. If you need anything, please let us know."

Anne thanked the man and wheeled the suitcases toward the elevators. As soon as she was out of sight of the front desk, she turned down a hallway and followed the exit signs to the back entrance. Outside, she spotted Candace's car backed into a parking slot with a hedge behind it.

She handed over the suitcases and the card. "You're in room four-fifteen. I left the departure date open. Told them I was having the house painted."

"This shouldn't take but a couple of days. Maybe three. With any luck, Eric and Missy will fumigate the house and be gone from the Inn by then.

"Good luck, oh, and make sure you use my name to sign any dining room or room service checks."

"I'll pay cash. The signatures won't match."

"I doubt if anyone will notice." She hugged her friend. "If you need anything, just call."

Candace smiled. "I will and thanks for everything."

With Candace safely tucked away at the new hotel Anne walked around to the front of the place to retrieve her car, and within minutes was on her way home. She hoped the woman was smart enough to leave and enter the hotel from the back entrance just in case things didn't go as planned. With any luck, Gil would have the killer in custody soon.

And speaking of Gil...why hasn't he called?

****

It was after ten when Anne walked into the kitchen. The TV in the living room told her at least one of her kids was still up.

"Hi, Mom," Ken said from the sofa when she entered. "Are you and Mrs. Warren all right?"

"We're fine." She looked at the screen and gasped. Reporters were gathered around parking lot of the country club like fleas on a hound in summer. Her misdirection of earlier had paid off. "Holy cow!"

"Yeah, the murder is the lead-off story."

As she watched, Eric and Missy emerged from the entrance. The reporters swarmed shouting questions. The couple could barely move in the throng. Finally, Eric took a swing at one of them.

"Leave us alone, goddammit! Get out of here!"

Missy smiled at the cameras.

"Do you think your ex-wife also killed Mrs. Lassiter? Did she make a mistake and mean to shoot you, Mrs. Warren?" one of them shouted louder than the rest.

"Of course, she did it! She's always hated me and now that she's out, she's going to kill me," she said with a toss of her blonde head.

"Missy, shut up!" Eric snapped.

"Don't you dare tell me to shut up! And quit defending her! How do you think that makes me feel? You're probably sorry it wasn't me floating in that pool."

"Is that true, Mr. Warren? Are you and Mrs. Warren having marital problems?"

"No! And shut the hell up!" Eric replied in a furious tone.

"How do you feel, Mrs. Warren?" another reporter asked.

The shapely blonde fluffed her hair and batted her eyelashes. "Angry that the police haven't arrested the bitch yet!"

Anne noted the new Mrs. Warren didn't look too angry for the cameras. *Probably thinks she's more attractive while vamping. In reality, she looks silly and sounds like a moron.*

Eric grabbed Missy's arm and dragged her through

the crowd. The swarm pursued them until the valet service arrived with the Warrens' car. Eric shoved Missy inside, got behind the wheel and peeled out.

From what she'd heard, it sounded as though Eric and Missy had had a slight difference of opinion regarding Candace's involvement.

Trouble in paradise? Was the marriage on the rocks? Lord, she hoped so. It would serve Eric right.

"Wow, I'll bet the country club is going nuts with all the turmoil outside," Ken said.

"All those rich old codgers like things predictable, that's for sure."

"You and Mrs. Warren—the real one—actually discovered another body?"

"Sad to say, yes. We thought it was Missy at first, but it wasn't." She didn't want to go into any more detail than necessary with her kids. "Where's Lisa?"

"Upstairs playing on her phone. Probably telling her friends how you found a body again."

"Oh, geez."

Her phone rang. It was Gil. *Finally!*

She walked into the kitchen as she answered. "Gil, have you found out anything new?"

"No, not really. Ms. Lassiter's phone is pretty well water-logged, so I'm not sure we'll get much from it. Forensics is trying to dry it out. The hair salon confirms the new Mrs. Warren was there between two and four-thirty. She chatted on her phone with numerous people. She volunteered to show us the outgoing call to Ms. Lassiter at one-fifty-six. According to Mrs. Warren, Ms. Lassiter stated she'd be there in ten minutes."

"Damn, I was hoping Missy wouldn't have an alibi. Wait a minute… You only have her word for it that this Barbara person answered the phone. Maybe Missy shot her at one-thirty and called on her way to the salon just to make it look good."

A heavy sigh sounded in her ear. "We're pulling phone records now, but it takes time. The signal would bounce off the nearest cell tower. That will tell us where both women were and how long the conversation took. Can't show that unless someone answers the phone. And why would Mrs. Warren want to shoot Ms. Lassiter?"

"I don't know. Maybe Barbara was trolling for Eric. Maybe she succeeded in reeling him in. Maybe Missy was pissed as hell. Investigate Eric. If he cheated on Candace, he may have cheated on his current wife, too."

"We are, just like we're also investigating the former Mrs. Warren, but as I said, it all takes time."

An alarm bell rang in Anne's head. "You're investigating Candace? Why? She was with me from a bit after four and had a bunch of people she was meeting before. And for Pete's sake, call her Candace. This Mrs. Warren thing is confusing."

"Given her history, not investigating would be ludicrous."

"Do you have a time of death yet?"

"If we take Mrs. Warren's word for when she called and spoke with the victim at two, and when you found the body at roughly four-fifteen, I'd say between two and four-fifteen, wouldn't you?"

"Gil, there's no need to be sarcastic."

"I'm sorry, honey, but don't let your friendship for Mrs. War…excuse me, Candace…get in the way of reality. One of the neighbors puts a white car in the driveway at the same time as Ms. Lassiter's black Lexus."

Anne drew in a sharp breath. Candace drove a white BMW. "When?"

"She's not sure. She lives across the street and was on her way to run errands, but didn't pay much attention."

"What color is Missy's car?"

"It's a silver Mercedes."

"That can easily be mistaken for white. And Eric pulled up in a light-colored car, too."

"He drives a white, late model Lexus."

"Ah-ha! What about the rest of the neighbors? Surely someone heard the shot and can give you an accurate time of death."

"The next-door neighbor to the west works and wasn't home. The one on the east said she may have heard something, but had the TV on as she was cleaning up the kitchen and thought it came from there. No time frame at all. The neighbor behind the Warrens' house was inside with the A/C on. She heard something, but dismissed it as kids with firecrackers."

"Kids? But the schools don't let out for another two weeks."

"I know, but the woman doesn't have kids at home anymore and didn't think about it. That seems to be the theme from everyone—some heard or saw something, others nothing, and no one has a specific time for anything."

"Well, from what I heard from Jen, Barbara was not afraid to spread her charms around the country club. Probably a lot of suspects there."

"We'll do our best. In the meantime, do you think

you can resist getting involved?"

"No. In fact, the Snoop Group is already on it."

Gil sighed. "Why is it that doesn't surprise me? Just be careful—please."

She liked a man who knew when to admit defeat. "I will. I always am."

"Uh-huh—Jackie Simmons, George Harrison, even Candace Warren. Need I say more?"

"Okay, you've made your point. I will be so discreet it will amaze you." She paused as a thought occurred. "Gil, the hair salon said Missy's appointment ended at four-thirty, yet she didn't show up at the house until almost five-thirty. Where the hell was she for an hour?"

"We asked and she said she stopped at a clothing store where she met a friend and chatted for a while."

"She went shopping when she was already late for our appointment? Do you buy that?"

Gil sighed. "We're checking. Look, honey, I'm tired and ready to go to bed. I'll talk to you tomorrow."

"Okay. Love ya."

"Love ya, too."

Anne sighed as she disconnected wondering if Gil's slightly irritated tone had stemmed from exhaustion or from fear that she and the group would get in over their heads. Probably the latter, but this time she swore she'd be the soul of discretion. *I'm actually getting pretty good at this investigating thing.*

She was about to pack it in for the day when Jen called.

"Anne, I've got a great idea. Suppose the Snoop Group meets for lunch tomorrow at the club? Candace, too. We can ask questions and do whatever we have to do."

"That's probably an awful idea, but I like it. We have to start somewhere. But I don't belong to the club. Neither does Rose. I'm not sure about Ellie or Candace."

"No problemo. I'm a member and can invite anyone I want. Are you in?"

"Yes, I'm in."

"Good. I'll call the others, but I don't have Candace's number anymore. I lost it when I upgraded my phone last year. Can you get a hold of her?"

"I'll call her now."

She hung up with Jen and called Candace.

"I'm not calling too late am I," she asked when her friend answered.

"No, I'm just sitting here watching a movie."

"How's everything? No reporters?"

"Not that I've seen. It's quiet, although I do peek through the curtains and look out the window every time a car pulls in."

Anne breathed a sigh of relief and told her of Jen's plan.

"Anne, I don't think that's a good idea."

"Why not?"

"Oh, not about the lunch, but me being there. After I was sent to prison, the country club revoked my membership. My turning up again, even as a guest, would cause problems for Jen and her husband. I'd hate to have that happen. Besides, I'm not sure exactly how much I can contribute. I didn't know this Barbara Lassiter at all, and I only know Missy from the totally unhealthy perspective of a bitter ex-wife."

Anne saw Candace's point. Her presence would

certainly raise eyebrows. People might not be willing to talk about Barbara Lassiter with her listening in.

"All right, I'll let Jen know."

"Don't tell her tonight. I don't want her calling and trying to talk me out of it this late. I'm beat. And to be perfectly honest, I don't see me adding any kind of positive input to this investigating thing."

"You could be right. And don't worry about Jen. I'll tell her in the morning. Don't hide in your room all day. Enjoy the beach and the dining room. Go shopping at that nearby mall. Give it a few days. By then the reporters will have someone new to hound."

"Let's hope so."

Anne wished Candace sweet dreams and hung up.

Poor Candace. If only she could have left for St. Pete last week. Then the police would have no reason to suspect her of killing Barbara Lassiter.

But the fact remained that somebody shot and killed the woman.

Chapter Five

Anne drove through the gates of the San Sebastian Country Club and wound her way along a serpentine driveway to the front entrance. She pulled up under the purple canopy emblazoned with "SBCC" in gold lettering. A valet opened her door. She exited, handed over her keys, took her receipt, and swept through the doors held open by a uniformed doorman. She felt like a queen or at least someone of importance.

She paused at the reception desk. "Hello, my name is Anne Jamieson. I believe Jennifer Swanson is expecting me."

The woman checked a list in front of her. "Yes, Ms. Jamieson, she's in the dining room. Andre, will you please escort Ms. Jamieson to the dining room and Mrs. Swanson's table?"

A young man, also in uniform, stepped forward. "Please, follow me."

Anne trailed after him admiring the stone fireplace, the marble tiled floors, and plush leather furniture in the lobby. For a weekday, the dining room was almost full. But then, for all she knew it was always like this. Jen waved from a table set up for five near the terrace windows. Anne thanked her escort who pulled out a chair. Rose was already seated.

"Hi. Did you have any trouble at the desk?" Jen asked.

"Nope. Sailed in like I belonged. You know, I've never been here before. I'm impressed. Very luxurious."

Jen snorted. "It should be for the monthly dues they charge."

"I'm lucky I made it through the front gate," Rose said with a laugh. "My minivan with all the child seats and trash on the floor isn't up to country club standards."

"They aren't picky about who gets in. Maintenance on this place is horrendous. The more members, the more money to keep it going. I'm just sorry Candace isn't coming."

Anne had called Jen earlier with their friend's reasoning for not attending.

"I can understand her point of view," Rose said. "It must be tough to start over after what she's been through."

"She told me the club had revoked her membership while she was in prison. She didn't want to cause any trouble."

Jen made a face. "Buncha hypocrites. Charlie Forsythe was convicted of insider trading and still has his membership. He and his wife dine here all the time."

"Insider trading isn't the same as murder," Rose told her.

"And Eric Warren pulls down an income that probably pays for a lot of the landscaping at this place in spite of a whopping divorce settlement," Anne added. "Candace was expendable."

Ellie, also escorted by Andre, walked up to the table. "Hi, am I late?"

"Not at all," Jen said. "Have a seat. It's only the four of us. Candace can't make it."

Ellie sat with a frown. "I'm not sure how comfortable I'd be around her anyway. I mean, I have no idea what to say to someone who just got out of prison."

"I understand," Anne said. "And I'm sure Candace would, too."

A waiter arrived, distributed leather-bound menus, and took their drink orders. White wine all around.

"What do you recommend, Jen?" Rose asked.

"Anything. I'll say this, the kitchen here is top-notch. The chef knows what he's doing. I guess those dues aren't all going to azalea bushes."

By the time their wine arrived, they had made up their minds and ordered.

"Now, exactly how is the Snoop Group going to work on this one?" Anne asked.

"Well, I got here early and asked a few questions of people who knew Barbara," Jen replied. "Don't worry, I was discreet. Just put on a shocked face and made comments along the lines of 'who on earth would want to kill her' type of thing. You'd be surprised at the answers I got."

"Like what?" Rose inquired taking a sip from her glass.

Jen leaned forward and lowered her voice. "A lot of people I spoke with named Candace as the culprit. Missy's tirade here last night probably contributed to that. However, others weren't so sure. Elaine English called Barbara a serial whore who went after anything in pants. I pretended not to understand and learned Barbara had put the moves on Elaine's husband, Bill, last fall. Same story with a couple of other women."

"But Barbara was killed at Missy's house. She was floating in Missy's pool," Anne reminded them. "Did any of them have a problem with Missy?"

"I'm not sure. If Missy was doing anyone here, I haven't heard about it—yet."

"I'm not sure how much help I can be in all of this," Ellie said. "I mean, I don't know any of the people involved and certainly don't know any members of the country club." She glanced around the room. "I take that back. There's Roberta Canfield."

They all shifted their gazes to a table along the far wall where a man and a woman sat. The woman waved. Ellie waved back.

"How do you know Bertie?" Jen asked.

"She's in my bridge group." She wiggled her fingers in the air again as the woman rose and made her way toward them.

"Ellie, what a surprise. Are you a member here?" Roberta asked.

"No. Jen invited us all to lunch. How's everything?"

"Just fine. Jen, it's good to see you. Haven't seen you on the tennis court in a while."

"No, been too busy, I guess." Jen introduced the rest of them, and then once again lowered her voice. "Isn't it awful about Barbara Lassiter? I swear to God, I don't know what this world is coming to."

Anne shot Jen a glance. This was not the most subtle of transitions.

Roberta stiffened. "Can't say as I'm surprised. That woman pissed off half the female members. I sometimes wondered if she and Missy had a contest going on who could bed the most men."

Jen's eyes widened. "Missy? Have a seat. Do tell."

The woman shook her head. "Well, I don't actually have any proof Missy Warren was having an affair—other than with Eric before he and Candace were divorced, but she and Barbara were good friends. Always lounging around the pool area in their skimpy bikinis, flirting with men in the bar, and laughing at the older women with the not-so-great figures. They also had a lot of guests—good-looking women with *unrealistic* figures." She made a face. "I heard it said that the Lassiters' membership was approved by her sleeping with then president of the club, Jerry Bedford."

Jen nodded. "That's right, I seem to remember Barbara having a husband. Don't recall seeing him lately."

"They divorced. I have no idea where Drew Lassiter is now. I think someone said California."

"Well, I just hope they catch whoever did it soon. I mean, someone sure hated Barbara enough to kill her. Maybe it was a member." Jen shivered in mock horror.

Roberta glanced at all of them. "Well, from what Missy said last night, Candace Warren and some other woman found the body. Or so they say. I had no idea she'd been released from prison. You were pretty good friends with her, weren't you, Jen?"

"Yes. Still am. In fact, I invited her to lunch here today, but she couldn't make it."

"I see." Roberta's voice took on a cool tone as she glanced at the man seated at her table. "I'd better get back. My husband's waiting. Nice chatting with you. See you next week for bridge, Ellie. If you and your husband would like to join the club, just let me know.

I'll sign a sponsorship. Talk to you later."

"Well, that was awkward," Rose said as the woman left.

"And not terribly informative, although it wasn't hard to figure out she sounded like she has first-hand experience," Anne added.

"Wes?" Jen said with a chuckle. "No way. He's like a lap dog."

"Well, we still didn't learn anything new."

"Oh, I don't know," Jen remarked. "We found out Barbara probably bedded Jerry Bedford. He's kind of a smooth operator, but low-key, if that makes any sense. In his early forties, I think. His wife heads the annual San Sebastian Country Club auction every year. The proceeds go to various charities. She's snooty and likes to let you know it's her money, not Jerry's."

"I found it interesting that this woman knew Barbara Lassiter's husband's name," Rose commented. "I mean, if they were divorced after joining and she has no idea where he is now, why would she remember his name? Were they good friends with the Lassiters?"

"Not that I know of, but you bring up a good point," Jen said. "I kind of remember when they joined, but have little recollection of him other than the fact he was damned good-looking. I'm not even sure when they became members."

"Candace didn't seem to know the name either," Anne told them. "So my guess is it was after she was sent to prison or shortly before."

"You know, thinking about it, why would Roberta volunteer this kind of information at all? Obviously, she didn't like Barbara Lassiter, but why go on about how she may or may not have slept with the then president of the club in order to guarantee membership? Is she a major gossipmonger?" Rose asked.

Jen sipped from her glass. "I've never heard her gossip. Roberta is usually on the quiet side. You're right, her behavior is odd."

"Not if she's hiding something," Anne commented. "Like maybe her husband *was* involved with the dead woman."

"That would explain the character assassination of Barbara Lassiter," Rose added.

"You know, I may be able to help after all," Ellie said. "I could call Roberta and pretend to be all interested in joining the club. Naturally, I'd ask questions along the way."

"Great idea," Rose chimed in. "She probably suspects Anne and I are friendly with Candace, but since you're relatively new to the area she might tell you things."

"And if anyone asks, just say that while you never met Candace Warren, the name sounds familiar," Anne added.

Their meals arrived and the conversation turned to their former critique group member.

"So, how is she doing after yesterday?" Jen asked.

Anne sighed and told them about the reporters and her subterfuge to get them to leave.

Jen giggled. "And you told them your name was Susan Lynch? That's too funny."

Rose laughed, too. "I hope they showed up on Susan's doorstep with all kinds of rude questions."

"And she probably directed them right back to Anne," Ellie said with a grin.

"I just feel sorry for Candace having to hide out

like that," Jen grumbled as she shoved a forkful of seafood salad into her mouth.

"Hopefully, it won't be for long."

If Eric and Missy continued to stay at the San Sebastian Inn, then maybe it was a good idea for Candace to stay where she was. Even though receiving a large divorce settlement from Eric and with the recent sale of the house, Anne wasn't sure if Candace had the funds to finance the Bonanza Beach Resort for more than a couple of weeks. *I'm not sure I do considering the bill is on my credit card, although I know she'll pay me back.*

"Funny how Missy set up the whole thing," Rose said. "I mean, if she hadn't complained about a strange smell, nobody would have been there. What was the odor anyway?"

Anne sipped from her wine glass. The Chardonnay was excellent.

"I have no idea, but it was foul. I smelled something the minute we walked into the foyer. It was stronger in the den, and downright overwhelming in the master bedroom."

"What on earth were you doing up there?" Ellie asked.

She told them how she and Candace had rung the doorbell, and then entered when they found the door unlocked. "Naturally, we looked around since we were late and expecting Missy to be there."

Jen and Rose ceased eating and stared. "Oh, my God," Jen breathed. "Just like with Dorie."

"Pretty much," Anne admitted.

"You mean you walked into an unlocked house and found a body before?" Ellie said with wide eyes.

Anne wasn't sure how much she wanted to tell their newest critique partner and tried to formulate a reasonable answer.

Jen, however, wasn't so hesitant. She explained how Anne, Nancy, and Candace had found Isadora Powell's bludgeoned body.

"But, Candace killed her, right?" Ellie asked.

Jen also explained about the stolen novel and Candace's drinking problem.

Anne jumped in before Jen could add that all of the group had been suspects and had lied to the police. Nor did she mention how Candace had tried to kill her, too.

"Candace really didn't remember doing it until later," Anne told her. "Most of her actions were fueled by alcohol. She's sober now."

Ellie frowned. "Do you think she could kill sober?"

"No," Rose stated. "Plus, I'm sure Candace has alibis for the afternoon. Remember? We overheard her talking to Eric when he called to bitch about the smell."

"I'm sure Candace will be exonerated," Jen said. "I think Missy was the target."

"And yet Barbara could have arranged to meet someone at the house when she found out Missy was going to be very late," Anne mused.

"Hmm, Barbara calls a man she's pursuing, invites him over for some extracurricular activity, they argue, and he kills her," Rose said in a speculative tone.

"Or if the guy was married, the wife waits until he leaves, and then walks in and kills her," Ellie added.

"Now, that's Snoop Group thinking," Jen told her with a grin.

The waiter came to clear their plates and offered coffee. Rose and Ellie opted for dessert.

Anne was about to ask Jen a question about the club when a couple stopped by the table.

"Jen, nice to see you," the woman said.

"Oh, hello Darlene. Yes, it's been a while since I've been in for lunch. Carl and I were here for dinner last night, though. Darlene, Jerry, these are my guests, Anne Jamieson, Rose Bennett, and Ellie Campion. Ladies, this is Darlene and Jerry Bedford. Jerry is a former president of the club."

Anne didn't need a roadmap to understand this was the man Roberta Canfield suggested Barbara had slept with.

"I enjoyed being president," Jerry said with a smile. "I was able to meet so many members I'd never met before."

"Yeah, I'll just bet," Jen replied. "Isn't it terrible about Barbara Lassiter? I didn't know her very well, but she seemed like a nice person."

Jerry's smile slipped. "Terrible, just terrible."

"So shocking," Darlene added. "I didn't have much to do with her, of course. I was too busy with various club committees. She didn't volunteer for any that I recall."

"That's right, she and her husband became members while you were in charge, didn't they, Jerry?"

"Yes, I believe so," he said.

His wife's fingers tightened around the strap of the purse hanging from her shoulder. Her lips thinned and her eyes narrowed slightly.

"I also heard rumors that she flirted with a lot of the men here."

"I don't know anything about that," Jerry said.

"And of course I have no love for Missy Warren

what with Candace and all," Jen continued. "Wouldn't be surprised if she was batting those eyelashes at other men either."

Darlene inhaled a ragged breath. "I don't engage in gossip, so I wouldn't know. Sorry, we have to be running. I've got a meeting with the concession stand committee in a few minutes, and Jerry tees off in a little while."

"Gotta hit the old practice green," he said with a strained smile.

Jen waved her hand. "Nice talking to you. Have a good game, and Darlene, I hope you can do something about the prices the concession stands charge."

"That was interesting," Anne said as the Bedfords moved off.

"Did you see the looks on their faces?" Ellie commented.

"Yeah, he looked uncomfortable as hell, and she was angry," Rose added. "Bet the rumors are true and he slept with this Barbara *and* his wife knows about it."

"You could be right," Jen said. "Think I'll stick around a while longer. Maybe smack a few balls on the driving range or on the tennis court. I can ask more questions."

Finished with the meal, the group walked back into the lobby. Anne was admiring the view of the eighteenth green as Jen pointed out the landscaping through the terrace windows when another woman strode up.

"Jennifer, I was just talking to Bertie Canfield and she said you told her you'd invited Candace Warren to lunch. Is that true?" Her tone was confrontational and loud.

"Yes, but she couldn't make it."

"Well, I for one am appalled. She has no business here, and if she does show up as your guest I will let the membership committee know of my displeasure."

"Oh, cram it, Lynne. I can invite whomever I want. It seems to me you and your husband often played golf and dined here with Eric and Candace. You also chummed around with Missy and him later, even though she broke up the marriage."

"That was before I knew the real Candace. Imagine, a killer! I'm proud to say I was one of the first people to suggest to Jerry Bedford that her membership be revoked."

"I'm not surprised. You also played racquetball on a regular basis with Barbara Lassiter, too."

"So what? She was a good player. And now it looks like Candace has struck again. Mistaken identity from what I heard. Thought Barbara was Missy."

"Nonsense. Candace has an alibi," Jen shot back.

The woman straightened her shoulders. "Just consider this a warning, if you show up here with that killer in tow, your days in this club are numbered."

"Who the hell was that?" Ellie asked as the irate woman stomped off.

"Lynne Nordstrom," Jen replied glaring at the woman's back. "She and her husband, Sam, joined about the same time as Carl and me. He's also the current president. She's opinionated and just plain nasty."

"Boy, I'll say." Rose glanced at her watch. "Geez, I have to get going. The kids will be home from school soon and I have to get the other two out of day care. Thanks for lunch, Jen."

Ellie and Anne also left. During the drive home, Anne tried to convince herself the killer was a club member. Goodness knows just this luncheon had provided two or three new suspects. But a voice in her head kept repeating a name she knew all too well.

Candace?

Chapter Six

Gil called a few minutes after six just as Anne was beginning to make dinner.

"Candace Warren is missing," he stated in a grim tone.

"Missing?"

"As in she checked out of the San Sebastian Inn last night and is nowhere to be found. Neither does she answer her cell."

She breathed a sigh of relief. "No, no, she's at the Bonanza Beach Resort. I helped her move." A long silence greeted this information. "Gil?"

"And you didn't think to inform me of this?"

"I guess I just forgot to tell you. I…I did it last night. And maybe she isn't answering her phone because it's out of charge or something."

"Why did she move?"

Anne explained about the reporters. "Candace didn't need that kind of stress, so I made a reservation under my name."

"She is a suspect and should have notified us of her new whereabouts immediately. You should have thought of that."

Lisa entered the kitchen.

"Well, excuse the hell out of me, *Detective* Collins. It was kind of a hectic day yesterday. I found another body. Remember?" Her voice rose.

Lisa turned and walked back out. Anne hated that her daughter had caught her arguing with Gil.

"I remember," he replied with a sigh. "And I also have to keep in mind that you aren't a cop."

Her irritation with him softened at his calmer tone. "Look, I'm just starting dinner. It's nothing fancy. Just burgers, frozen peas, and boxed au gratin potatoes. Would you like to join us?"

"I can't. I need to talk to Candace Warren again."

"Why?"

"Her alibi isn't as strong as it should be."

"What do you mean? She picked me up a few minutes before four and we found Barbara around four-fifteen."

"And Ms. Lassiter was killed sometime between two o'clock and when you discovered her floating in the pool."

"But Candace had appointments in the afternoon. Jen, Rose, Ellie, and I heard her tell that to Eric when he called."

"Her one o'clock appointment with her parole officer lasted ten minutes. She arrived early for her appointment with her lawyer and he confirms that she left at two-fifteen. That leaves a gap of well over an hour for her to have gone to the house waited until she thought she saw Melissa Warren arrive, follow her inside, shoot, and then leave."

Anne's spirits took a nosedive. "I refuse to believe that. Besides, why would Candace show up at the house that early?"

"To kill Missy Warren."

"And then come pick me up all calm, cool, and collected? I don't think so."

"Seems to me she did much the same thing with Isadora Powell."

"She killed Dorie in an alcoholic haze. Candace was stone-cold sober when we found Barbara."

"And she was stone-cold sober when you found Isadora Powell's body, too. Hungover, but sober."

"I still refuse to believe it."

"And I still have to ask her where she was. You know that. And I want to get this over with. I'm leaving now. I'll talk to you later."

She hung up and caught her lower lip between her teeth. This did not bode well for Candace. Could her soon-to-be collaborator have done as Gil speculated?

No, I just don't believe she could have killed and been so rational when she picked me up.

Lisa walked back into the room. "Um, sorry, I didn't mean to eavesdrop."

"You didn't. Gil and I were having a difference of opinion, that's all. Happens to married people all the time—and those who are almost married. Your dad and I tried to keep our arguments behind closed doors so you kids wouldn't hear us."

"I guess that's why the divorce was so hard to accept. Everything seemed normal to me. Sometimes, I think it's better for the kids to hear things like that."

Anne marveled at Lisa's ability to put things into an adult perspective. The kid had her head on straight. A bubble of pride swelled in her chest. She'd done a good job of raising her daughter—and son.

Ken joined them. "When's dinner? I'm starved."

"About twenty or thirty minutes. Why don't the two of you set the table while I get going?"

As she ate, her mind stayed busy imagining Gil

questioning Candace again. Did he call her down to the station or go the hotel? She hoped Candace had called her attorney. Should she have given her friend a heads-up that Gil wanted to talk to her again? No, that would have been interfering with an investigation. In view of her recent conversation with him, Anne didn't need that. He was already irritated with her as it was.

"Mom, are you all right?" Lisa asked as she helped clean up the dishes.

"I'm fine. Just tired."

"Don't let a little spat worry you. Gil loves you."

If only it were that simple. "I won't. You know, if you can finish up here, I'd like to go upstairs and try to get a few more pages written."

"No problem."

But once seated at her desk the words refused to come. She worried about Candace and was concerned that Gil hadn't called to give her any information on the latest round of questions.

Finally, her phone rang at ten o'clock. It was Candace.

"Candace, are you all right?" She had to phrase her question carefully. She didn't want her friend to know Gil had told her of his plans.

A ragged breath on the other end told her things were not well.

"Oh, Anne, I've just come back from the police station. Gil brought me in for more questioning."

"Did you call your lawyer?"

"Immediately."

"Where are you now?"

"At the hotel."

"Well, that's better than in jail."

"I suppose, but I'm so tempted to go down to the bar. Could…could you come and keep me company for a while."

"Of course. Call room service and order every flavor of ice cream they have in stock. We'll talk and eat. I'll be there in twenty minutes."

Candace made a noise between a sob and a laugh. "All right, and Anne…thanks."

"Hang in there."

Anne hurried downstairs, told the kids she'd be out for a while with Candace, and then ran to the car. A train, a drawbridge, and a minor accident on the main route to the hotel made her late. She arrived at Candace's hotel room the same time as the ice cream.

Settled in the chair with mint chocolate chip, she spooned some into her mouth and asked, "So, tell me what happened."

"Your detective showed up here around six-thirty and read me the riot act about not informing the police of my change in hotels. Honestly, it never occurred to me to tell him. I was just so glad those reporters were gone, I didn't think about it." She shoveled vanilla fudge swirl into her mouth.

"He could have called you to find out where you were. He had your cell number from yesterday." Anne had to tread lightly.

"I turned it off when I went down to the pool this afternoon. I was still upset and didn't want to talk to anyone. I totally forgot to turn it back on. I don't know how he found me and don't care."

"So did he escort you to the station?"

Candace nodded. "As soon as he said he wanted me downtown, I called my lawyer. He met us there."

"And what did Gil ask?"

Her friend licked the spoon and frowned. "He had reservations about my alibi. My appointments didn't run very long and I had a lot of time before I picked you up."

"What did you do?"

"I ran errands for the most part. I stopped at the drugstore for some toothpaste and shampoo. I went to the grocery store for some of my favorite flavored water. Just errands. I also drove around looking at San Sebastian. I've been away a long time and wanted to see what had changed."

Candace finished the vanilla fudge swirl and reached for the strawberry ice cream. Anne did the same with the mint chocolate chip and lifted a bowl containing salted caramel.

"That sounds reasonable to me."

Candace set the bowl on the table and buried her face in her hands. "Except that isn't quite true. Oh God, Anne, I went to the house."

She burst into tears. Anne's bowl landed on the table with a sharp click as dread descended on her.

"When?" she asked in a hushed tone.

"Along about three or so. I pulled into the driveway, next to a black car. I figured it was Missy. I waited a couple of minutes, thought about what you'd said about not meeting her alone, and then left. I don't think anyone saw me. I drove around a bit more before picking you up."

"Did you tell Gil this?"

She shook her head. "I didn't exactly lie, but I didn't tell the truth either. What am I going to do? I'm so scared."

"Does your lawyer know?"

"No."

"Candace, you have to tell them both."

"I swear before all that is holy, I didn't kill Barbara Lassiter—by mistake or otherwise."

"Remember all the lies we told when Dorie died? Gil eventually found out about them and there was hell to pay. Call your lawyer first, and do what he recommends. I'm certain he'll tell you to come clean. If so, then I'll go the police station with you."

Candace sniffed. "All right."

Anne studied her friend's face. The expressions ranged from confused to scared to sad. She couldn't bring herself to eat another spoonful of ice cream. Her stomach was on the verge of rebellion and her worst fears confirmed.

Much as she didn't want to believe it, Candace could have killed again.

****

"I have something I need to tell you," Candace said to Gil.

She sat in front of his desk flanked by her attorney.

Anne had a seat near the back of the room. She was only here because Candace had insisted she be present and Gil had made her promise not to say anything. It was late. She was tired and hoped her fiancé wouldn't keep her friend long.

"I thought you might," Gil replied pulling out a notepad and a recorder. "What is it you want to say?"

Candace took a deep breath, glanced at her lawyer who nodded, and told Gil about her afternoon. "And then…then I went to the house. But I didn't go in. I stayed in the car and left after a couple of minutes. I swear."

The attorney nodded. "I already confirmed that my client left my office at two-fifteen."

"What time did you get there?"

Candace frowned. "Three o'clock, three-fifteen or so. Maybe later. I'm not sure."

"So, you didn't go in, but just left. Where were you from the time you left your attorney's and where did you go after you left the house?"

She reminded him about her errands.

"That still doesn't account for all your time. What did you do?"

"I just drove around."

Gil's eyebrows rose. "Around where?"

"Just around. Detective Collins, I've been away for two years. I'm about to make a permanent move to St. Petersburg. I lived in San Sebastian for a long time. I parked in the lot near the soccer fields where my kids played on Saturdays. I stopped near the park where I took them when they were toddlers. I was nostalgic and sad. I'm leaving a good chunk of my life behind. I sat in the car and cried for a while before picking up Anne. Now, I'm just plain scared. I swear to you, I didn't kill Barbara Lassiter."

Gil shrugged. "I suspected you may have been there. A neighbor says she saw a white car in the driveway around that time. You could have entered the house, killed who you thought was the new Mrs. Warren, and driven away."

"But I didn't."

The attorney leaned forward. "Detective Collins, my client is scared to death of being sent back to prison. That's why she didn't come clean with the full story of her whereabouts that afternoon. Thank goodness she called Ms. Jamieson who immediately urged her to inform me and you of the truth. She realized it was the only thing to do."

Candace ran a hand through her hair. "I…I understand how this looks, but it's the truth. Are…are you going to arrest me?"

Anne also leaned forward and studied Gil's face, but detected nothing except a stern expression. She held her breath when he made eye contact with her. Would he arrest Candace?

His gaze shifted back to Candace. "Not at this time, but I have to warn you that I don't want you to leave town. Also stay away from your ex-husband and his wife. No personal or phone contact. Is that clear?"

"Crystal," she replied visibly relieved. Her posture relaxed as she inhaled a shaky breath.

"I'm sure that won't be a problem," the lawyer said. "The current Mrs. Warren has been accusing my client of murder on more than one occasion in public forums. Tomorrow I'm serving her and her husband with an injunction to cease all such activity."

"That's your business, not mine." Gil rose. "Let me get this typed up. You can sign it, and then leave."

"I take it you haven't found the murder weapon yet," the attorney said.

"No, not yet. Anne, may I speak with you outside?"

Anne followed Gil into the hallway. "I think it would be a good idea for you to not be alone with Candace Warren until this is cleared up. She's dangerous and I don't want you in any kind of danger."

"Gil, I appreciate how you feel, but Candace is my

friend—in spite of what happened in the past. She's scared and very much alone. I can't and won't abandon her. I know what she did looks bad—real bad. I'm not afraid. She may have hated Missy at one point in time, but I doubt she still does. Killing Missy wouldn't bring Eric back to her. I don't think she'd even want him now. She's ready to move on with her life."

"Just be careful."

"I will. Have you heard anything new from the neighbors?"

"No. I'll try to jog their memories some more tomorrow. Dinner out tomorrow night?"

"Sounds good. How long will you keep Candace? I drove her over here."

Gil brushed her cheek with his lips. "Wait in the lobby. This won't take but a few minutes."

It was Friday night and the lobby was full of people, all waiting for something, most with taciturn expressions. Anne chose a chair as far away from the disgruntled occupants as possible. The few minutes turned into thirty. Finally, Candace and her attorney emerged.

"Thank goodness that's over," Candace said as Anne hugged her.

"You're damned lucky he didn't arrest you," her attorney stated in a stern voice. "Don't ever withhold information from me again. If you do, I'm off the case. If they arrest you, I can't mount a defense if the police know things I don't during a trial."

"I won't. I promise."

Anne dropped Candace off at the back entrance to the hotel and waited until she was safely inside before heading for home. All she wanted was her bed and a good night's sleep.

It was after one when she entered the kitchen with a soft step. All was quiet telling her the kids had gone to bed. Anne climbed the stairs determined to do the same.

But sleep was elusive. She tossed and turned, her mind churning with theories on why Barbara Lassiter had been killed and by whom. It had to have been a case of mistaken identity. The murderer thought he or she was taking out Missy. The common denominator was the country club. They were both members and friends. And apparently it was well known Barbara slept around. Plus one of the women from lunch today had suggested Missy did, too. On that subject, however, she had no proof. Still it made the most sense. Unfortunately, the person with the best motive so far was Candace.

Anne was ninety-nine percent sure her friend was innocent, yet that final one percent gave her pause. That and the missing time created problems. And Isadora Powell hovered at the edge of her mind, too. Could Candace have gone there early like she said, but instead of driving away, entered the house, shot who she thought was Missy, and then left?

And she was late in picking me up. No, the killer has to be from the country club. But since I'm not a member, chatting up possible suspects will be difficult.

That left only one person who could ask questions—Jen. And Jen wasn't always subtle, but there was no other choice.

I'll call her in the morning.

Anne rolled over and sighed. Finding the killer might prove to be harder than at first thought. *But then, it's never easy.* This time the suspect list could be enormous.

****

Anne's phone rang at the unlikely hour of seven-thirty before she'd even finished her first cup of coffee. She'd had a lousy night's sleep. Caller ID told her it was Jen.

"Hi, you're up with the birds this morning."

"Do you play tennis?" Jen asked.

"Not in a long time. Why?"

"Well, last night I thought I'd start my sleuthing duties by playing doubles with Bertie and Wes Canfield, so I reserved a court for eleven only my husband, Carl, can't make it, so I thought you might sub. We planned on lunch afterward."

"Why me?"

"Because you'd know what questions to ask and would probably do it a lot better than I could."

Anne swallowed the last of her coffee. "Won't it seem odd that I'm lunching with you two days in a row? Don't they have limits on the number of guests and how often they attend?"

"Supposedly, but I've got that all figured out. I'll just tell anybody who asks that you're interested in joining and they won't raise a stink. I told you, the club needs the money."

A second cup of coffee was in order. Anne poured it. "I'm not even sure I have a tennis outfit. And I have no clue where my racket is."

"No problemo. Just wear a pair of shorts. No one is that fussy—well, mostly no one. And I can lend you one of my rackets. So how about it?"

"All right. Should I come to your place or directly

to the club?"

"Stop by here around ten-thirty. I'll drive."

Anne hung up. Her problem of how to access the club was solved—at least for today. She finished her coffee, ate a couple of slices of toast, and headed upstairs to find something suitable for the courts.

Later, back in the kitchen, Ken ambled in wearing a rumpled T-shirt and a pair of shorts.

"Morning, Mom. What are you dressed up for?"

"I'm playing tennis with Jen at eleven."

"Tennis? Seems I remember you and dad playing occasionally when we went to the park."

"It's been a while, but when she asked it sounded like a good idea. I need more exercise. I'll be having lunch afterward, so I'm not sure what time I'll be home. Oh, and I'm having dinner out with Gil tonight. Can you and Lisa cope?"

"Sure. Patty Wainwright is throwing an end-of-school party this afternoon complete with burgers and pizza. Lisa and I are invited. Not sure when we'll be home either."

"Will her parents be there?"

"As far as I know."

"Well, just be careful driving and as tempting as it might be—no beer."

"Patty's pretty straight about that, so you don't have to worry."

"I'm a mother. I'm supposed to worry about my kids, especially behind the wheel of a car and at a party."

Last winter she'd splurged and bought her sixteen-year-old son a used car. It was nothing fancy and got him from point A to point B with no trouble.

“I’m careful.”

Anne glanced at the clock. “I’d better head over to Jen’s. Have a good time and if you need me just call.”

“Same to you.”

She chucked a small duffle bag with a change of clothes in it into the back seat of her car and left. On the drive to Jen’s, she marveled at how grown up her kids had become in the past couple of years. Both had level heads and did the right things. Anne didn’t really worry about them drinking and driving or doing drugs. And both pulled down good grades.

She parked on the street and walked up to Jen’s front door. Jen opened before she had chance to ring the doorbell. She wore a white tennis skirt and a white sleeveless top with navy piping along the collar, armholes, and V-neck.

“Hey, come on in. I found a fairly good racket for you. I had it restrung last year, so it shouldn’t be too spongy.”

“Thanks. I hope these shorts are all right. At least they’re white.”

“You look fine. I thought if we got there a little early, you and I could smack a few balls around just to warm up. I haven’t played in over a month.”

“Let’s go. It’s time to start asking questions about Barbara Lassiter and Melissa Warren.”

“And who they may or may not have been sleeping with,” Jen added.

For Candace’s sake, Anne hoped for a lot of men to crop up as possible lovers. And while she didn’t like poking her nose into strangers’ lives, she suspected the number of affairs might be staggering.

Chapter Seven

Driving with Jen was always an adventure. She talked a mile a minute and frequently got lost. Today, however, she focused on the road and listened as Anne told her about Candace's side trip to her former residence.

"Good Lord, what is wrong with that woman? I mean, why do something that dumb?"

"Well, it's not like she knew there was a body floating in the pool," Anne replied hoping that was the case.

"And while she didn't quite lie, she didn't tell the truth either. What does Gil say? Is she a serious suspect?"

"He didn't come right out and say so, and she wasn't arrested, but I'd have to say she is. I'm having dinner with him tonight. I hope he has more information."

"Anne, what if…I mean…suppose she did it. She really hated Missy."

"I know, but prison mellowed her out. She's changing her life, so I can't see her jeopardizing all of that just to off her ex's new squeeze. Now, tell me more about the people we're playing tennis with today. Bertie Canfield—she's the woman who stopped by the table yesterday. Ellie's friend."

"Yes. Bertie's okay, but her husband Wes is a bit

of a dolt. Fairly good tennis player and golfer, but one of those people who sometimes speaks before he thinks and says dumb things." Jen shot her a glance and grinned. "Worse than me."

Anne laughed. "Sometimes I think there is a distinct method in your madness."

They pulled into the members' parking lot at the club and made their way toward the tennis courts. While Jen checked them in, Anne scanned the playing surface. The hard-packed clay looked in good condition. Jen joined her and they batted some balls across the net to warm up. It wasn't long before Bertie and Wes joined them.

"I met you yesterday, didn't I?" Bertie asked as she shook hands with Anne.

"Yes, I'm recently engaged and my fiancé and I are thinking about joining. We decided we needed exercise and this seems like a perfect setting."

"Oh, without a doubt," Wes stated with a laugh. "I get a lot of exercise running away from all the good-looking women."

His wife glared at him before turning to Jen. "So, how about you and me against Wes and Anne?"

"Fine with me," Jen replied.

"I'm game if you are, Wes. I haven't played in a while. Hope I don't embarrass myself or disappoint you."

"Just a friendly game, so it doesn't matter."

The arrangement suited Anne. Between plays and sets, she could ask innocent questions of Wes.

"Oops, sorry about that net ball," she said as they lost the first point.

"Not to worry. Bertie's serving and that's not her

strong suit."

Sure enough, the score was soon tied fifteen all. Anne concentrated on the game. No need to rush into an interrogation. Let Wes Canfield feel comfortable with her. They lost the first set to Jen and Bertie six-four.

As they switched sides of the court, Anne smiled at her partner.

"I like this place. It seems to be well-run."

"Oh, yes, Jerry Bedford kept on top of things. He was president two years running, and still sits on the board. Our current president, Sam Nordstrom isn't as conscientious, but does a pretty good job."

She lowered her voice. "I hear one of your members was murdered a few days ago."

"That would be Barbara Lassiter," he replied as they took their positions on the court. "Your serve, Anne."

Anne served and thanks to some hustle by Wes they won the point.

"Do the police know who did it? I mean, I'd love to join, but suppose the killer is a member? That would be awful. Did you know her? Did she play tennis?"

"Tough luck, Bertie. You're still serving low," he called out to his wife as the ball slapped into the net. "Yes, she was quite a good tennis player. I partnered with her for club tournaments on a couple of occasions."

This time Bertie's serve cleared the net and headed straight for Anne. She slashed it back. Jen returned it to Wes. The volley lasted for several strokes before ending.

The past few minutes had shown her how out of

shape she's become. Her breath rasped in and out of her lungs and her legs felt like lead. And was it her imagination or did the sun seem to get hotter and more intense every time she hit the ball?

She was grateful when Jen took her time to gather up some loose balls.

"Did you and Ms. Lassiter win?" Anne asked Wes when she'd regained her breath.

"What? Win? Oh, you mean in the tournaments? No. Always ended up playing the best couple in the club. Had fun though. I'll miss Barbara. She was a nice person. Beautiful woman. Pleasant personality. Often met up with her and Missy Warren in the bar after a game."

Jen and Bertie won the next point.

"It's always so sad when someone young and vibrant is cut down before their time. I guess she must have had an enemy," Anne said.

"Other than Missy and a few of their friends they had as guests, she was mostly in the company of men. I know a lot of the women didn't like her. Jealousy, pure and simple. But don't let something like that deter you from joining. We're wonderful once you get to know us."

The game continued until they were tied at one set each. Anne's legs and shortness of breath continued to let her know she needed to do this more often. She and Wes lost the last set six-two.

After a quick shower and changing clothes, she and Jen joined Wes and Bertie near the practice green.

"Sorry, I didn't do too well," Anne apologized as they walked toward the terrace dining area.

"You did fine," Bertie said. "My serve sucks. I

need to take a few lessons from our tennis pro, Adam."

They were shown to a table. After ordering drinks, Anne plunged in with questions to Bertie.

"I take it the club has both tennis and golf pros."

"Adam Jefferies is the tennis pro. Ted Saunders takes care of golf lessons. Both are good."

"Glad to hear that. I'd like to learn how to golf. My fiancé loves to play." She had no idea if this was true. Gil never seemed to have the free time for sports.

"Well, speak of the devil." Wes waved.

A handsome young man in tennis clothes approached the table. "Wes, Bertie, Jen, good to see you."

Wes performed introductions. "Anne, this is our tennis pro, Adam Jefferies. Adam, this is Anne Jamieson. She and her fiancé are thinking of joining."

Adam smiled. "Welcome, Ms. Jamieson. I hope you decide to join. Have you seen the courts yet?"

"Yes, just finished a match," Wes told him.

The pro eyed Anne. "How was your game?"

"I'm woefully out of practice," Anne said. "I could probably use a few lessons to get back up to snuff."

"My serve hasn't improved at all. I may contact you about some more lessons next week," Bertie informed him.

"Give me a call and we'll find a time."

Jen leaned toward Adam and lowered her voice to ask, "Wasn't it awful about Barbara Lassiter?"

The tennis pro's face changed from smiling to guarded. "Yes, a terrible tragedy. Hope the cops get the killer soon."

"Didn't the two of you date for a while last winter?" Jen continued with a sad look on her face.

"Briefly. She was a nice lady. Pretty good player, too."

"I saw Missy Warren on the court a month or so ago. Her game has definitely improved. You gave her lessons, too, right?"

"Yes, her game has improved." His voice had taken on a cool tone.

"There, you see, Anne, if you join you'll be in good hands with Adam. He'll have you on top of your game in no time." Jen flashed him a dazzling smile.

The smile he returned was strained. "I'll do my best. Now, if you'll excuse me I have to grab a bite before my next lesson." He nodded and left.

Throughout the exchange Anne noted that Bertie's gaze hadn't moved from the garden foliage just below the terrace. Wes stared at a shapely brunette seated a few tables away. Neither said a word.

The waitress returned with their drinks and took food orders. Anne was famished after all the exercise and selected the Lobster Newburg. As the others placed their selections, she gulped her iced tea.

"Nothing like a game of tennis to make iced tea taste so good," she commented turning her attention back to Wes. "You mentioned someone named Bedford. I think I met the Bedfords yesterday when I was here. They seemed nice."

"Jerry was our president. His wife, Darlene, heads up a lot of our committees and such," Bertie said.

"I also met a woman named Nordstrom. She was not overly pleasant."

Bertie snorted. "Lynne Nordstrom. Her husband is our current president. He was just elected six months ago. She seems to think that being his wife gives her the right to try and influence policy. She's incredibly power hungry and very opinionated."

"I swear that if she runs for president and wins, I'll drop my membership," Jen added.

Anne homed her gaze in on Bertie's husband. "Is he a good leader for the Club?"

"He likes to give orders for sure," Wes said. "He's good with the money end of things, but has no people or communications skills. Rubs some the wrong way. Likes to delegate issues he doesn't want to deal with to others, and then doesn't follow up."

His wife frowned. "Wonderful way to talk up the club to prospective members, dear."

"Oh! That's just my opinion. All in all Sam is very, ah, efficient."

Bertie cleared her throat. "So how do the two of you know Ellie Campion?"

"She's a member of our writers group, the Southeast Florida chapter of the Writers Association of America," Jen explained. "She's also our critique partner."

Wes turned toward Anne. "What is it exactly that you write?"

"Romance for the most part," Anne replied.

"Oh." He stared blankly.

Anne shot a glance toward Jen. They were accustomed to getting that reaction.

"Ellie has a lot of potential," Jen hastened to add.

"Well, she plays an excellent hand of bridge." Bertie eyed Anne. "Do you play?"

"I can, but to be honest, just never liked it that much. Some people can be cutthroat about it."

"I never had the patience to even learn the game."

Jen made a face. “All that bidding confused me.”

“Tell us a little about yourself, Anne,” Bertie said.

Anne spent the next few minutes telling them about Gil, her kids, and her work.

A man clutching a glass of amber liquid stopped by the table as she finished. “Well, well, the Canfields and Mrs. Swanson. So nice to see you. I don’t believe I’ve had the pleasure of meeting this lady,” he said staring at Anne.

“This is Anne Jamieson. Anne, meet Sam Nordstrom, the Club president.” Jen went into the she-might-be-joining spiel.

“Excellent, excellent. Mind if I join you?”

Without waiting for a reply, he signaled a waiter for another chair while the others scooted closer together.

Anne shot a look at Jen who shrugged. He was as pushy as his wife was abrasive.

Seated, Sam turned a smarmy smile on Anne. “What makes you want to join us?”

It was an odd question. However, before she could answer their food arrived. For the next few minutes, she sampled her Lobster Newburg as the rest made small talk. If she thought Sam Nordstrom would forget he’d asked her a question or have the good taste to leave, she was mistaken. To her displeasure, the man’s wife, Lynne, appeared and stood behind him with a frown on her face.

“Hello, dear. Pull up a chair,” he said.

“Can’t. I’m due on the first tee in a few minutes.”

Anne took the brief respite to eat more of her excellent lunch. It was perfection, but she wasn’t given much time to enjoy it.

Sam shrugged and turned his attention back to Anne. "Now where was I? Oh, yes. Why do you want to join the San Sebastian Country Club, Ms. Jamieson?"

"Well, my fiancé plays golf and I like tennis. Plus Jen and Carl are members. Jen often mentions the club, so I decided to take advantage of a few of the amenities as her guest to see if it's what we want."

He frowned as if that wasn't what he wanted to hear.

Before he could say anything, his wife commented, "I hope you make up your minds soon. We have a limit of four visits per guest in a year."

Nordstrum waved his hand. "Nonsense, Lynne. That's not important. Have you considered our trial membership?"

"Trial membership?" Jen asked. "What's that?"

"We instated it a couple of months ago. For a small fee, prospective members can try us on for size, so to speak, for a month. In addition to golf and tennis, there are indoor and outdoor pools, Jacuzzis, and a fitness center. It's not huge, but seems to go over big with members."

Anne heaved a sigh. "That sounds like a good idea. Um, how much is the fee?"

Nordstrum quoted a price that sounded a bit above "ouch", yet below "breaking-the-bank."

"I see. Well, let me talk to my fiancé and see what he says."

"And what does your fiancé do for a living?" Lynne asked.

Anne took another bite of food, then smiled and decided to let them both have it right between the eyes. "He's a homicide detective with the San Sebastian

Police Department."

Wes jerked and stared. Bertie drew in a sharp breath. Jen grinned. Other than raising his eyebrows, Sam's expression didn't change. Lynne's nostrils flared.

"How interesting. I don't believe we've ever had a police officer as a member before," he said.

Anne kept her smile in place and bit her tongue. His tone suggested that accepting a policeman as a member lowered the club standards.

"Maybe he'll be the one to solve Barbara Lassiter's murder. That would certainly add to the club's image," Jen said with a saccharine sweet smile.

Sam turned a hard stare onto her. "Lynne told me how you had invited Candace Warren here as a guest. That would most certainly not enhance the image of the club." He drained his glass, pushed back his chair and rose. "Now if you'll excuse me, I have some club business to attend to."

"Bastard," Jen muttered as he strode from the dining room with Lynne right behind him.

"Well, inviting Candace Warren here was a bit out of line, Jen," Bertie said.

"Maybe," her husband replied. "But I'm sorry you had to hear any of that, Anne. As I said, he has no people skills."

"His wife doesn't seem to either," Anne replied. "I wonder how he got elected president."

Wes shook his head. "He plays a lot of golf and volunteers for quite a few events. Plus he was treasurer and has been a member for years. I'm sure you and your fiancé would be assets to the club."

Anne ate the rest of her lunch while the Canfields

discussed the club and its advantages in an effort to sell her on the idea of a membership. She made all the appropriate responses, but didn't really listen. Jen was also unusually silent.

A short time later, she and Jen left the terrace and parted company with Bertie and Wes.

"Lord, thank goodness that's over," Jen said heaving a huge sigh. "And the sad part is I don't think we gleaned any kind of information."

Anne shrugged. "Wes seemed to think Barbara was okay and the women who didn't like her were simply jealous. Said he often partnered with her for club tennis tournaments and intimated he hung out with her and Missy in the bar."

Jen snorted. "Wes Canfield is dull as ditch water and wouldn't have the guts to have an affair with either of them—assuming they were interested. I suppose even *they* must have standards. Besides, Bertie keeps him on a tight leash."

"Sometimes leashes are slipped. And all the while you and the tennis guy were talking Wes was ogling some babe sipping a mimosa not far away. I didn't know the club had so many amenities. I mean real ones, not just good-looking brunettes."

"I didn't know the club had a trial membership. Guess I should read the newsletter once in a while. I suppose it is a way to bring in a bit more money. You going to do the trial thing?"

"I may. It would certainly get me in the front door for a while."

"Well, if you want, I'll sign the sponsorship papers to get the ball rolling."

"Thanks, Jen. Do you ever use the pools or the

gym?

Her friend shook her head. “We have a pool at home and a treadmill along with some free weights in the bonus room.”

“I wonder if I get my money back if I decided not to join.”

“Probably not, but it may be applied to your membership fees if you do.”

“I’ll be eating hamburger for months if I do the trial thing,” Anne replied in a dry tone.

“I can help out. You can pay me back later,” Jen offered.

Anne hugged her. “Thanks, but that’s not necessary.”

On the drive home, Anne did some quick mental math. A trial membership would put a hefty dent into her checking account. On the other hand, if she didn’t join her access to the people who knew both Barbara and Missy would be nonexistent.

Then her logical mind stepped up. *I wonder if I can write a couple of scenes set in the country club into a future work in progress, and then deduct the fee as a business expense on my taxes. I’ll talk to Gil. Maybe he would like to go halfsies with me. He might actually like the club.*

On the other hand, he might object to spending that kind of money just so she could play detective again. *For all I know, he hates golf and tennis. I’ll tackle him about it tonight at dinner.*

****

“I think it’s a terrible idea and a disgusting waste of money,” Gil said emphatically as they waited for their cocktails to arrive.

Anne had broached the subject of the trial membership as soon as the server had left.

"So, I take it you aren't interested in golf or tennis?"

"I've swung both a golf club and a tennis racket in my time, but never got a whole lot of pleasure out of it."

"But it's the only way I have to legitimately ask members questions."

"You don't need to ask members any questions. That's my job." His tone turned testy.

"And exactly what questions will you ask? And of whom? I met the tennis pro today and he definitely didn't want to discuss Barbara Lassiter."

Gil sighed. "Anne, one of these days sleuthing will get you killed. You're an amateur playing in a pro game. You didn't even know the victim."

"But I know Candace. And may I remind you she and I found the body? Plus Missy accused both of us of killing Barbara. That kind of makes it my business."

She wanted to scream in frustration. Didn't he understand that in all of the cases she and the Snoop Group had helped solve they'd been helpful to the police? Or did he understand and was just ignoring her?

"Is this negative attitude new because we're now engaged?" Anne demanded.

"Partially. I just can't help but think how you've put *yourself* in danger every time you guys help out. You might not be so lucky next time." His hard expression softened as he placed his hand over hers. "Honey, I'm not sure I could stand losing you."

Anne blinked tears from her eyes. "Gil, I love you. You're not going to lose me. I promise. But I want to help. Candace is a friend who's been through a rough time."

"She's also a convicted killer."

"She was also acting under the influence. I don't think she meant to kill Dorie that night. It just happened."

"And she tried to kill you," he insisted.

"Not really. Well, all right, the thought may have crossed her mind," she amended as his expression changed from stern to an outright scowl. "But I never could bring myself to think of her in that term—'convicted killer.' I don't think she killed Barbara either. Do you?"

"She had the motive and the opportunity. And I shouldn't be discussing any of this with you. It's an open investigation."

"But you are discussing it."

His expression clearly showed a level of frustration equal to Anne's.

Their drinks arrived and they took a moment to order their meal. When the waiter left, she decided to take another tack. "I assume you've searched Barbara's house by now. Did you find anything helpful?"

"Not much. We're pulling credit card receipts along with phone and financial records." He sat back and stared. "You're going to take out that trial membership, aren't you, in spite of my objections?"

Anne looked him straight in the eye. "Yes."

Gil sighed and shook his head. "Just please be careful. And report all conversations to me, is that clear?"

"As a bell."

"Isn't that a cliché?" he asked with a smile.

"Yes, it is. Guess some of my profession has rubbed off on you, too," she replied with a chuckle.

"Now, can we discuss wedding plans instead of murder?"

Now that she had gotten her way, Anne's mood improved to downright playful. Slipping off her sandal, she rubbed her bare foot up Gil's leg to his thigh.

He jerked upright and grabbed her ankle before she got to his crotch.

"Behave yourself."

"Nobody can see. The tablecloth hides everything."

She tried to inch along his thigh, but his grip tightened as he gently pushed her foot in the opposite direction.

He drew in a ragged breath. "Can you contain yourself until after dinner?"

She pushed her lips out in a faux pout and pulled her foot away. "Oh, if you insist. But let's eat fast."

Gil chuckled. "Your place or mine?"

"Definitely yours."

Anne leaned her chin on her hand and gave him a look that she hoped promised something better than dessert.

At his house, they made their way to the bedroom. Clothing hit the floor.

Gil ran his hands up and down her torso from chest to hips stopping occasionally to caress her breasts. A light pinch had her nipples hardening.

She drew in a ragged breath and slid her hand around his erection, stroking softly. Both of them groaned and sank onto the bed. Hands kneaded. Lips glided across skin. Teeth nipped—sometimes gently, sometimes not.

As Gil nestled between her legs, Anne drifted in a sea of pleasure. Wave after wave of heat washed over her. She wanted him now and forever.

He obliged by sliding into her warmth. A pause, and then they began the age-old motion that never changed. Her legs tightened around his waist. Their bodies continued rocking and thrusting harder and harder as the passion grew. The fires built and burned hotter until finally exploding with an intensity that left her breathless.

As Gil rolled onto his side, she slipped her hand into his. He squeezed. She squeezed back with a satiated sigh.

"I love you," he whispered.

"And I love you."

They needed no other words.

****

Ellie called the next morning before Anne had finished her second cup of coffee.

"Anne, I don't know if this is relevant, but I subbed in a bridge group yesterday afternoon. One of the women was a former member of the country club, so I asked a few discreet questions about Barbara and Missy. You know, making comments about how awful it must have been to know a murder victim and all that. The conversation was interesting, to say the least."

"Oh? Who was the woman and how interesting?"

"Her name was Gloria Townsend, and she had little nice to say about either Barbara or Missy. They always had guests at the club, both men and women. All young, all good-looking. They'd congregate in the bar or around the pool."

"That doesn't sound out of the ordinary. Members

can invite anyone they want provided it's not too often. I think the visitations are limited to four a year or something along those lines."

"I know, but according to this Gloria, that rule was often overlooked by Jerry Bedford and now by Sam Nordstrum. She also said that Barbara had no problem coming on to men at the club even when their wives were present. And while Missy may have flirted a bit that was apparently as far as it went. The whole bar and pool scene was nothing more than an enormous meet and greet."

So, the shapely younger women received special treatment where guests were concerned.

"I'm not surprised," Anne replied. "Anything else?"

"When Gloria complained to Jerry, she got the brush off, so when Sam Nordstrum was installed as president, she went to him. Same thing. She claims the last straw was when one of Missy's friends got Gloria's husband drunk and laid a big, fat wet one on his lips with Gloria watching. She and her husband didn't renew their membership this year."

"Thanks for the update, Ellie. It's looking more and more like the entire female membership of the San Sebastian Country Club had reason to kill Barbara or Missy or both."

"I'm glad I could help in some way."

Anne hung up and thought about this new information.

I wonder if this Gloria's husband took a kiss to the next level. And how angry would she be if he did.

Chapter Eight

Saturday proved to be a huge bust. Gil had to cancel their intended cookout at his place when a new case landed on his desk. Anne tried to work, but the people at the country club refused to leave her mind.

The more she had listened to comments from members, the more she learned that Barbara was generally hated. Missy was an irritant to many, but so far, there was no evidence she generated the loathing her friend did, which meant Missy wasn't likely the target.

"Jerry and Darlene Bedford, Roberta and Wes Canfield, the tennis pro and Lord only knows who else could have done it," she murmured out loud.

She needed another sounding board. A call to Rose sounded like a good idea.

"I'm not sure what to tell you," Rose said. "From what you've been told, it appears Missy and Barbara managed to create havoc wherever they went. And I wouldn't count Missy out of the equation so fast. She just might have been more discreet than her friend."

"So, Missy may have put the moves on a husband…"

"Who responded," Rose added.

"Who responded, felt remorse, and confessed to an irate wife who in turn decides to kill the other woman, only mistakes Barbara for Missy. Yeah, I can see that."

She then told Rose about her tennis game with Jen and the Canfields.

"Do you think either of them could have done it?"

"I don't know. Wes gives the appearance of being kind of clueless, but Roberta seems to know what's what. Jen says she keeps him close to home."

"Every hour of every day?"

"Good point," Anne agreed. "I also met the current president, Sam Nordstrum. Jen's right, he's a jerk, but he did tell me about this trial membership thing."

"Trial membership?"

She explained how it worked. "I think I'm going to do it. How else can I question suspects?"

"Well, just be careful."

"I don't intend to put myself in danger."

"You've said that before. Let me make a few calls. I know a couple of people who are members. I can always ask questions on the excuse that Jack and I are thinking of applying for a membership." A cry in the background signaled the conversation was about to end. "Sorry, the baby just woke up. I'll talk to you later."

Anne hung up and contemplated her next move. In spite of Gil's objections, she saw no other choice than to join the country club on a temporary basis. Not only would it gain her access to possible information, but she also liked the idea of the whole atmosphere—a place to exercise and dine amidst friends.

Anne spent the next day, Sunday, working on her book and lazing around the house. Ken and Lisa had joined some friends for a trip to a nearby state park and wouldn't be back until late. Gil had driven up to Jacksonville to attend a conference on Monday. He'd be back sometime tomorrow night, but the next couple of days loomed long and boring without him.

Rose called in the late afternoon.

"I talked to my friends about the club. Bill and Midge Holman have been members for three or four years. Midge said she'd never heard of Barbara Lassiter or Missy Warren. I have the impression the Holmans play golf and golf only. I had better luck with Joanne Randolph. She didn't much care for either Barbara or Missy. Called Missy a homewrecker. I assumed she referred to Candace's marriage. At any rate, she says the friends Missy brought to the club were—how did she put it—subtle sluts."

"What does that mean?" Anne recalled Ellie's information about someone else calling Barbara a serial whore.

"I'm not sure, but I think a lot of flirting and sexual innuendo combined with booze in the bar entered into it."

"Did anyone mention Barbara's ex-husband, Drew Lassiter?"

"Yeah, Joanne said he was good-looking with a killer smile. Also said he spent a lot of time with the guys in the bar and on the golf course."

"So he may not have been aware of his wife's antics. I need to ask Gil if he knows where he is now."

"I didn't think to ask questions about him," Rose said.

"Probably doesn't make any difference anyway."

"Wish I had more to tell you, but if you want my opinion, I think Barbara and Missy were up to no good. Anybody who garners that kind of animosity is a candidate for shady business of some sort."

"You could be right. Thanks for helping. I'll talk to

you again later. I'm going to take out that trial membership tomorrow."

Anne disconnected and sighed. Few liked Missy and most hated Barbara. With that last thought on the subject, she pulled some chicken breasts out of the fridge and got down to the job of making dinner for when the kids returned home.

Dinner was easy, but thoughts on who killed Barbara Lassiter were more problematic.

****

Monday dawned with rain and a forecast of more to come. She finally called Jen shortly after noon. "I'm taking out that trial membership."

"Good. Want to do it now? Carl left today for a seminar in Dallas and I'm at loose ends."

"I've got a few things to do this afternoon. Want to have dinner there? Gil is at some conference, and the kids know how to order in."

"Sounds good to me. My kids know the number of the nearest pizza place, too. I've got an idea. Suppose we meet there around five and scope out the fitness center? I have it on good authority that Barbara and Missy spent a lot of time in there. Maybe we can pry some information out of whoever's in charge."

"Good idea. Meet you in the lobby at five."

"Don't forget your swimsuit. We'll finish off in the pool and hot tub."

Anne hung up and tapped her finger on her lips. Her mind envisioned Barbara and Missy crushing bowling balls with their thighs, using the Stairmaster without breaking a sweat, and giggling at the less than perfect bodies of everyone else in the place.

"Bitches," she said out loud.

Shaking her head, Anne headed upstairs to her office where she made a quick call to Candace to bring her up to date.

"How are you doing?"

"Not bad, considering. I haven't heard any more from the police. My lawyer called earlier with the news that Missy and Eric have been served with an injunction to stop bad-mouthing me, and I haven't seen a reporter in days. How about you?"

Anne told her of the decision to take out a trial membership.

"Actually, the trial membership thing sounds like a winner. If I recall, Sam had good ideas, but didn't always follow through. Are you seriously considering joining on a permanent basis?"

"Probably not, but it gives me an excuse to nose around. What can you tell me about the Nordstrums? Jen seemed to think the wife didn't have many friends."

"Lynne is one of those people who has an opinion about everything and isn't afraid to share it. She's not what you'd call warm and cuddly."

Anne recalled the abrasiveness of the woman in front of strangers when she'd spoken to Jen.

"How about the tennis and golf pros?"

"Adam Jefferies and Ted Saunders? I didn't play much tennis, so I'm not sure about Adam, but I took several lessons from Ted Saunders. He's a nice guy. Married—or at least he was when I knew him. Seems to me he had a couple of kids."

"Jen and I are going to check out the fitness center. I heard Barbara and Missy were regulars."

"Can't tell you anything about it. That's one place I avoided like the plague. I don't like sweating and I'm lazy," Candace said with a chuckle.

"Well, I'm glad you seem in better spirits."

"I am. So much so, in fact, that I'm thinking of checking out tomorrow and moving back to the San Sebastian Inn. And this time I'll inform my attorney and Gil."

"Good girl. I'll call you with how our workout goes and what new information we can uncover."

Anne hung up and refocused on her work in progress. With any luck, she might get that chapter finished and have her heroine find another body.

Four hours later, she shut down her computer satisfied that the story was progressing the way she wanted.

Now what do I wear to the fitness center?

She shifted through her drawers before finally finding a pair of loose shorts, a sports bra, a tank top, and running shoes. Anne stuffed them into a tote bag along with her swimsuit, flip-flops, and a towel, then dressed in a skirt and blouse to look presentable for applying for membership—even a temporary one.

"Okay, kids, I'm off," she called out as she came downstairs. "There's money on the hall table for whatever you order in. Do any homework you have and I'll see you later."

"Have a good time, Mom," Lisa replied.

"Get all fit and trim," Ken added.

"Sore and half-crippled is more likely."

"Shame this membership doesn't include us. I could use a little time lounging around a pool," Lisa said with raised eyebrows.

"I'll check into that if and when I go whole hog on this thing."

Fifteen minutes later she pulled up under the canopy and handed her car keys over to the valet. Jen met her inside.

"So, are you all ready to become a member of the San Sebastian Country Club?"

"As ready as I'll ever be, I suppose—at least on a temporary basis."

The whole process was relatively painless, until it came time to write the check. Anne's hand trembled slightly as she wrote. *This is a hell of a lot of money to spend for a murder investigation.* She did it anyway.

"Thank you, Ms. Jamieson," the club secretary said. "Welcome and if you have any questions, please feel free to ask."

"Well, I was wondering if I could see the fitness center. Maybe get in a little workout before dinner."

"Certainly. Let me call down to Bobby Lanier. He's our fitness guru, so to speak. He can show you the equipment and such."

"I can show her the way," Jen offered.

"Do you know the way?" Anne asked.

"I know the way to the locker room. The pool, hot tub, and gym are nearby. Not even I can get lost."

Jen led her off down a hallway, into the lobby area, down another corridor, and then through a pair of large double doors. Anne instantly inhaled the odors of chlorine and disinfectant.

"The pool and hot tub are through those doors," Jen said indicating another set of glass doors. The blue water of the pool gently lapped at the sides of the gunite and tile. "There are racquetball courts down that hallway. The women's locker room is through here." Jen opened a door.

For a locker room, it wasn't bad. Rows of lockers lined two of the walls. The toilets, sinks, and an area for blow drying hair were through an archway to her right. The showers were to her left. It took only a few minutes to change into workout gear.

"Well, let's get this road on the show," Jen misquoted with a grin.

"Ladies, my name is Bobby. Welcome," a lean, but heavily muscled man said as they entered the fitness center.

"Thank you. I'm Anne Jamieson, and I just took out a trial membership."

"Good idea. Get an idea of what to expect before shelling out for an entire year."

"I'm Jennifer Swanson. My husband and I are members, but I have to confess, I've never used this facility before."

"Well, let me show you around."

The room had the usual complement of stationary bikes, treadmills, stair-steppers, free weights, and machines Anne assumed were designed more as instruments of torture than anything else.

Bobby showed them how to adjust the weight of each machine and the proper way to use them.

"Oh my God," Anne groaned as she ended her reps on the ab machine before moving on to the seated leg curls. "I'm expecting instant results with this one."

"A few months of this and I should be able to crush beer cans between my biceps and forearm," Jen replied. "I feel like a wimp with only ten pounds on the bicep machine."

Bobby laughed. "Don't worry. It gets better the more you do it."

Anne decided it was time to probe. "I imagine there are some members who look like gods."

"Or goddesses," Jen added. "Do you have many women taking advantage of this?"

"Oh, yes. Younger women want to look good in their bikinis and older women want to keep in shape, too."

"I'll bet Missy Warren is in here all the time," Anne ventured between grunts as she hefted twenty pounds on the leg curl. Her thighs burned.

"Just about every morning," the guru answered. "She and Barbara Lassiter were workout buddies. Never missed a session."

"Boy, I was sure surprised about Barbara." Jen pulled down on some contraption designed to tone the shoulders.

"Same here," Bobby agreed with a guarded look on his face.

"Wasn't that the one who was murdered?" Anne asked. She headed for the leg press machine.

"Yes, she and Missy were great friends," Jen replied for effect. "Did she and Missy have regular workouts with other friends?"

Bobby shot her a sharp glance and frowned. "I really couldn't say. She and Mrs. Warren often stopped to rest during their routines to chat with other members. This is a country club, after all. Being sociable is part of the atmosphere."

Anne huffed and puffed as she pushed the weights on the leg press. "Well, I've heard enough gossip to suggest that Barbara wasn't liked all that well by some people. She was young, beautiful, and divorced. Must have given more than one middle-aged married woman a sense of unease."

"If a middle-aged man is the subject of attention from a young woman, then I'm sure there's a smidgeon of misinterpretation," Jen added.

"I don't listen to gossip." Bobby looked at his watch. "I have a client due in a few minutes for some personal training. Think you can cope with the bikes and the treadmills on your own?"

"Sure, no problem, and thanks again. I'll be back," Anne assured him.

He nodded and left quickly.

"Well, that was abrupt." Jen stared after him.

"He didn't want to talk about Barbara or Missy, that's a fact. Nobody around here does."

"I think those two hit on anything male that came along. Now that Barbara is dead, no one will admit to what may or may not have been going on. Self-preservation, I guess. Wanna give the treadmills a try?"

Anne shook her head. "Not me. I don't like treadmills. I'll do the bike instead."

"Treadmills are no big deal. You can set the speed for whatever you want."

"No way. They scare the crap out of me."

"Scare you?" Jen said with a laugh. "I've never heard of anyone afraid of a treadmill before. What's so scary?"

"If you must know, I have this fear that I'll trip over my own two feet, fall face down, shoot backwards into the aisle where some little old lady walking by trips over my prone body and breaks a hip. Then I get sued."

Jen laughed harder. In a few seconds, Anne laughed with her. It was a silly fear, but everybody had at least one.

In the end, Jen chose the treadmill while Anne pedaled fast and furious to nowhere for the next thirty minutes.

"Okay, I'm whipped," she said wiping sweat from her forehead as she got off the bike.

"Me, too. It's almost seven-thirty. Let's hit the pool, the hot tub, and then the showers before we have a go at dinner."

"Sounds like a plan to me. I'll probably eat like the old proverbial horse."

They exited the fitness center and headed for the locker room. Anne admitted her entire body was telling her she needed to do this more often. She also noticed that neither Bobby nor his client were anywhere in sight.

Obviously an excuse to leave. *Our questions and comments must have made him nervous. Had he been involved with either Missy or Barbara on a personal level?*

Jen pulled open the door to the locker room and literally ran into Lynne Nordstrom.

"Oh, Lynne, I'm so sorry."

The other woman backed away with an annoyed expression. "Maybe you shouldn't be in such a hurry."

"I didn't think I was in a rush. It might be a good idea to do away with the frosted glass. That way accidents can be avoided," Jen retorted.

Lynne shifted her gaze to Anne, and then back to Jen. "I really must protest on the way you impose on the club rules concerning guests."

"*Your husband* assured me the other day that it was inconsequential."

"Well, it isn't, nor should it be."

Jen arched an eyebrow. "Yeah? Well, he's the president, not you."

Anne quickly jumped in. "No rules have been broken, Mrs. Nordstrum. On your husband's advice I took out a trial membership earlier today."

"I see. In that case, I hope you enjoy the experience."

Jen eyed the woman and her tote bag. A pair of shorts peeked out from under a couple of running shoes. "I was just showing Anne the gym. We didn't see you in there."

Lynne frowned and shifted the bag higher on her shoulder. "I was playing racquetball and decided to unwind in the sauna before taking a shower. Now, if you'll excuse me, I'm due to meet Sam in the dining room."

Anne noted the woman wore a nice skirt and top. "We'll probably see you there, but right now we're going to check out the pool and hot tub."

Lynne gave a short, jerky nod and moved past them.

"Whew, the personality of a prickly pear," Anne said.

"She was always overbearing, but it's gotten worse since Sam became club president. She's suddenly become a stickler for rules and regulations. Sometimes I think she has the impression she's running the show."

"I remember you saying something about canceling your membership if she became president."

"I would, too. She's incredibly judgmental and narrow-minded. Her comments to me the other day about inviting Candace as my guest prove that."

"Does she have any friends here?" Anne asked.

"A few of the older set."

"I wonder who her partner was for racquetball."

Jen shrugged. "I didn't know she played, and theoretically, racquetball doesn't require a partner. You can serve the ball to yourself. I've seen plenty of people do it. Now, let's hit that pool and hot tub."

She and Jen quickly changed into their swimsuits and made a beeline for the pool.

Anne opened the door to the indoor pool area and let her gaze wander from one end to the other.

"It's deserted. We're the only ones here," she said as Jen joined her.

"I'm not surprised. It's almost eight. Any water aerobic classes are done for the day and most members have gone home. Not even the lifeguards are on duty. Besides, the weather sucks. People either didn't bother to come in today or left early."

"Well, at least you're the only one who'll see my flab. I don't know what it is about a swimming suit that causes a shapely, mostly in-shape woman to suddenly hate her body."

Jen grinned. "Because women are aware of every bump and bulge. Men never get past our chests. And you're not flabby. Come on, let's do some laps, and then relax in the whirlpool." She walked over to a large bin and grabbed a flotation noodle. "I'm a lazy swimmer."

They dropped their beach towels on a bench against the wall. A door marked "Towel Room" was off to the side.

"I see they have towels available, too."

Jen glanced over. "Yeah, they used to be free, but from what I heard they're now charging. My suggestion is to bring your own. The ones here aren't very thick." She turned the knob, but it was locked. "Guess they're closed for the night."

Walking to the steps, Anne tested the water with her foot. The temperature was delightfully warm. Inhaling a deep breath, she used the steps to descend into the water.

She swam the length of the pool and back again five times with a slow easy crawl. Winded, she stood in the shallow end, leaning back against the side of the pool, her arms resting on the tiled coping. Jen had draped the noodle across her shoulders and was idly kicking back and forth.

The warm water combined with all the exercise guaranteed she'd sleep well tonight. Determined to make the most of her time, Anne swam another five laps down and back before heading for the steps. Looking around, she noted Jen had also exited the pool and was replacing the noodle in the bin.

"Don't know about you, but the workout and the laps have just about done me in," Anne said squeezing the water from her hair.

"Same here. Ready for the whirlpool?" Jen asked.

"I could go for some hot, frothing bubbles. Where is it?"

"Over there."

Jen led her to a secluded alcove with a white railing resembling a picket fence separating it from the pool deck. They entered through a gate and draped the towels over the railing.

The lights in the area were turned off, but Anne had no problem hearing the jets gushing air into the water at a high rate of speed. The hot tub was large enough to accommodate at least ten people. At the moment, only one man was sitting on the underwater bench, his chin down almost touching his chest. He looked vaguely familiar, but in the dim light, she didn't recognize him.

"Why the hell are the lights off?" Jen said walking over to flip them on before descending into the warm agitated water. She looked at the man. "Hi, Jerry, mind if we join you?"

Anne descended onto the first step and now recognized Jerry Bedford.

When Jerry didn't answer, Jen waded over and poked him in the shoulder. "Jerry, are you asleep? Wake up. It's not good to fall asleep in the hot tub."

Jerry still didn't answer. Instead, he rolled to the side and fell face-first into the water. Within seconds, the strong jets bobbed his body to the surface.

Jen gasped and backed away.

Anne gripped the handrail and stared. In spite of the hot water, a numbing coldness swept over her.

Jerry Bedford was definitely dead.

Chapter Nine

Jen scrambled for the steps as Anne stared in consternation, the water frothing around her ankles. She climbed out a second later.

Why is it always me?

Standing on the edge of the tub, Jen kept a death grip on the handrail. “Oh, shit! He’s really, really dead. What do we do now?”

“We call nine-one-one and notify the club.”

Jen’s teeth chattered. “Yeah, right, call the cops. Our phones are in the locker room. Let’s get the hell out of here.”

“One of us should stay here with the body.”

“Why? He’s dead!”

“In case someone else comes in and finds him. It would look bad if we weren’t here.”

“Well, it’s not gonna be me. I’ll make the call, you stay here.”

“Fine. I’ll stay with the dead man. You make the call. Hurry!” Her breath came in short, rapids puffs.

Jen nodded and stumbled toward the gate, pushed it open, and ran from the area.

Alone with the late Jerry Bedford, Anne shivered in spite of the heated atmosphere. She grabbed her towel from the railing and wrapped it around her body.

A minute ago the rushing water seemed soothing. Now it sounded like Niagara Falls. The powerful jets pushed the body against one side of the tub where another jet pushed it back. She looked around the small enclosure and saw a panel of buttons next to the light switch. She walked over and pushed the one marked "Off" under the heading of Whirlpool. The noise ceased. A quick glance at the hot tub showed Jerry semi-submerged in the middle.

Anne backed away and through the gate. The comparative silence was even more unnerving than the noise of the bubbles. The lapping of the water against the side of the pool reminded her of footsteps. She scanned the area, but was as alone as before. Time seemed to stand still.

Hurry up, Jen. What's taking so long?

An exhaust fan in the ceiling clicked on. Anne whirled with a gasp, her heart pounding, and then breathed a deep breath.

Get a hold of yourself. It's not like this is an unusual experience for you. You're alone, dummy.

She glanced at the clock on the wall. *Eight-ten? Is that all? Where is Jen?*

In reality, she had no clue how long her friend had been gone.

What a time for Gil to be out of town. She could sure use his strength about now.

She almost screamed when two security guards burst through the doors.

"Lady, are you all right?" one of them asked.

Anne nodded and pointed toward the whirlpool. "I'm fine, but I can't say the same for Mr. Bedford."

Panting, Jen ran into the area, still in her swimming suit.

"Where have you been? You were gone forever."

"Are you kidding? I ran all the way, even into the lobby in my swimsuit. I banged the bell on the desk until my hand was sore. Finally, some guy came. I told him what happened. He called nine-one-one and notified security. It took less than ten minutes." Jen grabbed her towel from the railing and mimicking Anne, wrapped it around her body.

The guards had entered the hot tub area. One of them retrieved a long-handled skimmer from the corner of the enclosure and pulled Jerry to the side. The other man helped heave the body out of the water and laid him face up on the deck. The guard dropped the skimmer, felt for a pulse in Bedford's neck before putting his ear to Bedford's chest.

Anne and Jen ventured closer.

"I can't get a pulse, hear a heartbeat, and there's no sign of breathing. He's dead. I'll try CPR anyway."

Guard number two pulled a radio from his belt and spoke into it.

Anne stared at the man administering the chest compressions on Bedford's body. In checking to see if he was still alive, the security guards had altered the crime scene, assuming there was a crime.

Sam and Lynne Nordstrum rushed into the pool area, along with another man carrying a medical bag.

"Good God, what happened?" Sam demanded.

"Anne and I came in to use the hot tub and saw Jerry. He looked like he was asleep, but when I poked him he fell into the water and didn't move."

"Didn't you try to give him CPR?" Lynne asked in an accusatory tone.

"The guard did. I don't know how," Anne replied.

"Me neither," Jen added.

The doctor who was examining Bedford raised his head. "Wouldn't have mattered. He's gone. Probably for a while. The hot water in the tub likely repressed rigor mortis. Coroner may have trouble fixing the time of death."

"You mean there's nothing anybody can do?" Sam asked.

"Not a thing."

The paramedics now joined the party, along with a couple of policemen and a man in plainclothes Anne assumed was a detective.

"Who are you?" Lynne asked in a sharp voice.

The man smiled. "Detective Frank Roberts. And you are?"

Her husband waved her silent. "I'm Sam Nordstrum, the club president. This is my wife, Lynne. That is Doctor Harold Greene. These ladies are Mrs. Swanson and…I'm sorry, I can't remember your name."

"Jamieson. Anne Jamieson."

"Gil Collins's fiancée?" the detective questioned.

"Yes."

"That's right, he's at that conference up in Jacksonville today, isn't he? Mrs. Swanson, this is Officer Peters. Will you go with him and tell him what happened?

Jen nodded and followed the policeman to the bench along the wall where she began the tale with lots of hand gestures.

"Now, Ms. Jamieson, want to tell me what happened from your point of view?"

"Why are you here?" she asked.

"Because whoever called in the nine-one-one alarm

said someone had been killed. They sent me along to save time if it wasn't an accident. Doesn't look like I'm necessary, but I can still help out by taking your statement."

Anne gave him the story from the time they entered the pool area until when they found the body. By now she knew where to shorten the story and to highlight the pertinent details.

She was just finishing when Jen returned.

Her friend shivered. "Can we go get dressed? I'm freezing."

In spite of the humid atmosphere, Anne was also chilled. *Shock, I guess.* She pulled her towel tighter.

"Yes. We may need to contact you later, but I doubt it."

The doctor approached. "Uh, Detective, there's something here you should see."

As Roberts moved off, Anne and Jen followed. No one stopped them. Sam had moved into the hallway with the security guards while Lynne talked on her phone several yards away from the men.

"What is it, doctor?"

He looked around before answering in a low tone. "Detective, this was no accident. At first, I thought he'd had a heart attack. Can happen if a person stays too long in the hot tub. Then I rolled him over. There's a large bruise at the base of his neck and a severe depression to the occipital bone just above the bruising."

"Could he have slipped and hit his head on the side of the tub or are you suggesting something a bit more sinister?"

"Definitely sinister. No blood anywhere. If he'd

fallen and cracked his head there more than likely would have been bleeding."

"Oh, my God," Jen said with a groan.

Detective Roberts turned. "Ladies, you shouldn't be here."

"But we are, and as I told you, when we found him, he was sitting on the underwater bench with his head bent forward. Somebody had to put him there," Anne insisted.

"Gil said you were good at this kind of thing. Keep this under your hats, all right?" He looked over to the paramedics. "Let's get him to the morgue. Autopsy will help determine time of death, and of course, there may have been other people in here earlier who saw him. Peters, you and Smith get the particulars of next of kin from the club president. As far as anyone knows it looks like a simple heart attack."

"Do you need us downtown to make a statement?" Anne asked.

"No, not right now. You gave me a very detailed statement, but I'll call you back later to make it official. Guess I am necessary now."

"Can we leave?" Jen questioned.

"Yes. Go home."

Neither Anne nor Jen spoke until they were in the locker room.

"Who the hell would want to kill Jerry Bedford?" Jen peeled off her suit and dried the last bit of moisture from her skin.

"You knew him better than I. How about his wife?"

"Darlene? I'm not even sure she knows where the pool is located. And how do you bash in someone's head without leaving a ton of blood?"

"I don't know, but I can attest that both Dorie and Alan Grayson were covered with it."

"Let's get out of here," Jen said. "I don't think dinner in the main dining room is on the agenda, do you?"

"Definitely not. Rafferty's?"

"That's what I was thinking. Simple and we won't know anyone. God, this is a nightmare."

Anne dressed quickly, jammed her gym clothing, towel, and only slightly damp swimsuit into her tote bag in record time.

Something tells me, I won't be taking out a permanent membership anytime soon.

****

It was close to ten o'clock when they got to Rafferty's. The bar was full of patrons watching a baseball game, but the dining room was almost empty. They chose a booth in an out-of-the-way corner. A waiter quickly welcomed them and asked for their drink orders. The reply was two white wines in large glasses.

"Oh Lord, what a night," Jen said with a groan as the man left. "Other than Dorie, I've never seen a violent death before."

"That's right, technically you found Dorie's body before Candace, Nancy, and I did."

"It was a sight I'll never forget, that's for sure. Thank God, there wasn't any blood this time around."

Anne sat back and rubbed her arms. She wasn't sure if the cold was the result of air conditioning or the aftereffects of finding Jerry Bedford.

"And that's odd. What on earth do you hit a person with that can crush his skull, but leave no trace of blood?"

"*And* perhaps kill him with other people nearby. That takes balls."

"Oh, I don't know. If others were swimming, would they notice who was in the hot tub or coming and going from it?" Anne asked.

"I suppose they might not. Would whacking someone in the head make much noise?"

"I have no idea. Would Jerry make any noise—cry out or something?"

Jen frowned. "Might not. If the base of his skull was crushed, he could have died instantly."

"And yet to make sure, the killer may have held his head underwater, then arranged the body to look like he was just sitting there."

"Possibly in full view of other members. Like I said, that took balls."

"I'm still working on the murder weapon," Anne muttered. "For the life of me, I can't imagine what could pack a wallop hard enough to kill, but leave nothing other than a bruise."

"Plus it would have to be something inconspicuous, something Jerry wouldn't be surprised to see if he happened to look up when the killer approached."

"Good point. You know, I never noticed if there were surveillance cameras in the pool area."

"Me neither. In fact, I don't recall seeing cameras anywhere even outside or in the parking lot. Ever. You'd think that would be the thing to do to make members feel safe," Jen said.

"Or maybe some members didn't like being spied on." Anne rubbed her arms again. "I guess we'll have to wait until the autopsy results to know for sure how he died. Are you hungry?"

"As callous as it sounds, yes, I am."

They picked up their menus and read the selections they practically knew by heart. The server arrived with the wine. Anne ordered a Shrimp Po'boy while Jen settled on a Philly Cheesesteak.

"I suppose I should call Rose and Ellie with the news," Anne commented.

"I don't think it needs to be done tonight." Jen hesitated. "I'm not sure how into this Snoop Group thing Ellie is. I mean, she seemed kind of upset that day she met Candace, and I don't think her heart was into asking questions of people."

"Well, she did come up with some information about Barbara and Missy, but I think you're right. I hate to involve her in something she feels uncomfortable doing."

"Should we more or less cut her out of the snooping loop?"

"I'll just give her the basics and tell her she doesn't need to help if she doesn't want to."

"I miss Nancy," Jen admitted. "Her analytical mind would be more than welcome right now."

Anne nodded as she sipped from her glass. Nancy's last email had been over a week ago from somewhere in the Fiji Islands. Her Internet connections were hit and miss in the more remote areas she and Brad had visited. At present, Brad was on the location of an active volcano on a small island in the Solomon's while Nancy had been forced to remain behind. Her friend was antsy and bored, but writing to pass the time.

"I should also warn Candace about this, too," she

said.

"Warn her?"

"This is the second club member to die under mysterious circumstances in less than a week. The media will have a field day with it. Reporters might swarm around her again."

"I never thought of that. Poor Candace can't seem to buy a break even though I doubt if she'd be a suspect in this."

On this point Anne wholeheartedly agreed. Good luck and Candace just didn't go hand in hand.

"I talked to her this morning." She told Jen about the conversation. "In fact, why don't I call her now? Just to give her a heads up."

She fished in her purse, found the phone, and called.

"Hi, Anne, what's up?"

"Uh, Candace, if I were you I wouldn't check out tomorrow."

"Why not?"

"Jerry Bedford was murdered tonight—at the club—in the hot tub."

"What? Oh no, how?"

Anne brought Candace up to date on the situation.

"God Almighty, what's going on anyway?"

"I have no clue, but my intuition suggests it's connected to Barbara Lassiter's murder."

"In what way?"

"I don't know. Just a hunch. How well did you know the Bedfords?"

"Enough to say hello and chat for a while, but Eric and I didn't really chum around with them. Jerry played golf, I think, but Darlene didn't involve herself with the sports angle. She was more into organizing bazaars and raffles—that kind of stuff. I think she played a lot of bridge, too. There are two or three groups who play a couple of times a week."

"What were they like personality-wise?"

"Jerry seemed to be a pleasant sort. You know, smiling, congenial. Darlene was more controlled. She liked being in control, which probably explains why she was so good at the organizing thing."

"Could she have bashed his head in?"

"Darlene? If she wanted to kill him, she sure as hell wouldn't do it in the club hot tub. She'd make certain to do it in the privacy of their home. Then she'd bury the body in the garden and tell everyone he'd left town."

"Candace, I hate to bring this up, but I hope you have an alibi for tonight. The police may want to talk to you."

"Thank God, I was having dinner in the dining room here at the hotel from six-thirty until almost eight. Besides, I'm no longer a member, so how would I get into the club?"

"I see your point. Oh, and don't tell anyone about this, okay? I don't think the police have released the details that he was murdered yet."

"I won't, don't worry," her friend assured her.

"Would you like to do lunch tomorrow?"

"Sounds good. What time and where?"

"How about The City Tavern at noon?"

Candace agreed to meet her there.

"Do you want to join us?" she asked Jen after hanging up.

"Might as well."

"Think I'll ask Rose to come, too." Anne grabbed

her cell again and called, giving Rose the news about Jerry Bedford.

"Good God, another one? What kind of place is this country club, anyway?" Rose asked in a shocked tone.

"Not the best of recruitment resumes, is it? Candace, Jen, and I are meeting for lunch tomorrow. Want to come along?

"Sure, I can drop Graham and Adam at Mothers Day Out while the rest are in school."

Anne gave her the time and place before hanging up. "She's good to go."

"What did Candace have to say about Jerry and Darlene?"

Anne relayed the information.

"That sounds close. Jerry was just a nice guy who liked most people. He was a popular club president. Darlene preferred to do her own thing. Seems to me she was also a little OCD. Had to have the same table in the dining room, sit in the same chaise out by the pool, that kind of thing. Almost territorial if you get my drift—*my* table, *my* chair."

"Wonder how she'll take her husband's death? She struck me as a bit standoffish when I met her the other day."

Jen shrugged. "She'll be controlled, almost uncaring, in public, but probably cry her eyes out at home. A lot of people are like that."

Their food arrived and for the next few minutes they concentrated on eating.

"Anne, why did you tell Candace to keep the fact Jerry was murdered to herself?"

"Well, it wasn't obvious that he was murdered. No

gunshot or knife wounds. No blood splashed about. And if we hadn't been there to overhear the doctor, we would have assumed it was a tragic accident."

"True enough, but the truth will come out as soon as the autopsy is done."

"But autopsy results can take days, even weeks if drugs are involved. Keeping it under wraps for even a few days gives the police a chance to investigate before people start lawyering up."

"Or suspecting *they* might be suspects. You know, Sam and Lynne weren't around when the doctor told us about the crushed skull, so my guess is they think it was natural causes, too. Shame Gil is out of town for this one."

"I'm sure he'll be brought up to date tomorrow morning at the station, and then get in touch with me."

Anne finished her sandwich, drank her remaining wine, and glanced at her watch. It was going on eleven o'clock. Time to get home and in bed. She hoped Gil would have more details. And she had the nagging suspicion the murders of Barbara Lassiter and Jerry Bedford were connected, although in what way was still a mystery.

Because of the gossip I heard concerning Barbara and Jerry having had an affair? All I have to do is figure out how—and who may have killed them.

****

Anne sat at the kitchen table, cell phone nearby, waiting for Gil to call. It was nine o'clock. Surely, he was or soon would be at the police station. Someone was bound to tell him of last night's events.

The call came in twenty minutes later.

"Hi, Gil. How was the seminar?"

"It was okay. Wanna tell me about what happened?"

She gave him the whole story, including the speculations she and Jen had discussed at dinner.

"So, do you have any more details?" she asked when finished.

"No. Detective Roberts gave me the report this morning. He said you knew Bedford didn't die a natural death."

"Does anybody else know besides him, the doctor, the paramedics, and Jen and me?"

"He specifically told them to keep it quiet until he could see if there are any surveillance tapes or witnesses. The autopsy will be done today, but the results will be held a bit longer."

"Jen and I discussed surveillance cameras last night Jen seems to think there aren't any *anywhere* in the club. Gil, do you or Detective Roberts have an idea about the murder weapon? Jen and I almost went nuts last night trying to figure it out."

"Don't know yet. I'll ask Frank to keep me abreast of things since Bedford was a member of the country club, too. After all, it is his case. First Barbara Lassiter and now Jerry Bedford. I don't like coincidences, especially in view of the rumors you heard about the two of them having an affair. I may tag along with him when he questions Mrs. Bedford."

Anne told him about her conversation with Candace regarding the Bedfords.

"Mrs. Warren will probably be interrogated by Frank, too. And before you get huffy, we have to cover all the bases. You know that."

"I wasn't getting huffy and I understand. So does

Candace. Jen, Rose, and I are having lunch with her at The City Tavern at noon. You're welcome to come along if you want. Kind of give you a chance to get a leg up on your end of the investigations."

"I'll think about it. I've got a lot to do today. Dinner tomorrow night?"

"Sure. Would you like to go to the club? Give you a chance to see the scene of the latest crime."

"I'll think about that, too. I've got to go, honey. I'll talk to you later."

She hung up none the wiser about Jerry Bedford's death or the investigation. She wondered if Gil would show up for lunch.

I hope so. I need my fix of Gil Collins.

Anne also needed answers. She may have taken out a membership in the Country Club of Death.

And who will be the next victim?

Chapter Ten

Anne met Candace at The City Tavern a few minutes after noon. No one else had appeared yet.

"Jen and Rose said they'd come, too," she told her as they took their seats at a table.

Candace took a deep breath. "Good. I'm looking forward to seeing Jen—and Rose."

"I haven't seen Rose since critique last week."

"Is her husband still a jerk?"

"He's coming around. She gave him an ultimatum after the last baby—either do his fair share around the house or no nookie," Anne said.

Candace grinned. "And is it working?"

"To a certain extent. It's a whole new world for him."

"Which—the no nookie or changing a diaper?"

"Probably both."

"I just hope Rose can find some time for herself."

"Rose's life is full steam ahead with five kids and her writing. I'm surprised she can breathe."

"How well I remember. And she writes erotic romance in the bargain. Might explain the five kids."

Anne chuckled, and then waved as Rose walked in. She quickly joined them.

"Candace, good to see you again. How are you holding up?"

"As well as expected, I guess."

“I think it’s only fair to warn you that I invited Gil to join us,” Anne admitted.

Candace shrugged and smiled. “That’s fine. For once I can prove where I was at the time of a murder. In fact, I have to meet with a Detective Roberts at the police station at three o’clock. He called early this morning.”

“I’m sure it’s all just routine,” Rose said in a soothing voice.

“Are you still at the resort under my name?” Anne asked.

“As of now. So far no reporters have tracked me down.”

“If the police don’t release the information that it was murder, then the reporters may not connect the dots. It’ll simply be a case of a man dying of a heart attack at the country club. I’m not even sure the country club was mentioned with Barbara Lassiter’s death, although thanks to me, they did show up there to harass Eric and Missy the other night.”

Candace heaved a sigh. “Lord, I hope they don’t make the connection.”

“I can’t see reporters being interested in a supposed heart attack death at the San Sebastian Country Club,” Rose added with a nod.

“I may go back to the Inn tonight. Of course, then I’d run the chance of seeing Eric and Missy. On the other hand, that could be fun if seeing me irritates them as much as seeing *them* irritates *me*.”

Rose laughed. “I’d love to bug the hell out of them.”

Jen rushed up and pulled out a chair. “Sorry, I’m late, but parking downtown is a pain in the ass. Hi,

Rose, Candace. How are you getting along through all of this?"

"Pretty well. Gil might be joining us also."

Jen shot her a surprised look. "Really? Is Candace a suspect for this one, too?"

Candace held up her hand and shook her head. "I swear I was nowhere near the country club last night. I had dinner in the hotel dining room and I'm sure my credit card receipts can bear that out."

"Ladies," Gil said standing behind the remaining chair.

Anne jerked her head in his direction surprised that she hadn't seen him enter the restaurant.

"Have a seat," she said.

He sat, and then nodded to the others. "Mrs. Bennett, Mrs. Swanson, Mrs. Warren, it's good to see you again."

"I thought we were past all that Missus stuff. I'm Jen."

"And I'm Rose."

"And two Mrs. Warren's is one too many. Just call me Candace."

The waiter arrived at the table. Everyone ordered iced tea and picked up menus.

"Any news about Jerry Bedford?" Anne asked getting to the point.

"Nothing you don't already know," he replied shooting Candace a look.

"You don't have to be discreet. Anne's already told me what happened. And for the record, I can prove where I was last night at the time of the murder. I'm going to give my statement to Detective Roberts later this afternoon."

Gil gave Anne an exasperated look. "I see you had no problem ignoring the order not to discuss the case."

"Oh, come on, it's the Snoop Group. Did you really expect me not to?"

"Did you talk to Jerry's wife, Darlene?" Jen questioned as she closed the menu.

"I didn't, but Frank did. He says she was shocked and couldn't understand why anyone would want to harm her husband."

"Shocked, but not grief stricken?" Anne asked.

"Trust me, Darlene isn't the sort to display her emotions," Jen interjected.

Gil continued. "She also stated that she was at the club at the time, too, but had left for home around seven-thirty."

"So they drove separately?" Anne said.

"According to her, she was playing bridge from one until four-thirty in the afternoon, and then stayed to chat with some friends in the lounge. Her husband arrived around five forty-five after work, stopped by to say hello to everyone, and then went on to use the gym. That's the last anyone saw of him."

"Until we found him," Jen added.

"Wait a minute, that's about the time we were in the gym. I didn't see him."

"Mrs. Bedford simply said that's what he told her."

"Wonder what he was doing—and with whom," Jen mused.

"What was she doing all that time? I mean, three hours is a long time to spend chatting with friends," Rose commented.

Gil nodded. "She said she had a light dinner around six, and that her husband claimed he had plans to meet 'some of the guys' for dinner later. Witnesses corroborate her statements. She was where she said she was. Haven't found out who Bedford was supposed to be meeting."

"Could be he skipped the gym and the dinner," Candace said. "Or lied about both to his wife."

"Well, we know he was in the hot tub around eight," Gil told them in a dry tone. He then heaved a sigh. "And why the hell am I telling you any of this?"

"Because we really do help every once in a while," Rose suggested.

"Witnesses or not, if she left the club around seven-thirty, then that would have given her enough time to track down Jerry and brain him in the hot tub," Jen said.

"Possibly," Gil admitted.

Their iced tea arrived and they took a few minutes to order.

"Any clues as to the murder weapon?" Candace asked when the group was once again alone.

"Not that I know of," Gil replied. "It was something heavy enough to crush the back of his skull just above the base of the neck, yet it didn't leave any broken skin. I'm thinking something like an old-fashioned blackjack."

"What's that?" Rose wanted to know.

"It's a weapon used by thugs years ago. Usually, a heavy hunk of wood, about six to eight inches long, with a leather or cloth covering and a wrist loop. Very easy to conceal."

"So, even if the pool had people in it, anyone could have waltzed into the hot tub area, nailed him, and walked out again with no one the wiser," Candace said.

"Who really pays all that much attention when you're swimming laps?"

"The killer took a chance, that's for sure," Jen commented with a frown. "Who on earth would have a blackjack just lying around?"

"Someone into violence," Candace replied, paused, and then added, "Or BDSM."

"Oh, my God, what a thought," Rose said. "A local country club with kinky members."

Jen waved a hand in the air. "At this stage of the game, nothing would surprise me."

"What about Barbara Lassiter? Anything new there?" Anne prodded.

Gil shook his head. "Not much. No murder weapon for that either. I did, however, talk to the neighbors again. One of them remembered seeing a light-colored car parked in the driveway next to the victim's car at one point in time. She says it was definitely before she heard the loud bang she thought had come from her TV."

"And Anne and I got there around four-fifteen, so that means the killer could have left just minutes before," Candace mused.

"I'm afraid not," Gil said. "Autopsy report states that Ms. Lassiter was likely killed sometime around three or three-thirty. Rigor mortis had begun to set in."

"Swell, and I got there around three to three-fifteen or so, give or take a few minutes," Candace said with a groan. "I guess that still makes me a suspect. And I drive a white car."

"And you could easily have arrived just after the killer left. Plus, the neighbor said a light-colored car," Anne reminded her

"Well, white is light," Gil stated.

"Look, I've done a lot of stupid things in my life, but after the past two years in prison, I can swear to you I would never do what I did to land me there again."

"You need to talk to people at the club," Jen told him. "A whole bunch of them had reason to hate Barbara Lassiter."

"I plan on doing that this afternoon," Gil replied looking at each of them in turn. "And before you ask, no I don't want any of you around while I'm interviewing people."

"I wasn't going to ask," Anne answered. "But I'm interested in who you're going to question."

"It's not a matter of questioning, but more like a background check of Barbara Lassiter. We might dig up something."

"What about the ex-husband?" Rose asked.

Gil shook his head. "No sign of him yet. In fact, we're having trouble finding anything on Barbara and Drew Lassiter prior to them moving here. And I mean nothing is coming up. We'll keep searching, but it's suspicious."

"Like they may have been using fake names?" Anne questioned. "Why would they do that?"

"When people start changing their names, that's a pretty good indication they're hiding something," he said.

Jen snapped her fingers. "I've got an idea. You're going to be at the club this afternoon. My husband, Carl, is due back in town tonight and he likes to unwind at the club. Why don't you and Anne join us for dinner? You can always say you're thinking of joining like Anne did or something along those lines."

"You know, that's a good idea," Anne said. "You can tell us what you learned from your interviews."

"I am not discussing this or any case in a crowded country club dining room. And I'm especially not discussing it with your husband around, Jen. I repeat; I shouldn't be discussing it now," Gil told them with a frown.

"No, I can see that, but you will get a good dinner," Jen replied with a smile.

Gil smiled and shook his head. "Okay, you talked me into it."

"You and Jack want to join us, Rose?"

"No thanks. I've got a pot roast in the slow cooker, but keep me in the loop, okay?"

Their food arrived and Anne wondered if Gil could find a nugget of truth amid all the rumors floating around the San Sebastian Country Club.

****

"Good to finally meet you, Gil. Jen's told me a lot about you," Carl Swanson said.

"Same here." Gil pulled out a chair as Anne sat in it. "I've been looking forward to this."

Anne decided Carl Swanson was one of those men who lived for his work. He loved Jen and the kids, but preferred to trade commodities on a worldwide scale from the comfort of his real office or from his laptop at home. Past conversations told her that he gave his wife a lot of leeway in running the house. Money wasn't an issue for the Swanson family. His good looks had held up over the years and at forty-five he stayed in shape.

"So, Jen tells me Anne has taken out a trial membership. How about you?"

"Not sure yet. I've never had a yen to swing either

a golf club or a tennis racket."

Carl laughed. "I'm not real big on the sports aspect, but do like to come for the food and such. Friday nights are often set aside for socializing. You know, a band, a dance floor, that kind of thing."

"Ah, now that appeals," Anne said casting a glance at Gil.

"I've been told I'm quite a good dancer," her fiancé said with a smile.

"Then you need to put your money where your mouth is," Jen replied.

A waiter arrived, handed them menus, and took drink orders. Anne was dying to know what Gil had learned from his interviews, but he'd refused to say anything on the ride over. "I'll tell you later" was the best she got.

The conversation began with menu recommendations from Jen and Carl. The waiter returned with their drinks and as they sipped and chatted, she tried to think of a way to bring up Barbara Lassiter and Jerry Bedford. She didn't have to, Carl did it for her.

"Terrible thing about Jerry Bedford. Can't tell you how many times I've been in that hot tub. Never occurred to me that a person could die in one."

"I guess the heat could get to someone or cause death if they had a heart condition," Jen replied.

"And they might not even know they had heart problems either," Anne added. *So Jen didn't tell her husband the whole truth.*

Carl shook his head. "I'm just sorry you and Jen were the ones who found him. Must have been rough after you and Candace discovering Barbara Lassiter's body last week."

The server approached and they ordered dinner. After he left, Carl glanced at Gil.

"I know you're a detective. Do you have anything to do with Barbara Lassiter's murder?"

"I'm lead detective on it," Gil replied sipping his vodka and tonic.

"Any suspects?"

"I really can't talk about it. It's an open case. I'm sure you must understand."

Carl nodded. "Yeah, I guess so. Kind of odd to actually know a murder victim, but I can't say I'm surprised it happened."

"Why is that?" Gil asked.

"You know how you meet a person and right away there's something about them that sends up a red flag? Well, that's the way it was with her. She just came off as being phony and, I don't know, pushy. She couldn't have a conversation without getting up close and personal. Standing close, touching an arm or a shoulder when she talked to you all the while batting her eyelashes and giving you a half smile. It made me uncomfortable."

"The bitch. I never knew this. She flirted with you?" Jen demanded with a scowl, her tone outraged.

"Frequently," Carl admitted. "I ignored her and stayed out of her way as much as possible."

"Did her husband notice?" Anne asked before Gil could.

"I think he did, but maybe it didn't bother him."

"How well did you know Mr. Lassiter?" Gil inquired.

"I met him occasionally at the dances. He seemed

nice enough. He golfed a lot from what I heard."

"Have you talked to him?" Jen asked.

Gil shook his head. "Can't find him yet. People I talked to aren't sure where he went after the divorce."

"Seems to me, someone said he moved to California," Anne told them.

"We're checking."

Anne understood enough by now to know that Drew Lassiter was MIA on the police radar screen. After all these months, at least a credit card receipt should have turned up.

Jen sent a glance in her direction. "Oh look, there's Ted Saunders, the golf pro. Didn't you want to talk to him about lessons, Anne?"

"Uh, yes, I did." She didn't have much interest in golf, but wanted to probe into his insight about the Lassiters.

Jen waved and motioned him over.

"Good evening, Mrs. Swanson, Mr. Swanson. How's everything?"

Jen sent him a dazzling smile. "Just fine, Ted. I'd like you to meet my friend, Anne Jamieson and her fiancé, Gil Collins. Anne's taken out a trial membership and wanted to know about some lessons."

Ted shook hands with both of them. He was average height and build with sandy hair and blue eyes. Anne recalled that someone had said he had a wife and family. She judged his age at somewhere around fifty.

"Of course, always glad to have a new pupil. How about you, Mr. Collins, do you golf—or want to?"

"I've played before but wasn't very good at it. Guess I don't have the patience."

"Ah, but once you do get good at it, it's like an

addiction," the pro said with a laugh. "In fact, it's an addiction even if you aren't good at it."

"I know this is short notice, but would you have time tomorrow?" Anne asked.

Saunders pulled out his cell phone. "Let me check my schedule." He swiped the screen a couple of times. "Actually, I do. According to the scheduler, I had a cancellation. How about ten o'clock?"

"That sounds fine."

"Do you mind if I tag along?" Jen queried. "I haven't played in ages and could use a couple of pointers. Maybe when we finish, we can hack out three or four holes, and then do lunch, Anne."

"I don't know about the three or four holes, but maybe we could take a few swings at the driving range and practice putting. Lunch sounds good."

"Lunch always sounds good to Jen," Carl quipped.

They all laughed as his wife made a face.

"Good, see you both out on the practice tee at ten tomorrow." Ted glanced at his watch. "Oops, I'm late for dinner. Nice to see the Swanson family again and to meet you, Mr. Collins and Ms. Jamieson."

He smiled and walked away to join another man at a table along the back wall of the dining room.

"Who's that he's with?" Jen asked Carl.

He twisted around in his chair. "Have no idea."

Anne happened to glance over at Gil who stared at the two men with raised eyebrows. From the expression on his face, she concluded he did know the other man. Experience, however, had taught her to not say anything.

Their food arrived—filet mignon for the men and seafood for the women. Anne had ordered the crab-stuffed grouper, while Jen indulged in lobster thermidor. This would not be a cheap meal.

To keep from discussing the Lassiters or Jerry Bedford, Anne asked Carl about his work. With Gil feeding in questions at the appropriate times, the conversation swirled from commodities to life at a country club.

They were just finishing their coffee and dessert when Eric and Missy walked in.

"Oh crap, just who I needed to see." Jen rolled her eyes.

"Then I suggest we have a nightcap in the bar." Carl's tone told them this wasn't his favorite couple either.

They paid the enormous bill and strolled across the corridor to the Nineteenth Hole Lounge. A round table for six was open in the corner. They slid into their seats.

Anne looked around and spotted Wes and Bertie Canfield a few spaces away. They waved at the new arrivals but made no effort to get up. In fact, Bertie's expression was one of total wariness and distrust.

"What's with Bertie? She looks odd."

"She didn't like being interviewed today," Gil answered.

"Why not?"

"She just didn't like the idea. As a result, she didn't have much to say. Her husband, however, babbled on and on about nothing."

The waiter came over and they all ordered drinks—an Amaretto for Carl, red wine for Gil, and white wine for the women.

"Did you find out anything useful?" Jen wanted to know.

“Not much,” he told her.

His guarded look suggested to Anne he thought otherwise.

Jen took the hint and changed the subject.

“Hope I didn’t put you in a tough spot with Ted. I mean about the golf lessons and all.”

“Not at all. I can ask some discreet questions while I learn something new.”

“Questions?” Carl asked.

Oops. She wasn’t sure how much Carl really knew about the Snoop Group’s sleuthing endeavors. The waiter brought their drinks. Anne hoped Carl would forget the question. No such luck.

“What questions?” he asked again as he sipped the Amaretto.

“Um, about the club and the members. What a nice room this is.”

“I like it,” he replied. “It’s bright during the day and dark enough at night to seem intimate.”

Actually, Anne hadn’t lied just to change the subject. The dark walnut wainscoting contrasted nicely with the cream-colored upper half of the walls. Artwork depicting golf and tennis scenes were abundant. The carpet was a deep red.

“I think they redid it a couple of years ago,” Jen added.

“Has a cozy atmosphere, yet at the same time seems spacious,” Gil remarked.

Anne shot him a glance as she sipped her wine. Small talk was not his forte. Her gaze once again swept the room stopping on the Canfields. Wes smiled and lifted his glass in a salute. She smiled back. Bertie frowned. Good grief, did the woman think she was flirting with the man?

She looked away. No need to get the woman upset.

"Oh Lord," Jen said with a groan. "It's Marian Talbot. And she's feeling no pain."

A tall, middle-aged woman with harshly dyed black hair wobbled up to their table.

"Hi, Jen, Carl, how's it going." She hiccupped slightly.

"Just fine, Marian," Carl said.

Without being asked, the woman pulled out one of the vacant seats and plunked her fanny in it, then stared pointedly at Anne. "Who's this?"

"Marian, this is Anne Jamieson and her fiancé, Gil Collins. Anne, Gil, this is Marian Talbot. Anne's taken out a trial membership."

Marian snorted. "I'm surprised anyone's interested in joining what with members dropping dead every few days."

Anne choked on her wine. Marian hadn't bothered to lower her voice and patrons at nearby tables ceased talking to stare. Luckily, the waiter arrived.

"Scotch, neat," the woman demanded.

"Uh, where's Frank?" Jen asked as the server returned to the bar.

"Playing bridge. The last rubber should be over soon. Heard you and some woman found Jerry Bedford."

"Yeah, poor man. Had no idea a hot tub could be so dangerous."

Marian's eyes narrowed. "Life can be dangerous. People need to pay attention to what they're doing. Why just the other day, I read where a guy was jaywalking and got nailed by a crosstown bus."

Anne looked at Gil who shrugged. She had no idea what to add to this conversation and wasn't about to admit she was with Jen when they found the body.

The waiter set Marian's drink in front of her and left.

"Here's to a good evening," she said in a booming voice and hefted the glass in a toast.

After taking a generous swallow, she set her gaze around the room.

"I see Bertie and Wes are here. Must have let him out of his cage for a while. They normally don't show up after dark. Especially in the bar. Of course, with that Lassiter woman biting the big one, I guess she figures it's safe to let him off the chain again."

The Canfields clearly heard. Wes coughed and looked into his glass, while Bertie glared.

"I take it Mr. Canfield was friends with the woman," Gil said in a smooth tone.

Marian laughed. "According to my sources, she flirted like crazy with him, but he was too chicken to do anything about it except boast about how he still had the power to attract younger women. Bet old Bertie was ready to kill him—or her."

Anne lowered her wine glass. Suppose he wasn't too chicken. Suppose he'd succumbed to Barbara's charms.

Would Bertie be pissed enough to do something about it? Like murder?

She dared another glance at the Canfields. Wes shifted in his chair while Bertie's face flamed red, but whether with embarrassment or temper, Anne wasn't sure.

A short, balding, overweight man ambled up to the

table and smiled at Marian.

"Ah, here you are, my dear. Are you ready to leave?"

She bolted the rest of her drink. "Yep. How'd the bridge game go?"

"Very good. Jeff and I won. We're thinking of teaming up in the tournament next month."

"Good. We can always use another trophy on the mantel." She rose and took the arm offered by her husband. "See you all later."

"What an odd conversation," Anne said as the couple left.

"Marian's an odd woman. She doesn't come with a filter and says whatever she wants. Her bluntness has pissed off more than a few people," Jen told her glancing at Wes and Bertie's table. "I'd say you can add the Canfields to that list."

Carl waved a hand. "She's irritating, but harmless."

"I guess a country club is like a small town. It has its fair share of quirky personalities and people you either like or dislike. If I do take out a full membership, I hope I can afford the monthly dues. They seemed a little steep," Anne said.

"I never thought of it in those terms, but you're right, and while the dues are high I wouldn't worry," Carl replied. "Several members have been late paying off and on over the years. Even the Nordstrums were late a couple of times earlier this year. It's no big deal, provided you don't let it go on too long."

"How do you know that?" Jen asked with a quizzical expression.

"Bill Janson, the treasurer, mentioned it once when we were having drinks here in the bar."

"I'd think he'd be more discreet about something like that," she replied.

Carl shrugged. "You'd think so, but he'd had a couple of belts."

"Well, I don't know about the rest of you, but I'm ready to call it a night," Gil said.

Anne finished her wine. "Me, too. This has been fun. We'll have to do it again sometime won't we, Gil."

"Definitely." His expression and tone suggested not a chance in hell. He signaled the waiter who came over immediately. "Check, please. This is on me."

"Nice of you, Gil," Carl said with a smile. He lifted his glass and shifted his gaze to the doorway, then froze with a stunned expression. "Holy shit!"

They all turned to stare at the man who had just entered.

Jen gasped. "Oh my God, isn't that…"

"Yep, that's Drew Lassiter."

Chapter Eleven

Out of the corner of her eye, Anne saw Gil's head swivel and his eyes narrow. Her appreciative gaze, however, was focused on the tall man who had just entered the bar. His physique was muscular, yet trim, showing he probably worked out on a regular basis. His dark hair was neatly combed and his deep tan told her he spent a lot of time outdoors. The navy-blue slacks and grass green polo shirt fit like the old proverbial glove.

He paused, scanned the room, waved to someone seated behind them, and then smiled. Anne remembered someone once saying he had a killer smile. They were drop dead right.

As he made his way between the tables, Gil rose and stepped in front of him.

"Drew Lassiter?"

The man stopped and looked at Gil with raised eyebrows. "Yes. Do I know you?"

"Not yet. My name is Gil Collins and I'm the detective in charge of your wife's murder case. I'd like to talk to you."

Drew's brows rose further. "Here? Now? I'm meeting some friends for dinner."

"No, no, not now. We can do it tomorrow at the police station. I'd like to ask you a few questions about your wife's friends and such."

"My ex-wife," he stated, then turned to indicate with hand signals to his friends that he would be stopping here for a few moments.

Anne noted that one of the friends was Ted Saunders.

Drew sat in the chair recently vacated by Marian Talbot as Gil resumed his seat.

"Hello, Carl Swanson, right? How's everything?"

"Fine, Drew. Kind of surprised to see you here."

"Oh, I'm still a member." He turned his attention back to Gil. "Now what is it you want to know?"

Gil smiled. "As I said, now's not the time or the place. We've been trying to get a hold of you for several days."

"I've been out of town. A friend of mine owns a small hotel on Castaway Beach in the Keys. He invited me down to help out with his deep-sea fishing charters. Just got back a while ago and heard the news."

"I see. First of all, I want to say how sorry I am for your loss."

The waiter came over and Drew ordered a scotch on the rocks. He turned back to Gil as the server left.

"Thank you, but Barbara and I didn't speak much after the divorce."

Anne would have given anything to have Gil start the interrogation, but knew she'd have to wait. Jen wasn't so reluctant.

"We heard you'd gone to California," she said.

"Naw, I like San Sebastian. But that doesn't mean I have to spend all my time here."

"Poor Barbara. You must have been as shocked as the rest of us by her death."

Anne had no idea how Jen managed to keep such a

sincere look on her face.

Drew shrugged. "She lived a free-wheelin' lifestyle. I did for a while, too."

"Free-wheeling?" Anne asked. Gil kicked her ankle, but she ignored him.

"She liked to do what she wanted, when she wanted, and with whom she wanted. Gradually decided I wanted to settle down, raise a family. Wasn't on her agenda, so we split. It was amicable."

His drink arrived. He nodded at the waiter and sipped.

"But you're still a member here?" Carl asked.

"I enjoy golfing and such. Got a little apartment not far from here in Port Rosa. Then my friend called and suggested I come down. Sounded like fun, so I decided why not and went for a month or so. I liked the change of scenery." He glanced at his watch and rose. "I'd better go. My friends are waiting."

"I'll be expecting you tomorrow at the police station, say about ten?" Gil said in a forceful tone.

Drew stared for a moment before answering. "Yeah, sure. Nice to meet you and good to see you again, Carl, Jen."

He walked away and joined Saunders and the other man.

"'Carl' and 'Jen'?" Anne asked. "I thought you said you didn't know him that well."

"We don't," Carl replied. "I'm surprised he knew my first name."

"Mine, too. Oh well, it's a country club. Sooner or later we tend to think of everyone as friends," Jen added.

"And now, we really have to get going, too," Gil

told them as he pushed back his chair and rose. "You ready, Anne?"

Anne was most definitely not ready, but nodded anyway.

"Jen, I'll meet you here around nine forty-five. I'm looking forward to learning golf."

Her friend shot a glance at Gil as if knowing Anne would discuss tonight with him.

"See you then."

Gil was silent until they got into the car and drove down the winding driveway to the street.

"And just what did you think you were doing talking about Barbara Lassiter to her ex-husband before I interrogated him?"

"Well, not talking about her would have seemed odd. I mean, surely, Drew Lassiter would have found it strange if we just started chatting about charter boats in the Keys."

"Don't do it again."

"All right, already." She took a deep breath. "Why was Bertie Canfield so uptight?"

"I don't think she's happy with you and Jen asking questions about the Lassiter woman. Mrs. Canfield claimed little contact with the victim and gave vague answers."

"I did tell them you were a detective and lead investigator on the case. Sam and Lynne Nordstrum were there when I said it, too."

"Why let them know that?" he asked.

"They wanted to know what you did for a living, so I told them. Why hide it? They'd find out sooner or later anyway."

"I wish it had been later."

Anne could tell from his tone he was not happy with her. However, that didn't stop her from plowing on with questions.

"Did you talk to Wes Canfield?"

"Yeah, he tap-danced around questions, too. Kept insisting he knew Ms. Lassiter casually and played tennis once in a while with her. Said she was pleasant enough."

"He told me he thought the rumors of her behavior were based in jealousy. Who was the man with Ted Saunders? You acted like you knew him."

"I've seen his mug shot on more than one occasion."

Anne drew in a sharp breath. "He's a criminal?"

"His name is Howard Sturgis. He's been arrested several times for fraud—investments that don't work out, real estate that isn't worth as much as he sells it for—that kind of thing. He's clever. His companies are always set up with partners, many of whom can't be found when the shit hits the fan. That's when he claims he was duped by unscrupulous people."

"No convictions?"

"Not yet. His victims either drop the charges or settle out of court."

"So what's he doing with Ted Saunders, the golf pro?"

"And Drew Lassiter. That's who he joined for dinner. Something's in the wind for sure. A country club with a lot of wealthy members is a fertile hunting ground."

Anne remained silent the rest of the drive home. She had a golf lesson in the morning. She'd ask a few discreet questions then.

****

"Oh dear, I barely hit it," Anne complained as the golf ball dribbled off the tee and bounced a mere thirty yards down the driving range.

"That's because you straightened up as you made contact. It's a natural instinct to do so. Makes the golfer think they're hitting the ball harder and lofting it farther. As a result, the face of the club only hits the top half of the ball. It's called topping the ball," the golf pro explained.

He gave her instructions on how to avoid the problem.

As she tried to implement the advice, Ted Saunders moved away to help Jen with her swing.

Anne whacked away and decided golf was not her sport. The scorching sun glared from a cloudless sky. Sweat slid down the sides of her face. She wiped it away and pulled her polo shirt from her damp back. Damn it was hot. No way were she and Jen playing a real game in this heat.

She hit another ball and winced as it sailed off to the right. What had Saunders called it? Oh yeah, a slice. She figured that if she ever did get on the course, she'd decapitate some poor duffer three fairways over—assuming she could hit it that far.

Saunders returned to her side. She hit again. This one went straight and dinged off a sign with a one hundred printed on it.

"Not bad, Ms. Jamieson, not bad. You made it to the hundred-yard marker. All it takes is practice." He glanced at his watch, and then smiled. "Time's almost up. Do you feel like you learned something?"

"Yeah, that I'm terrible at this."

He laughed. "You'll get better. How about lesson number two on Friday? Same time all right with you?"

"I guess so."

Jen jammed her driver into her golf bag and joined them. "So, do you want to play a couple of holes?"

Anne fanned her face. "Not a chance in hell."

Saunders replaced Anne's club in her bag. "In that case, let me walk you back to the clubhouse and the pro shop. See about getting you some clubs."

Anne had borrowed an old set from Jen and had no intention of spending yet another fortune on golf clubs she'd never use. But the walk would give her time to ask questions.

She and Jen wheeled the little portable carts with the bags on them along the path. Saunders walked between them. Before he could discuss golf, Jen plunged in.

"Sure was awful about Barbara Lassiter, wasn't it?"

"Terrible tragedy. Had dinner last night with Drew. He's as dumbfounded as the rest of us."

"Did she play golf?" Anne asked.

"Some. Was pretty good, too, but she preferred tennis. Now Drew is a golfer. Shoots consistently in the low eighties."

Anne had told Jen about her and Gil's conversation on the way home last night, so it didn't surprise her when her friend continued.

"Yes, he stopped by our table last night. Who was the other man you met? He looked familiar, but I can't quite place him. Is he a member?"

"He's a friend of Drew's. Name's Sturgis. Some kind of investment banker." Saunders's answer was short as if he didn't want to talk about Sturgis.

"I guess he must have known Barbara, too."

Saunders shot Jen a quick glance. "I have no idea."

"Stands to reason, I suppose. I seem to remember Barbara once talking about her portfolio. Hmmm, maybe my husband, Carl, can look him up and see what kind of investments he's in."

"Perhaps." The golf pro frowned as he opened the clubhouse doors. "So, Ms. Jamieson, would you like to look at some clubs today?"

"Not just yet. Let me make sure I know I'm going to play before spending that much money."

He nodded. "Makes sense. I'll see you on Friday at ten. Will you be joining us, too, Mrs. Swanson?"

"No, I don't think so. I'll just take what you told me today and work on it."

"Golf's not your game either?" Anne asked as Saunders entered the pro shop.

"He gave me a lesson free of charge today. If I'd said yes, he'd have charged me. How much is he gouging you for?"

Anne heaved a sigh. "A hundred and fifty bucks per lesson."

"That sounds reasonable. He's a certified teaching pro. Belongs to the PGA. Lunch?"

"Definitely. You know, I got kind of a thrill when I finally hit a ball straight and long. Maybe golf isn't so bad after all."

"Do you like it enough to make this temporary membership permanent?"

"I'm not sure. It's expensive and I don't think Gil is on board with the social end of things."

They spent time poking around the pro shop. As far

as Anne was concerned everything for sale was overpriced. Seventy dollars for a golf shirt, a hundred-and-forty bucks for a tennis outfit, and the equipment costs were in the stratosphere. She was getting a quick lesson in how the other half lived.

Jen pulled her tank top away from her chest. “Whew, I could use a shower before lunch. How about you?”

“I could use a few minutes in the sauna or steam room to relax before I do. I’m still sore from that workout the other day.”

“Why not just use the hot tub?”

“I didn’t bring a swimsuit, and besides, I’m not real fond of hot tubs at the moment. I do, however, have a nice oversized towel in my locker along with a change of clothes.” Anne rotated her right arm. “Swinging that golf club let me know my shoulders will be stiff tomorrow. Ten minutes in the steam followed by a quick shower will make me feel better.”

“Well, in spite of Jerry Bedford, I have no aversion to the hot tub. I did bring my suit, so I think I’ll go have fun in the bubbles.”

“From our discussion last night, I have to assume you haven’t told Carl about the Snoop Group.”

“He doesn’t need to know everything I do.” Jen shot her a lopsided smile. “Besides, I don’t think he’d approve.”

They stashed their golf bags in a secure area before making their way into the main building and the locker room where Jen quickly changed.

“Don’t stay in the steam room too long. I’ll meet you back here in say fifteen or twenty minutes. Okay?”

“Fine.”

Anne undressed and wrapped her huge towel around her body, then sat on the bench. Saunders didn't really have much to say about Barbara Lassiter, although he apparently was well-acquainted with Drew. Still he tried to avoid discussion about the dead woman. Maybe he thought the questions had been pushy. Or he may have been reticent given Barbara's penchant for adultery. *I wonder if he was one of the notches on the woman's bed post.*

She mentally counted off suspects or at least the ones she knew about so far. Any or all of them could have committed murder. And Missy Warren may have been the target after all.

Missy is nasty and a liar. Perhaps she was having an affair with someone and the wife found out, then nailed the wrong bimbo.

Anne sighed. How long had she been sitting here? She fished her phone from her purse to check the time—eleven forty-five. She had no idea when Jen had left. She rose and pushed open the door leading to the showers. The sauna was located to her right at the end of the room. The steam room was on the opposite side. A sign on the door warned users to limit their time inside to no more than fifteen minutes.

She opted for the steam room, pulled open the frosted glass door and entered the hot, humid area. Condensation rolled down the glass. A hissing noise from her left followed by a billow of steam slapped her in the face. Several deep concrete benches lined the walls. Removing her towel and placing it on the stone, she lay down and breathed in the eucalyptus scented steam.

Closing her eyes, she let her mind drift back again

to her conversation with the golf pro, Ted Saunders. He seemed like a nice enough guy, but like Adam Jefferies, the tennis pro, and the workout instructor, Bobby Lanier, he hadn't wanted to talk about the Lassiters. *Circling the wagons?*

Anne wondered how she could approach Drew Lassiter to ask questions. His admission at dinner last night that he'd never left the San Sebastian area had been surprising. From all that she'd heard, he was supposed to have gone to California.

Maybe the logical way to do it is to ask about the funeral. I could pretend to have met his wife and gotten to know her pretty well.

A noise from the door had her turning her head, but no one entered. With a mental shrug, she resumed her train of thought.

Yes, the funeral was the way to go. Express condolences, offer to help with cleaning out Barbara's condo, which would likely be refused, and then ask some discreet questions about his ex's social activities. Now, she needed to figure out how to get a hold of him.

Drew had said that his membership was still valid, so perhaps he planned on returning now that his ex-wife was no longer in the picture.

I guess I just have to hang around the club until he shows up. She didn't like the idea of stalking him, but couldn't think of any other way.

Another hiss and burst of steam brought her out of her thoughts. How long had she been in here? Five minutes? Ten? She had no idea, but her sweat streaked body glistened in the dim lighting that glowed through the swirling moisture.

Anne sat up instantly becoming lightheaded.

Taking as deep a breath as she could, she waited for the feeling to subside. It did within a few seconds, but she knew it was time to go.

Wrapping the towel around her, she walked to the door and pushed. It jammed, refusing to open. She pushed again, and then pulled. Nothing. Again—with the same results. She pounded on the glass.

"Help! Can anyone hear me? I can't get out."

No one came. Her stomach clenched and her breathing became labored. Her hands shook and the towel came loose dropping to the floor. She repeated the pounding and yelled at the top of her lungs. The dizziness returned. Slowly, Anne sank to her knees.

"Help me, somebody, please help me." She realized she no longer screamed. Her voice was barely a whisper.

Jerry Bedford flashed across her mind.

I'm going to die.

Then darkness enveloped her as she could no longer keep her eyes open.

****

Air. Cool, refreshing air. Anne inhaled a deep breath and opened her eyes. Jen's frightened face along with that of another woman swam into view.

"Good God, are you all right?" Jen said in a wavering voice.

"Yes, I think so." She realized she was lying on the concrete floor, her towel covering her like a blanket. She struggled to sit up clutching it to her chest.

"I swear to God, I don't know what happened," the other woman said. She gulped as tears filled her eyes. Ear buds dangled from a cell phone in her shirt pocket. "I pushed the cleaning cart against the wall for just a moment while I went to get some supplies from the closet around the corner. I was only gone a few minutes."

Anne sat up and maneuvered her body to lean against the wall. "I'm not sure I understand what happened."

Jen took a ragged breath. "When you didn't come back to the locker room, I went searching for you. This lady was pulling you out of the steam room."

"I was cleaning the showers. It's lunchtime, and Wednesdays are slow anyway, so I decided to scrub down the sauna and steam rooms, too," the woman said. "I…I must have forgotten to set the brake. When I came back, the cart had moved and the mop handle somehow fell through the door pull. Then I saw what looked like a body huddled on the floor against the glass."

Anne looked at the door handle and then the mop. *Somehow fell through the door pull? Bullshit!*

"I remember pounding on the door and yelling."

The cleaning woman fingered the ear buds. "I was listening to music. It makes the day go faster. I guess I didn't hear you. I'm so sorry. Are…are you going to report me?"

With Jen and the lady's help, Anne struggled to her feet, secured the towel around her body, and stared. "I should. What you did was very careless."

"I know, and I'm so, so sorry. Oh, God, please, I really need this job."

Anne took another deep breath. "Maybe the next time you should check the room first, and then prop the door open while you get supplies."

"You're absolutely right and I promise to do so in

the future."

"How do you feel?" Jen asked.

"I'm fine. All I need is a shower and lunch."

"Are you sure? You could have heat stroke or something. Maybe I should take you to the emergency room."

"No, I'm okay." She felt perfectly normal now that the air had cooled her. "I think I was more scared than anything."

"Are you sure?" Jen repeated.

Anne nodded and took a moment to inspect the steam room door. "Let's get out of here."

"Are…are you going to report me?" the woman asked in a scared tone.

"No. It was an accident, but I'm thinking safety lessons should be part of your job orientation."

"Yes, ma'am. I'll bring that up to my supervisor."

"You really should have reported her." Jen helped Anne toward the locker room. "What if I hadn't come along or what if she decided to take a smoke break or something? You could have died."

Anne wanted to clear her head before she brought up her suspicions about the incident not being an accident.

"But I didn't, and having her lose her job wouldn't help matters. What time is it?"

"A little after twelve."

"I remember looking at my phone before I left the locker room. It was eleven forty-five, so I wasn't in there that long. Like I said, I think I was more scared than anything."

A cool shower helped Anne regain her composure. She sighed as she dressed under Jen's eagle eye.

"Jen, I'm fine. Honest. I don't feel dizzy or weak in the knees. All I am is hungry."

"If you say so," her friend muttered. "But I still say it was one weird accident."

As they made their way to the dining room, Anne knew differently. This was no accident.

Chapter Twelve

Anne didn't pick up the menu, but instead stared out the windows of the dining room at the terrace. She didn't see the terrace either. Her mind was busy sorting through the events of the last hour.

"Are you sure you're all right?" Jen asked.

"Hmm… What? Oh yes, I'm fine. I was just thinking. This was not an accident."

"You mean someone did it deliberately?"

"Yes. But it was meant as a warning. I've been asking questions, and those questions must be making someone very nervous."

Jen closed the menu and leaned forward. "Okay. Explain."

"I took a good look at the handle of the steam room. It's attached at both the top and the bottom. There's no way a mop handle could wedge itself through the grasp accidentally. Plus, how would a service cart roll down a non-sloping passageway and just happen to stop at the steam room door?"

"You're right, it couldn't," Jen replied sitting back again.

"I think someone followed me to the steam room, saw the cart and seized an opportunity."

"They were taking one hell of a chance."

"Not necessarily. Maybe that someone saw the cleaning lady leave the cart and go to the supply room.

The perpetrator may have figured she'd be back soon."

"But how could he or she have known that you would try to leave the steam room while locked in?"

"Could be they waited, trying to form a plan to attack me in the steam room when a better circumstance presented itself."

"So in other words, it was a spur of the moment kind of thing."

Anne nodded. "Plus, we didn't exactly keep our plans a secret when we were in the locker room. Anyone could have overheard us."

A waiter arrived to take their orders. Both women requested iced tea and the seafood salad.

"Jen, do you remember who was in the locker room with us and what time we got there?"

"Oh Lord, let me think." Her forehead wrinkled. "I remember that there were several people around. I just didn't pay attention as to *who* was there. I think a couple of water aerobics classes had just finished because I had to step around puddles of water by the door. And when I changed, I noticed two or three yoga mats on one of the benches, so I assume one of those let out, too."

The waiter brought their iced tea and said the salads would be out soon.

Anne sipped from her glass and let the cold liquid slide down her parched throat. She swallowed more. What was it that made her throat so dry? The exercise? The heat? Fear? Or all three?

She shifted her attention back to Jen.

"Do you have any idea when you left the locker room?"

"I glanced at the clock in the pool area when I

walked in. It said about eleven thirty-five. I was the only one in the hot tub, so I set the timer for seven minutes. I didn't want to keep you waiting. I came back, took a quick shower, dressed, and decided to come looking for you. I turned the corner and saw the cleaning lady dragging you out of the steam room."

"I don't think I was in there longer than ten minutes when I realized I was trapped. I have no idea how long I was unconscious. I wish there was some way to know what classes were held and who attended."

Jen snapped her fingers. "The club has a daily schedule posted at the front desk. Maybe I can match suspects to activities." She pushed her chair back and rose. "I'll be right back."

As Jen dashed from the room, Anne sat back and gazed out the window again. She was convinced her attacker had to have been in the locker room.

Damn, why didn't I stop to look around and see who was there when I left?

She had no answer for that. Maybe the person had been in the shower and seen her enter the steam room. But in that case, how did she see the cleaning lady leave the cart and why wait so long to move it? Anne recalled hearing movement outside the door not long before she decided to leave the steam room. That had to have been when the cart was moved and the mop jammed into the door handle.

A couple at the dining room door caught her attention. It was Wes and Bertie Canfield. Since her and Jen's table was located near the entryway, the couple had no choice but to pass by.

Anne waved. Wes waved back. Bertie frowned.

"Hello," Wes said as they walked up. "Good to see you again."

"Nice to see you, too."

"I see you're taking full advantage of your trial membership," Bertie commented in a frosty tone.

"I've only got a month, so I might as well sample all they have to offer. Jen and I had a golf lesson this morning. What have you guys been up to?"

"Not much," Wes replied with a laugh. "Worked on my putting while Bertie had a tennis lesson, then we…"

His wife interrupted. "Wes, the hostess is waiting to seat us."

"Oh, don't let me keep you," Anne said. "And by the way, I want to apologize for the behavior of that awful woman last night. I have no idea who she was, but she was certainly rude."

Wes shifted from foot to foot. "Oh…I didn't really pay much attention."

"Marian Talbot is a drunken bitch whose privileges should be suspended. In fact, I'm going to talk to Sam about it as soon as possible. Now, if you'll excuse us." Bertie pulled on her husband's arm and led him away.

Anne wanted to laugh. She had the feeling Bertie would not be in favor of her joining the Sam Sebastian Country Club on a permanent basis. The urge was stifled when Drew Lassiter strolled through the doorway and made a beeline for a table along the far wall. As he pulled out his chair she noticed his luncheon companions were the Sturgis man and another couple.

Lassiter's presence reminded her that he was supposed to have gone to the police station and give his statement. Anne was tempted to call Gil, but decided against it. He'd tell her what was said sooner or later.

She glanced at Sturgis. He was smiling and talking to the others. Was he using the country club as a hunting ground for potential investment victims? Sure looked like it. Or was he a member? The only thought that came to mind was a cliché—*talk about letting the fox loose in the hen house.*

The waiter arrived with the salads. Anne speared a shrimp and popped it into her mouth. What was taking Jen so long? At that moment a grinning Jen bounced back into the room with a slip of paper in her hand.

"Got it!" she said resuming her seat. "Let's see, between nine-thirty and eleven-thirty, there were two yoga classes and one water aerobics. To be honest, I don't know of anybody on our suspect list who'd do either. But, I did have the presence of mind to ask a couple of questions."

"Like?"

Jen forked some salad into her mouth and took a sip from her iced tea glass.

"Well, a lot of the suspects are the more active type, so I asked the concierge about the racquetball and tennis courts and if anyone had reserved them for that time frame."

"Did they?"

"He said the racquetball courts are supposed to be reserved, but not that many people play, so they tend to just go ahead and use them—except for this morning. Lynne and Sam Nordstrum, and we know Lynne is a stickler for rules, so she reserved the court—were playing for an hour starting at ten-fifteen."

Anne sat back and sipped her tea. "That's

interesting. Did you see her in the locker room?"

"No, but then I wasn't particularly looking either. The tennis courts, however, are another story. They must be reserved. And guess which couple were batting the ball back and forth beginning at nine-thirty—Wes and Bertie. If they played a three-game set, that would put her in the locker room at about the same time." Jen sat back with a self-satisfied smirk. "And that's not all. As I was looking over the daily schedule, this woman came up and asked where to find Bobby Lanier. She had a training session with him at one. The concierge informed her that Bobby Lanier no longer worked at the club. He resigned last Monday evening with the excuse he had accepted a better job in Tallahassee."

"Monday? That's the day we found Jerry Bedford and were in the gym. Remember? He left abruptly and said he had a client. Only we never saw him again."

"I'll bet he went straight to the office and quit. We must have scared him about something."

"I wonder if his so-called client was really Jerry Bedford," Anne mused.

"Could be that Jerry was in the gym just before us. Maybe they had an argument. Maybe Jerry was a creature of habit, so Bobby knew exactly where to find him. He kills Jerry, and then splits for who-knows-where. I doubt if he got a job in Tallahassee."

"And I'm sure he's miles away from San Sebastian by now. By the way, Wes and Bertie came in while you were gone. She was decidedly, shall I say, reserved. Wes said he was on the practice green and that Bertie had a tennis lesson. Would she have played a full match, and then had a lesson?"

"Seems like it would have been the other way

around. Maybe it was and Wes was just jabbering."

"Then look who arrived." Anne lifted her chin in Drew Lassiter's direction.

Jen's head swiveled. She turned back with a shrug. "Guess he must have answered Gil's questions the right way."

Anne told her about Gil's assessment of Howard Sturgis.

"Hmmm. I can see that happening. Many of our members are older, retired, and have a few extra bucks stashed away. And I'm damned certain he's not a member."

They finished their lunch, paid the bill, and rose to leave when Jen put a hand on Anne's arm.

"I've got an outrageous idea. Follow me."

She led them to Drew's table. Anne held her breath. When her friend got an outrageous idea, it was usually, well, outrageous.

"Drew, I'm sorry to interrupt, but I just wanted to tell you again how sorry I am about Barbara. It was such a shock."

Jen really should have been an actress.

"Uh, thank you, Jen. I'm still reeling from it all."

Anne wanted to roll her eyes. He hadn't seemed in the least bit concerned about his ex-wife's murder last night.

Jen continued. "I can imagine. Do you know when the funeral is? I, and I'm sure many of the members, would like to come pay their respects."

"Not…not at the moment. I'll certainly let the club know when all the arrangements are final."

"Thank you." Jen shifted her gaze to the other couple. "My goodness, Phyllis and Lars, it's been a long time since I've seen you guys here."

The woman smiled. "When Lars retired last year, we decided to travel."

"Oh, really? Where did you go?"

"Europe, the Far East. We just got back from a cruise to Alaska," her husband answered.

"How thrilling. We must do lunch soon so you can tell me all about it." Now Jen turned her attention to Sturgis. "Hello, I don't believe we've met. I'm Jennifer Swanson."

Anne marveled at how authentic her friend sounded.

"Howard Sturgis. Nice to meet you."

"Are you a member? I'm so bad about keeping up with who's new and such."

"Not yet, but I'm thinking about it."

"Wonderful. What do you do for a living, Mr. Sturgis?"

Anne's stomach tightened as the man narrowed his eyes.

"I'm in investment banking."

"How interesting. My husband is in commodities. We should all get together soon. Well, I won't interrupt you any further. Have a good day."

"I can't believe you did that," Anne said in a low tone as they walked away.

"I can't either. Investment banking my ass. That's what that con artist in New York with the Ponzi scheme was nailed for. He bilked billions from anyone who fell for the thirty-percent-return-on-their-investment line. You may be right about him fishing in fresh waters."

"Who was the couple with him?"

"Lars and Phyllis Allen. Nice couple. They golf

and enjoy the social aspects of the club. I probably should warn Sam Nordstrum and the Allens about this Sturgis dude. I'd hate to see some of my friends get taken."

They made their way through the club lobby to retrieve the golf clubs when a woman wearing yoga pants, an over-sized T-shirt, and carrying a large black gym bag crossed in front of them.

Jen stopped in her tracks. "Darlene! What are you doing here?"

Anne wondered that, too. The woman had been a widow less than forty-eight hours, but looked incredibly well put together. Not a hair out of place and her make-up immaculate.

"Oh hi, Jen. I came to pick up Jerry's things. One of the attendants cleaned out his locker this morning while I was in a yoga class."

"Yoga? I didn't know you were into that."

"It helps relieve the stress, and Lord knows, I've had a lot of stress the last couple of days," Darlene said, her chin quivering.

"I understand. It must have been an awful shock to hear Jerry died of a heart attack while in the hot tub. I know it was a shock finding him. I'm so sorry."

"Thank you." Darlene darted a glance at Anne.

"We met very briefly the other day. I'm Anne Jamieson. I was with Jen when we found your husband. My deepest condolences."

"Thank you," she repeated in a dull tone.

Anne eyed the gym bag, surprised the police hadn't confiscated the locker contents, but couldn't think of a way to bring up the subject. Other than the cops and presumably Darlene, no one was supposed to know

Bedford had been murdered.

"When is the funeral?" Jen asked.

"Friday afternoon, one o'clock at Webber Funeral Home."

"I'll be there, and if there's anything Carl or I can do, just let us know."

Darlene nodded and walked away.

"Yoga classes," Anne murmured.

Jen whipped the schedule from her purse. "Yoga classes this morning…let's see, one at nine-fifteen, and one at ten-fifteen. And another at noon. That could have put her in the locker room either just getting out of class or preparing to go in around the time we were there."

"Why on earth would Darlene want to harm me?"

"Maybe she didn't like your questions. A bridge table is a great place to hear the latest gossip and Darlene plays a lot of bridge."

Anne told Jen about her concerns regarding the gym bag.

"Maybe they looked through the locker and found nothing suspicious. Not much to find with a pair of slacks, a shirt, socks, shoes, and underwear."

"He probably had things like a wallet, money, and such in his pockets."

"Like I said, there might not have been anything of interest. I'll say this, she seemed awfully composed for the wife of a murdered man."

"I wonder how much she liked her husband."

Jen shook her head. "I don't know, but the suspect list just keeps getting longer and longer."

****

By four o'clock, Anne couldn't stand it any longer. She called Gil.

"So, how did the interview with Drew Lassiter go?" she asked immediately.

"About what I expected. Said he was on a boat in the Keys and had no clue as to why anyone would want to kill his ex-wife. He shrugged off their lifestyle as an open marriage and the divorce as a matter of moving on."

"Do you buy it?"

"No reason not to at the moment. I'm checking out his alibi. He gave me the number of his friend with the charter boat, but warned me that he may be out to sea for several days. Apparently, the boat goes out, they fish all day and put in at small islands for the night. Rarely any cell service."

"Well, I had an interesting day." She told him about the golf lesson and seeing Drew Lassiter at lunch, carefully leaving out her experience in the steam room. *No need to worry him and besides, he'll insist I butt out. Only I don't want to.*

"I wonder if Sturgis has taken out a trial membership, too," he said. "He's definitely up to something. I also wonder how he and Lassiter hooked up."

"Maybe he's an investor already and is helping to find new ones."

"Maybe. What about the other couple?"

She gave him the information Jen and supplied. "Oh, and here's something else. The trainer at the gym has left town supposedly for a new job in Tallahassee."

"I'll ask around."

"Maybe I'll go into the gym tomorrow and do the same."

"Anne…" his voice held a warning note.

"I'll be discreet. After all, I'm new to the club and don't really know the members. I might be able to get one or two of them to comment."

Gil sighed. "I really wish you wouldn't."

"Can you stop me?"

"Short of chaining you to the wall of a dungeon, no, I guess not."

She hung up with only a twinge of guilt about not telling Gil about the steam room. Maybe she'd do it when the case was solved.

Her phone rang as she was contemplating dinner preparations. Caller ID told her it was Rose.

"Hey, Rose, what's up?"

"I don't know if this is anything we don't already know, but Jack saw Jerry Bedford's obituary in the paper this morning and remembered he was a customer."

"What? Jerry Bedford didn't get his golf clubs from the pro shop?"

"According to Jack, Mr. Bedford was incredibly cheap. Refused to pay the inflated club prices. Or maybe that made him smart. Not sure. At any rate, Jack said Bedford was in the store about a month ago with his wife. He was buying a new putter or something."

"Whoa, wait a minute. From what I've heard about Darlene Bedford, she wouldn't be anywhere close to a sporting goods store. Yoga and bridge are her fortes."

"Considering what *we* heard about Barbara Lassiter, I asked Jack what the woman looked like. He said she was blonde, had boobs to die for, and a nice rear-end. I didn't know whether to be pissed that he noticed or glad that he did so he could definitely *not* describe the woman we met at lunch last week."

"So, he was with Barbara," Anne said.

"Or Missy—or even someone else for all we know. I also asked if he remembered what they said to each other, but he gave me a look that clearly said who the hell remembers something like that. He also asked why I wanted to know."

"I take it he doesn't know about the Snoop Group."

"Are you kidding? He'd kill me." Rose replied with a snort. "I'm getting the feeling there's a lot of crap going on at the country club, and that most members don't have a clue about it."

"I think you're right."

"I was thinking it might be time to put the squeeze on the new Mrs. Warren."

"How?" Anne asked.

"I don't know, but if she was a good friend of the Lassiter woman, then she must know the more intimate details of her life. Details she might not discuss with the cops."

"Hmmm. I was told that she and Barbara were regulars at the gym just about every day. I was going to go in for a light workout tomorrow. I'll hang around until she shows up. Of course, she'll probably tell us to go to hell and refuse to talk about it."

"Take a page from the Gil Collins book of police tactics. Scare her a little."

Anne hung up.

Scare her a little? Missy Warren would probably laugh in her face, but it was worth a try.

Someone had killed Barbara Lassiter and Jerry Bedford. And someone had said something to make Bobby Lanier take off for Tallahassee—or parts unknown.

And someone fired a warning shot across my bow in the steam room.

Chapter Thirteen

Anne called Candace, Jen, and Rose the next morning asking each if they were free for a dinner out that night.

"I have an idea that might help the Snoop Group with the case."

"What is it you hope to accomplish?" Candace asked.

"With any luck I'll be able to convince Missy to join us for dinner."

"Good God, why?"

"Because she knows a hell of a lot more about Barbara Lassiter than we do. I want that information. It's been a week since the murder and no arrest. Plus, Gil still has you on his suspect list."

"All right, I'll come, but don't expect me to enjoy the meal. Just thinking of dining with Missy makes me nauseous."

Anne suggested a restaurant near the beach and a time. She next called Jen.

"Of course, I'll come," Jen said immediately. "But convincing Missy could be a monumental task."

"I'll use diplomacy, tact, and if that doesn't work I'll threaten her." She gave Jen the place and time.

Rose was excited by the prospect of just having dinner in a real restaurant without kids.

"I'll tell Jack it's a girls' night out and he'll have to

watch the kids and make dinner. He won't like it, but he'll do it."

Anne chuckled. Jack Bennett wasn't really into babysitting, food preparation, or any other kind of household chore. She suspected the kids would be plunked down in front of the TV with ordered in pizza.

"How are you going to get Missy to come?"

"Curiosity, if nothing else. Plus I think she'll jump at the chance of a free meal at a classy restaurant."

"How classy?"

"The Passageway."

"Whooo, that's expensive."

"It's the only bait I can think to use."

"I'll bust the budget. What time?"

"Seven?"

"Fine, see you there."

Anne hung up satisfied with the arrangements so far. *Now, all I have to do is wheedle Missy into agreeing.*

She grabbed her workout clothes and car keys. It was time to see if the new Mrs. Warren was working out this morning.

Luck was with her. She entered the gym a little before ten and saw her quarry on the stair-step machine. Taking a deep breath Anne approached the younger woman.

"Missy, we need to talk."

"About what?" she replied without pausing in climbing stairs to nowhere.

"Barbara Lassiter."

"Not a chance in hell."

"Please, it's important, but not here at the club. Too many ears. Let's meet at The Passageway. It's a nice restaurant on the inlet to the bay."

"I repeat, not a chance in hell."

"Look, Barbara is dead. Jerry Bedford is dead. And neither was an accident."

Missy finally ceased climbing and gave her a startled look. "What are you talking about? I thought Jerry stayed too long in the hot tub and had a heart attack."

Anne hesitated, not wanting to reveal too much. "There were indications to suggest otherwise. How about seven o'clock? My treat. We really have to talk to you."

"We? We who?"

Again Anne hesitated, mentally cursing herself for the slip. "Candace, Jen Swanson, and another friend of ours, Rose Bennett."

"Just how stupid do you think I am? Are you trying to set me up to be murdered, too? Which one of you drew the short straw? The convicted killer? Or are the rest of you branching out?"

She gritted her teeth. "No, just the opposite. We're hoping to find out more about Barbara. Seven o'clock at The Passageway, okay? It's a very public place, so you needn't feel threatened."

Missy glared, and then shrugged. "Oh, all right. At least you have the class to choose a good restaurant, but I'm letting you know I'm telling Eric exactly where I'll be and with whom."

"Suit yourself."

Anne turned and walked away. Maybe an hour in the gym and a few laps in the pool would help her formulate what she, Candace, Jen, and Rose had to say.

Missy finished her workout, but not without

sending several curious glances in Anne's direction. She figured the new Mrs. Warren was dying to know more about Jerry Bedford.

****

"It's seven-fifteen," Jen said checking her watch for the third time in five minutes. "She's not coming."

"Give her the benefit of the doubt," Anne replied.

Candace shook her head. "It's me. She's not going to haul ass anywhere I am."

"She strikes me as the kind who is chronically late," Rose added. "You have to admit, Jen, you often aren't on time."

Jen rolled her eyes. "Touché. I guess I'm just anxious to hear what she has to say. The deaths of two country club members in less than a week have *all* members on edge. And don't forget Anne's little episode."

Jen had enlightened the rest of the steam room adventure.

Anne glanced toward the restaurant entrance just as Missy walked through the doors. She spoke to the hostess who immediately led her to their table.

"Hello, Missy," Anne greeted. "Have a seat."

The young woman stared at each of them in turn, and then pulled out the chair.

"I don't think you've ever met our friend, Rose Bennett," Anne began. "Rose, this is Missy Warren. Missy, this is Rose."

"Hello, Missy."

Missy nodded, unfolded her napkin, and placed it on her lap. "Okay, I'm here. What do you want?"

"Why don't we order some drinks and relax first?" Anne suggested.

"Relax? I feel like a duck in a shooting gallery." She cast a sharp glance at Candace.

"Nobody here wants to harm you," Jen told her. "We just need to know more about Barbara Lassiter—and Jerry Bedford."

"Strictly off the record," Rose added.

Missy rolled her eyes. "Yeah, right. Ms. Nosy Parker here is dating a cop. My guess is he'll know whatever I say in a heartbeat."

"Only if it could help find your friend's killer," Anne said. "You do want to know that, don't you?"

The younger woman shot another glance at Candace, but made no reply.

The waiter arrived to take their drink orders—white wine all around except for Candace who requested club soda with a lime twist.

"What makes you think I know anything more about Barbara or Jerry?" She hesitated. "Was he really murdered, too?"

Jen nodded. "Definitely. Someone nailed him with a blow to the head, and then may have held him underwater until he drowned. That was probably unnecessary since he was likely dead from the blow."

"What did they hit him with?"

"As far as we know it was some type of makeshift blackjack," Anne said.

"A what?"

"A blackjack," Candace replied. "It's kind of a leather-bound club—short and not hard to conceal. It's easy to make out of a couple of socks filled with a solid material. It's also called a cosh. The socks act as cushioning so the blow doesn't break the skin."

Missy stared with a dubious expression. "How do

you know about something like that?"

"I was in prison, remember? I learned a lot of things. And before you open your mouth, I didn't kill either Barbara or Jerry."

"In other words, someone put something heavy in some socks, nailed Jerry, held him under, and then walked away with no one the wiser," Rose said.

"Well, it wasn't me," Missy declared.

"No one is saying it was," Anne told her.

"Look, I still don't know what you want from me."

"Just information about Barbara and Jerry—Barbara mostly," Jen said.

Their drinks arrived, cutting off conversation. The server announced the dinner specials, and then left with the promise to return in a few minutes. They all picked up the menus and read. When the waiter came back, they ordered.

"Now, about Barbara and Jerry," Anne said.

"The only thing I can tell you about Jerry is that he was one hen-pecked son of a bitch."

"Hen-pecked? Really? He didn't look submissive," Jen said with wide eyes.

"Trust me, if Darlene said jump, he jumped."

"Did he resent it?" Candace asked.

"How should I know? I didn't see her too often, but I listened when other men talked in the bar. They laughed behind his back."

"Did Jerry know this?" Rose said.

"I don't know," she replied with a shrug. "I mean, he was a nice enough guy. He liked things to go smoothly. No bumps in the road. But then I barely knew Jerry Bedford."

"Not quite what I heard," Jen murmured.

Missy shot her a dirty look, but said nothing.

Anne took a deep breath. Time to begin. "Now, what can you tell us about Barbara Lassiter?"

Missy drank a large portion of her wine. "Barbara and I were pretty good friends for a while.

"What do you mean you were good friends for a while?" Rose asked.

Missy gave a half-shrug. "We weren't all that close the past six months or so."

"You mean after her divorce?" Anne probed. "What happened?"

"It's really none of your business, lady. None of this is."

Rose leaned forward. "Look, *lady*, I don't think you get how serious this is."

"Of course I do. She was a friend, murdered in my house, and found by my husband's ex-wife and her cohort. I still believe one of you did it and I can't think of a single good reason to think otherwise. Jesus, why am I even here tonight?" She took another large gulp of wine.

"Because you wanted an expensive dinner on someone else's credit card," Jen told her.

Rose narrowed her eyes. "You're here because we want information and to keep you alive, although I'm not sure why."

Missy glared back at her. "What do you mean, keep me alive?"

"That first day when we found the body, you suggested it was a case of mistaken identity," Anne reminded her.

"Yeah, so?"

Candace leaned forward her eyes staring daggers at

her ex's new wife. "Well, don't you think by now the killer—who isn't me or Anne—knows that? Don't you think that if you *were* the target, the killer realizes he or she made a mistake and is even now making plans to rectify the error?"

Missy's angry expression slowly changed to one of horror. Her eyes opened wide and she sat back in her chair.

"Oh my God," she mumbled, and then drained her glass.

"That's right," Jen added. "As we talk, the killer may be charting a course to take a second crack at you."

"So, we need to know all we can about Barbara Lassiter," Anne pressed.

"And about why you and she weren't the best friends you were a few months ago," Rose said.

Jen raised an eyebrow. "And all about her relationship with Jerry Bedford."

Missy swallowed hard and signaled the waiter who came over immediately.

"I need a refill. Fast."

The man nodded, looked at the others who shook their heads, and then left. The silence stretched.

"Well?" Jen finally asked.

"You really think someone was after me? Do the cops?"

Anne shrugged. "I imagine they're covering all the bases. I'm sure they've been interviewing your mutual friends, especially at the club."

She didn't mind using scare tactics to pry information out of Missy. Gil had already concluded that Barbara was the likely target. With her eye for the men, she made a lot of enemies. The only thing Missy was guilty of was stupidity.

The other woman's reaction to Anne's comment was to widen her eyes further and say with a groan, "Oh shit, they're talking to club members?"

The four women looked at each other, and then back to Missy.

Rose stared the younger woman right in the eyes. "Exactly, what was going on?"

"We heard Barbara was—shall we say—promiscuous," Anne added.

Missy's brow furrowed. "She was what?"

Candace smirked. "She screwed anything in pants."

"And then some," Jen contributed.

"Yeah, Barbara was always on the lookout for another conquest."

"Is that why she and Drew got divorced? I mean, I met and talked with him the other night and he didn't sound too broken up about his ex-wife's death. Was it that nasty a divorce?" Anne said.

The server returned with the wine and informed them their meals would be out shortly.

Missy sighed, buried her head in her hands, and then looked back up, grabbed her glass, downing half of it in one gulp.

Candace raised an eyebrow. "How friendly were you with Drew Lassiter?"

"Candace," Anne admonished not wanting to start an argument.

"Look you, I never cheated on Eric. He may have cheated on you, but I never did on him," she snapped.

Rose blew out an exasperated breath. "Let's get back to Barbara and Drew. Did they get a divorce because of her extra-marital activities?"

Missy groaned again. "Oh hell, I suppose this will all come out eventually, but the truth is Barbara and Drew were never married. They only said they were because Barbara needed to get into the country club and she wanted to make sure she succeeded. A married couple stands a better chance than a single woman."

"Needed to get into the club?" Jen probed.

Missy grimaced. "Okay, wanted. Is that better?"

"They just lived together? That's no big deal anymore," Anne said wanting to move on.

Rose shrugged. "It might have been to some of those snooty country club members."

Jen continued the questioning. "How long had they been an item?"

"I don't know." Missy sighed. "I didn't ask for details. For all I know their relationship was an open-ended kind of thing. She did who she wanted. Same for him."

"No wonder he wasn't upset at her death," Anne said. "So, if he wasn't a husband or even a loving significant other, who was he? A friend with benefits?"

"Kind of."

Now it was Jen's turn to release an irritated breath. "Missy, do we have to pull it out of you word by word? What the hell is 'kind of'?"

"Barbara and Drew were business partners."

"What kind of business partners?" Rose's tone was less than patient.

"They ran a little, ah, service-oriented business."

"Service oriented?" Anne persisted. "What type of service?"

Missy squirmed in her chair and refused to make

eye contact.

"Missy, come on. You've gone this far, you may as well tell us the rest before the police ask you," Jen demanded.

"It was personal. A kind of dating thing."

Candace leaned forward with a look of astonishment on her face. "A dating thing? Are you saying she and her fake husband ran a prostitution ring?"

Missy straightened her shoulders as if trying to maintain some dignity.

"Please, it was an escort service. They called it Reliable Escorts for All Occasions."

"Wait a minute. I heard from several people that you often had very attractive female guests at the club. Were you part of this scheme?" Anne asked.

"They explained to me what they had in mind and asked if I knew any good-looking women who might want to earn extra money. Whether or not sex was involved would be left up to them. For every woman who made a date, I got a small cut—a finder's fee. I only went along with it because it sounded like fun—a way to make a few extra bucks my husband wouldn't know about. And before you ask, I was never one of the girls. I'm telling the truth about being faithful."

"You were running an escort service out of the country club?" Jen questioned her voice rising several octaves. "Jeez, no wonder Barbara 'needed' to get into the club. It was the perfect hunting grounds. Did Jerry Bedford know?"

"I'm not sure, but yeah, I'd have to think he knew—maybe even got a cut like me. Barbara kept him laid and with a smile on his face as a distraction. She was good at that."

"I'll bet," Rose said.

"He doesn't sound so hen-pecked to me if he had time and the wherewithal for a little bump-and-run. Did Darlene know about his affair with Barbara?" Anne asked.

"I have no idea."

Candace skewered Missy with a single glance. "How did this business work?"

"Barbara hung out in the bar and flirted with the men. She also took tennis and golf lessons. Drew would chat up the members on the golf course or tennis courts. Find out how solid their marriages were, and if they were single or divorced, how they would react to a little female companionship. Crap like that. You'd be surprised how many men are in the danger zone age of thirty-five to fifty-five. They want to think of themselves as still young and virile, then look at their aging wives and decide to try younger models."

"Yeah, I can relate to that firsthand," Candace said in a dry tone. "Other than you, where did the other women come from?"

"I told you, I was not one of the other women." Missy paused. "This apparently was not Barbie and Drew's first rodeo. They came to San Sebastian from Baltimore. Before that, I have no clue. Barbara brought some of her friends with her. In fact, I'm not even sure Lassiter was a real name. I was once at their condo and saw an envelope addressed to Barbara Taylor."

"Why on earth would they use a fake name?" Rose asked.

"Because maybe they had police records, or warrants out in their real names," Candace told them.

"People with shady backgrounds can always come up with new identities—fake birth certificates, driver's licenses, social security numbers. All it takes is the right forger and some bucks."

"So, why did Drew leave?" Anne wondered.

Missy shook her head. "I'm not sure. By that time I had very little to do with the supply end of things. I ran out of willing, good-looking friends."

"Yet you and Barbara had some kind of falling out?" Jen pressed.

"Barbara started sleeping around with members a few months before Drew split, and she wasn't very discreet about it. She even made a play for Eric. I told her I didn't appreciate it, so she backed off." She stared down into the depths of her wine glass.

"What aren't you telling us?" Rose said in a tone difficult to ignore.

Anne leaned forward. "If you don't come clean there's the possibility of you being charged with aiding and abetting prostitution."

She had no idea if this was the case, but gave it a shot anyway.

Missy licked her lips and cast glances at all of them. "Look, I have no real proof of this, only what Barbara told me one day after several glasses of wine. Okay? I still didn't completely trust her after she came on to my husband, but decided to patch things up a bit. I don't have all that many friends at the country club. At any rate, the booze loosened her tongue and she said she discovered a new sideline—blackmail."

Jen drew a sharp breath. "Blackmail!"

Anne and Rose exchanged looks. Thanks to Isadora Powell, they knew all about blackmail.

"Yeah, Barbara would come on to a member, do him, and catch the whole thing on a hidden camera in her bedroom. She said they were making money hand over fist."

"So, why did Drew take off from such a profitable enterprise?" Candace wanted to know.

"Like I said, I'm not sure. All Barbara would say was that she had a new business partner, and that between them they were really going to rake in the bucks."

"Who was the new partner?" Jen asked.

Missy shrugged. "I have no idea and didn't ask."

Anne sat back not liking the direction this investigation was taking.

"Missy, if I were you, I'd be very careful. Barbara may have recalled the next day that she'd let things slip. She also might have confessed to her new partner who wanted to make sure you didn't repeat anything," she counseled.

"On the other hand, her new partner may have decided Barbie was the one that needed to be silenced," the young woman deduced with a hopeful expression.

"And kill the goose that laid the golden egg?" Jen replied. "I don't think so. He or she would tell Barbara to shut the hell up and do her job."

"Maybe I should just take a nice long vacation."

"So now that Barbara is dead, is the escort service still in operation?" Rose asked.

Missy shrugged. "I don't know, but I haven't seen many of the women she recruited in the bar lately. Things began slowing up about three months ago."

"After the divorce and Drew's supposed departure for California," Anne murmured.

“I had no idea Drew was still in town.”

Jen folded her arms across her chest. “When did Barbara make a play for Eric?”

“Not long after the split.”

“Sounds like she and the new partner were trying to set up your husband as a new contributor to their income,” Candace said.

“That thought never occurred to me. The bitch! And to think I wanted to kiss and make up.”

The waiter arrived with their meals. Missy took one look at it and shuddered.

“No way, can I eat now. Waiter, would you put this in a box? I need to go. I don’t feel so hot.”

He nodded and whisked her plate away as the others poked at their food.

“I suppose you’re going to go tattle to your cop boyfriend with all of this,” the younger woman said in a snide tone.

“I’ll have to. You just gave the police one hell of a motive. I’ll try to keep your part in the scheme out of it, but can’t promise.”

Conversation ceased. The man returned a few minutes later with the box and a check. Missy pushed back her chair and rose sliding the bill toward Anne.

“Here, this is yours. And if you say one word of this to anybody at the club, I’ll publicly call you all liars.”

On those parting words, she whirled and left.

“Oh, my God, I don’t know whether to believe this or not,” Jen said. “By the way, did anyone else notice Missy’s speech is riddled with clichés?”

“Yes, I noticed, and I believe what she said,” Rose countered. “It makes sense. The Lassiters were scum and it explains all the good-looking women as guests."

Anne sighed. "I think she's telling the truth as far as she knows it. Missy was scared when I told her Jerry Bedford had been murdered. That may be part of why she showed up."

"I wonder what excuse she gave Eric for dining out," Candace said, and then chuckled. "I get a laugh out of how all those upstanding country club members who demanded I get the boot will react to knowing their precious establishment was at the center of a call-girl racket."

Anne didn't see anything funny about it. And blackmail was a dangerous game—a very dangerous game.

Chapter Fourteen

Anne saw the kids off to school the next morning, and then took a cup of coffee onto the patio to think. Missy had dropped a nuclear bomb in their laps last night.

Imagine. An escort service being run out of the San Sebastian Country Club. Male members who were clients obviously knew about it. What about their wives or girlfriends? How many of them had suspicions about those get-togethers in the bar? She doubted the clients would tell anyone, especially if blackmail was involved.

It upped the suspect list by the dozens. Now, what to do with the information. She immediately called Gil, but got his voice mail, left a message to call her as soon as he could, along with a dinner invite that evening. She assumed he was busy with another case. The San Sebastian homicide detectives sometimes doubled in other departments, which tended to keep them busy. Oh well, she'd tell Gil when he came to dinner tonight, but how on earth were she and the Snoop Group supposed to ask discreet questions about this?

Hi, Darlene, Roberta, Lynne, fill-in-the-blank, what can you tell me about the Lassiters' escort service and its connection the club?

Oh, yeah, like that would go over well.

On the other hand, she did have another golf lesson

with Ted Saunders this morning, and today she'd be on her own. Jen had several appointments, one of them being Jerry Bedford's funeral. Another chat with the tennis pro, Adam Jefferies, might yield something new. Anne just hoped her bank account could take the hit with all this private instruction.

She finished her coffee, then went upstairs to change and write a few more pages of her latest work in progress. If nothing else, she was gathering plot lines to last a lifetime.

****

Anne squared her shoulders, gripped the golf club tightly, took a deep breath, and swung. The solid dink of the ball hitting the club face told her she'd hit a decent shot. She looked up to see the ball sailing down the driving range with only a slight curve to the right.

"Excellent, Ms. Jamieson. I'd say that was close to a hundred-fifty yards. You may have found a new sport," Ted Saunders said with enthusiasm.

"That one was rather good, wasn't it?"

"I suggest you play nine holes to see how you do on a real course. I noticed you were on the practice green earlier this morning. How's the putting going?"

"Not bad. I also tried the little area for short shots. Didn't do too well there."

"Chipping and your short game will come the more you play. Now, let's hit another one."

Anne banged away at the bucket of balls for a few more minutes with Ted giving advice along the way. *Time to pry some more information out of him about the Lassiters.*

She stood and shielded her eyes while watching the trajectory of her last shot.

"You know, I'm really liking the club. I mean, I can play tennis, work out, swim, golf, and get a great meal without having the hassle of driving from place to place. Wish I had discovered all this years ago. My ex-husband would have enjoyed it."

"You're never too old to learn, Ms. Jamieson."

"Ah, to be twenty-something again," she said with a small laugh. "I had dinner last night with Missy Warren. I have to admit, I'm envious of her. She looks great."

"She keeps fit, that's for sure." He shot her a guarded look. "You had dinner with her?"

"Yes, she and I got to talking in the gym yesterday. She's really missing Barbara Lassiter. I guess they did a lot together. She didn't seem to think much of Drew."

"Drew's an okay guy."

Anne shoved her driver back into the bag. Her hour was almost up.

"I guess it's only natural for Missy to take her friend's side in the case of a divorce."

"I wouldn't know about that." His tone was cool.

"I met him in the lounge the other night and again in the dining room yesterday. He was with that investment man. What does Mr. Lassiter do for a living?"

"He's an entrepreneur. He's got a lot of irons in the fire from what I hear. His latest is this financial thing with Mr. Sturgis."

Yeah, he's an entrepreneur all right.

"I've always wondered what an entrepreneur does. Do you know of any other businesses he's in?"

Saunders checked his watch. "Time's up for today, Ms. Jamieson. Would you like to schedule another lesson?"

"I would, but let me check my agenda for next week first."

"Fine. Just give the pro shop a call when you're ready. I have another engagement. Can you find your way back?"

"Yes, of course. And thank you."

He nodded, turned, and walked away quickly.

He knows something. He just isn't going to discuss it.

She sighed and pulled her golf bag along the path to the pro shop. Next stop, the gym. Maybe somebody there would know more about Bobby Lanier's sudden departure.

****

The gym was surprisingly busy for eleven-fifteen. Anne scanned the room noting that Missy was not among the exercisers. Maybe she'd already come and gone.

Not sure which apparatus to use first, she gravitated toward the stationary bikes choosing one next to an older gentleman. He pedaled at a moderate pace. A slight sheen of perspiration glistened on his bald head.

"Good morning," she said climbing on the seat and adjusting the time and difficulty levels. "Guess it's time to pedal to nowhere."

The man laughed. "Yep, gotta get the old heart pumping. You new here?"

"Yes, took out a trial membership last week. My friends Missy Warren and Barb Lassiter had been after me for months to give it a whirl. Wasn't it awful about Barbara? I mean, I knew her in a casual kind of way through Missy."

"Terrible tragedy. Just hope the cops can find the killer soon."

"I don't see Missy here. To hear them talk about it, she and Barbara were the workout queens."

"Missy is usually on the machines for a couple of hours in the morning. A real gym rat. Barbara not so much. She'd work out, and then stop to socialize. She loved flirting with the men, that's for sure."

Anne forced a chuckle and pedaled faster. "That she did. Heard she had more than a couple of conquests, too."

"Rumor mill was rife about that, but you know rumors."

"Right, some are true and others not so much."

"And I hate to say something bad about your friend, but I never approved of Mrs. Lassiter. Just too chummy with married men."

"Sometimes married men are the easiest to pick off."

"I'm afraid I was raised to respect your marriage vows. I'm seventy-four, love my wife, and wouldn't dream of flirting with someone else. Causes trouble for everybody."

"I agree. I also heard that Bobby Lanier no longer is with the club. Missy recommended him to me as a personal trainer."

"Yeah, someone told me he got another job out of town and just took off. Here one day and gone the next." The elderly man stopped pedaling. "Ah, good heart rate. Not bad for thirty minutes. Nice talking to you. Have a good workout." He smiled and walked toward a treadmill.

Anne continued on the bike until the timer dinged signaling her twenty minutes were up. She walked across the room to the machines taking the opportunity to chat with various people as she did. She garnered no new information. Bobby was gone—that's all anyone knew. Then she got lucky while on the biceps machine. Two men stood nearby and their conversation dealt with Bobby and Barbara.

"I told Bobby he was playing with fire when it came to the Lassiter woman," one man said. "She was a man-eater. Always coming on to the men."

"I wonder if he was involved in any of her, shall we say, extracurricular activities," his companion asked.

"My guess is yes. Bobby tried to hook me up with some friend of hers once. He wasn't even subtle about it. Said if I was looking for a good time, I should meet Barbara in the bar around five. She could introduce us. I'm a happily married man. Told him so in no uncertain terms."

"He made the same pitch to me about six or seven months ago," the second man said. "I have to admit that after my divorce the idea was intriguing and Barbara's friends were damned good-looking. Even went so far as to meet the woman, but I backed out of an actual date. The whole set up just didn't sound right, if you get my drift."

"After they got divorced the women seemed to stop showing up for happy hour."

"Never liked Drew Lassiter. Too good-looking, too buff, too hearty for my taste. Always had the feeling he was after something."

If Anne did one more biceps curl her arms would

fall off. She stopped, got off the machine, flexed her arms and winced. Damn, she'd feel this tomorrow.

The conversation near her also ceased as the men realized they'd been overheard.

Ignoring them, she headed for the locker room. If nothing else, she learned that at least some of the members of the San Sebastian Country Club suspected the Lassiters' activities were not on the up and up.

****

Twelve-fifteen on a Friday was not the best time to walk into the dining room of the club without a reservation. Luckily, the maitre d' found Anne a table for two along the wall. She opened the menu and mentally groaned. Between the cost of the trial membership, the golf lessons, and the dining room, her budget would soon be blown out the window. She ordered iced tea and the cheapest thing on the menu, a chef's salad—and it wasn't all that cheap.

Her tea arrived within a few minutes. She thought as she sipped. The two men in the gym had confirmed Missy's account of the Lassiters.

The point is how many others knew about the couple's business dealings? Jerry Bedford? Probably. Sam Nordstrum? Possible.

She'd also have to say that Bobby Lanier, Adam Jefferies, and Ted Saunders were also in the loop along with the bar manager. But what parts did they play? Talk up members while they were working out or smacking tennis and golf balls? Did any of them get a cut of the action? Did the bar manager turn a blind eye to what was going on for a few added bucks?

And don't forget the female angle. Did Darlene know what was going on? Possibly. On the other hand, her main concern would have been not an escort service, but her husband's affair with Barbara. Lynne? She strikes me as a moralistic tight-ass. If she knew about the Lassiter's enterprise, she'd have raised holy hell. Her reaction to learning about Jen's inviting Candace to lunch proved that.

The problem was this escort service thing had opened up the suspect list to include a large part of the country club—at least as far as Barbara's murder was concerned.

The motive for Jerry Bedford's death was another matter. Had the past club president been more involved with the Lassiters than she thought? And if what Missy said about Barbara having a new business partner was true, then could it have been Jerry? Or did the new partner consider Bedford a threat—someone who knew too much?

Her salad arrived. So this is what a seventeen-dollar Chef's Salad looked like. She poured the balsamic vinaigrette dressing over the top and forked a hunk of lettuce into her mouth. It tasted like any other Chef's salad, but honestly—seventeen dollars?

While eating, she plotted what she'd make for dinner with Gil tonight. It was just the two of them since this was her ex's weekend with the kids. Now that her son was sixteen, he drove the two-and-a-half hours to and from Orlando. She worried, but realized she had to let him have some independence.

"Well, well, Anne, mind if I join you?"

Startled, she looked up to see Wes Canfield standing next to the table.

"No, not at all. Where's Bertie?"

He pulled out the chair and flopped into it. "Oh,

she had a tennis lesson, and then decided to do some cardio in the gym. I didn't want to sit at home, so came along to see if we could get a court later. Like to make sure I'm getting my money's worth from Jefferies' tutoring."

The server stopped by the table. "I'll have two double vodka martinis and the open-faced shaved filet sandwich with a baked potato—with all the toppings—and a small salad. And bring the drinks together."

Anne had to wonder how effective he'd be on the tennis court with that much booze and a heavy meal in his stomach.

"You seem to be making good use of the club. How do you like us so far?"

She gave him the usual spiel about all the activities the facility offered.

"Yes, we do have an excellent assortment of things to do."

The statement made Anne pause. It suggested he knew of activities not on the club brochure—like escort services.

His drinks arrived and he quickly downed one of them. "Thank you for letting me join you. I hate to eat alone, don't you? Never know where to look."

"It can be awkward," she agreed.

He gulped a sizeable portion of drink number two and leaned toward her.

"Well, today is my lucky day. I'm fortunate to be dining with a beautiful young woman." He winked and slipped one of his hands under the tablecloth.

The next thing Anne felt was his hand on her knee. Good God, he was coming on to her! She almost dropped her fork and moved her leg out of the way.

"Behave yourself, Mr. Canfield. What would your wife say?"

"Oh, Bertie's okay. Just a little too possessive at times. Sometimes I like to get away from her for a while." He winked again.

"Yeah, well, I'm engaged and don't appreciate your actions."

He straightened and shrugged. "Whatever. Won't happen again. So, are you planning on joining on a permanent basis?"

"Haven't decided yet." She placed her fork in the almost empty salad bowl and pushed it away. The temptation to stab Wes with it was strong.

"I like the atmosphere. Can make a lot of social and business contacts over a drink, dinner, and on the courts or course, among other places."

Again his comment hinted at something.

"Since you seem to be here a lot, I assume you don't have a job," he said with what could only be described as a leer.

"I'm an author. I write romantic suspense." She looked around for the waiter, found him and signaled for him to come over.

"Oh, that's right. I remember you telling me that." He winked again. "Romance, huh? Lots of sex?"

Anne gave him a frosty stare. Why did people automatically think romance equated to porn? She was about to give him a piece of her mind when the waiter appeared.

"Check, please." Her dining companion ordered another drink. The server nodded and left.

"Leaving so soon? Stay and keep me company while I eat."

"I need to get back home."

The waiter brought her check. She flipped out her credit card. He once again disappeared.

An awkward silence fell as Wes finished drink number two. All Anne wanted at this point was to get the hell away from the man. The waiter returned, handed back her card, and Wes drink number three. She signed the receipt.

"Have a good lunch, Wes. See you…"

"Well, isn't this a cozy setting," a woman's voice interrupted.

Anne looked up and groaned inwardly. Bertie.

"Bertie, hello, how are you?"

Bertie ignored Anne and glared at her husband. "I thought you said you had some business to attend to this morning."

"I did," he mumbled. "Got finished and came here to find you. Maybe we can get in a quick set."

That was definitely *not* the story he'd told Anne.

His wife eyed the martini glasses on the table. "I see happy hour has already begun."

"Bertie, Wes is expecting his food any minute. Why don't you take my seat? I'm finished."

The woman shot a decidedly unfriendly glance at her. "And how did you come to be dining with *my* husband?"

"Really, Bertie, lower your voice. People are beginning to stare," Wes said.

Anne glanced at the nearby tables. He was right. A few members were staring.

"The dining room was crowded," Wes continued. "I saw Anne and asked to join her. You know I don't like to eat alone."

"There are a lot of things you don't like to do alone," she shot back.

Anne rose. "Here, Bertie. Have lunch with *your* husband? I'll see you later."

Without another word, she walked as quickly as she could to the door. It wasn't until she was in the lobby that she breathed again.

What the hell just happened in there? Wes Canfield was anything but hen-pecked. He'd come on rather strong to her. No wonder Bertie kept him on a leash. The old so-and-so had a wandering eye. *And I wonder if it strayed to Barbara Lassiter.*

Anne hurried to the pro shop to pick up Jen's golf clubs. She gave her parking ticket to the valet and was amused to see Bertie shoving Wes into a dark blue Mercedes, then tossing a take-home bag from the restaurant onto his lap. She then got behind the wheel and peeled out.

In spite of it all, Anne had to chuckle. *Wait until I tell Jen and Candace about this!*

****

Anne called Jen later that afternoon. "He did what?" Jen crowed as she laughed.

"Honest to God, he made a clumsy pass at me."

"I can't believe it. Stodgy old Wes Canfield?" Jen's laughter increased.

"And that's not all." Anne told her of Bertie's arrival and the Canfields' departure.

"I'd have paid to see that! I can now see why people say she keeps him on a short leash. I wonder how many other women he's tried that tired old routine on."

"Who knows? But his wife certainly seemed to be

clued in to his peccadilloes. She also glared at me like it was all *my* fault. He was the one who approached me and asked to sit down." Anne didn't know whether to sound amused or outraged. "The whole thing was bizarre."

"With a capital 'B'."

"All I know is I'm going to avoid both of the Canfields from now on. By the way, what does Wes do for a living or is he retired? I had him pegged as in his early sixties."

"You know, I'm not sure. I've known them for several years—played tennis with them—and no, he never hit on me, but it seems like they spend a lot of day time at the club."

"Could be he had a lucrative profession and took an early retirement at fifty-five or something."

"Or maybe they won the lottery. Wes doesn't strike me as being the brightest bulb in the pack. You know, slow-witted, on the dull side, and always saying the wrong thing at the wrong time."

"And yet, he had the presence of mind to squeeze my knee. He also made veiled comments that make me wonder if he knew about the escort service."

"It's possible if he spent any time in the bar, especially after four o'clock. You know, Bertie's playing tennis and he sneaks in the opportunity of a couple of martinis without her being any the wiser."

"Well, he certainly sneaked in more than one opportunity today."

Jen laughed again. "How did your golf lesson go?"

She relayed her conversations with Ted Saunders and the man in the gym. "I wanted to chat with Adam Jeffries, too, but never saw him. And Missy who is as regular at the gym as the sun rising wasn't anywhere in sight today."

"Hmmm. Could be our discussion last night threw a scare into her. Maybe she'd hiding under the bed. And an escort service would resonate with younger members, but the older generation like the man in the gym wouldn't approve of it at all."

"That would narrow down their field of operations."

"And yet their clientele could include a lot of members. So when do we go back to ask more questions?" Jen said.

"I'm not sure we have anybody left to ask. Most people are clamming up whenever Barbara Lassiter's name is mentioned. I'm more interested in Drew Lassiter at the moment. His business partner gets offed and suddenly he's back in town and doing new business with a known con man."

"Let me see if I can get a hold of Phyllis Allen, the woman who was at lunch with Drew and the con man the other day. She's pretty sharp. Maybe she can give me some info on this Sturgis guy and Drew Lassiter. Perhaps you, me, and Phyllis can do lunch tomorrow."

"Not a bad idea, but would she open up with me around? After all, I'm a stranger."

"You could be right."

"Maybe I'll see if I can glean any more out of Adam Jeffries while you're at lunch. Then we could meet later and compare notes."

"Great! I'll call Phyllis and set it up. Talk to you later."

Jen hung up and Anne sat back in her office chair. Gil was due to come by tonight for dinner and whatever else was on the horizon. She chuckled at what his reaction would be when she told him about Wes Canfield. Then the laughter abruptly ceased as a sudden thought.

Suppose Wes had come on to Barbara Lassiter. What if Barbara had accepted his advances—and caught it on camera. Had she been blackmailing him? And did Bertie know about it?

Barbara and Wes? Naw, not possible. Or is it?

Chapter Fifteen

With the costs at the country club adding up, Anne's dinner budget was shrinking. Tonight she was going to serve tuna casserole with a salad and rolls. She didn't really like tuna casserole. Gil wasn't fussy, but tonight's menu was totally uninspiring.

He arrived fifteen minutes late, very unusual for him.

"Hi, sorry I'm late, but it's been a helluva day. Had a bunch of burglaries and I needed to help out. Also sorry for not getting back to you earlier. Just wasn't time."

"That's all right, but I do have some information that you need to know."

She led him into the kitchen, poured them each a glass of Pinot Grigio and gave him the lowdown on the Snoop Group's dinner with Missy.

"They had a what!"

"You heard me. We couldn't believe it either, but it opens up a whole new line of investigation. An escort service and blackmail could involve dozens of new suspects."

Gil whipped out his phone and scrolled until finding a number, then dialed.

"Mr. Lassiter, this Detective Gil Collins with the San Sebastian Police Department. We spoke earlier this week regarding you ex-wife's death. I need you to contact me immediately. New information has developed and I want to discuss it with you. Please call me back at this number to set up a time."

He hung up. "Why didn't you call me last night with this?"

"After Missy left, the rest of us had dinner and talked. I then helped Candace move back to the San Sebastian Inn. Did she call to inform you? Said she was. At any rate, I didn't get home until close to midnight."

"Yes, she called and left a message this morning. But you should have let me know immediately. Time has been lost."

"I'm sorry. Don't be angry, but I didn't see how a few hours would make a difference since one of the principles is dead and Missy seemed to think the whole enterprise was down the tubes."

"I think I need to talk to the new Mrs. Warren again, too."

"Can you keep her name on the QT? She was just doing it for a lark and a way to earn a few bucks her husband didn't know about. I don't think she killed either Barbara or Jerry Bedford."

"She was contributing to a prostitution ring!"

"Gil, Missy is scared. She didn't show up at the gym today and she's always there Monday through Friday. Give her a break. If she tells you the same story she told us what's the harm. Couldn't you just tell Lassiter you got the information from an anonymous tip?"

"Since when do you care about Melissa Warren?"

Anne had asked herself the same question earlier.

"I don't know. I…I guess I feel sorry for her."

"What?"

"I know, it sounds silly given she's such a bitch, but I think she's lonely. Stop rolling your eyes. Most people don't like her and it sounds as though Barbara Lassiter was her only real friend at the club. Could be she feels out of place with the members. They're older, better educated, come from money, or at least earned it the old-fashioned way by working legitimate jobs, traveled to places she's only read about—that kind of thing."

"Psychology 101?" Gil drawled.

"Oh, go ahead and make fun of me, but it's just an impression I got. Can you keep her name out of it? Please?"

"I'll think about it. Besides, that's up to the prosecutor. All I want are the names of her willing friends. Now, what's for dinner?"

Anne sighed. He wasn't a happy camper and she didn't blame him. She probably should have called him first thing after dinner last night with the information.

"Tuna casserole, salad, and rolls. The country club is sucking money out of me faster than a vacuum cleaner."

"I told you not to join."

"I know, I know. Can we change the subject? Dinner's ready."

They filled their plates from the stove and countertop and ate in the kitchen. The white wine was the only nod to elegance.

"Have you got anything new on Barbara's murder?" Anne asked.

"I interviewed the neighbors again yesterday. The woman who was running errands said she left her house at about two-thirty and there was a light-colored car in the driveway next to what turned out to be the Lassiter woman's. It was gone when she returned at three-thirty. We found a neighbor down the street who was walking her dog around three-thirty. She remembers seeing a white car pull out of the driveway, but isn't sure of exactly when."

"Candace? She admits to being there around that time, but swears she never got out of the car."

"Possibly. I also finally got a hold of the homeowner next door to the Warrens. She was out of town and said she noticed two dark-colored cars in the driveway when she left for the airport a little after three."

"A dark-colored car? Other than Barbara's? Any idea who it belongs to?"

"None."

"What color car did Jerry Bedford drive?" she asked.

"A white SUV, and the neighbor says this was definitely not an SUV, but a sedan and not white."

"So, let me get this straight. We have a light-colored car in the driveway at two-thirty, but gone by three-thirty, driver unknown. We also have a dark-colored car, in addition to Barbara's, in the drive a little after three, driver again unknown. Then we have Candace in her white BMW in the driveway at about the same time or later, give or take a few minutes. The place should have had valet parking."

"That's about it," he replied with a smug look on his face.

"What is it you're not telling me? Wait a minute. How do you know what kind of car Jerry Bedford drove?"

"Barbara Lassiter's cell phone was too water-damaged from being at the bottom of the pool to get anything, but we pulled her phone records. She called Jerry Bedford at two-oh-three, just a few minutes after Mrs. Warren called to say she wouldn't be there until four. I found that significant and checked."

Anne leaned forward. "I don't suppose the neighbor running the errands happened to notice if the light-colored car in the drive at two-thirty was an SUV."

Gil smiled. "Happens she did and it was."

"So Barbara finds herself with a couple of hours on her hands and calls Jerry to come over to Missy's for a quickie?"

"We don't know and probably won't. She also had a couple of incoming calls, but the last call on her phone—the one right before she was shot—was to a disposable cell. No name, just a number."

"Do you think Jerry Bedford was her new partner?"

He shook his head. "From what you've told me people had to say about Bedford, I'd have to say no. But that disposable cell is sure looking interesting." He cleaned his plate and pushed it away. "So anything else happen to you I should know about?"

"Well, I had a golf lesson with Ted Saunders this morning. I'm getting better at it. But he's not talking much about the Lassiters other than to say Drew is now touting investment banking with Howard Sturgis, and that he really didn't like Barbara very much. He refused to go into details."

"Somebody needs to give the San Sebastian

Country Club a heads-up concerning Mr. Sturgis."

"Jen's going to put the bug in some ears tomorrow. I also had an interesting talk with a man in the gym. He didn't approve of Barbara, but was too old to be a prospective escort service client."

"Trust me, you're never too old." He rose. "Let me help you clean up."

As they carried their plates to the sink, Anne chuckled remembering Wes. Her encounter would certainly be classified as interesting.

"What are you giggling about?" he asked.

"I don't giggle."

"Yes, you do. What's so funny?"

She gave him the tale of her lunch with Wes.

"Why, that horny old son of a bitch!"

"The funny part was watching Bertie frog march him out of the club and into the car, then peeling out like a teenager."

"I got news for you. We ain't joining this country club!" He grinned and pulled her into his arms. "Now suppose we go upstairs for dessert."

She wound her arms around his neck and kissed him hard. "That seems like a sensible suggestion."

****

Anne didn't really want a tennis lesson. Not only did she have no intention of joining the club, the costs of all the extras were irritating. However, she decided to take one last try at learning if the tennis pro had any information about the Lassiters and an escort service. Unfortunately, the only time available was nine-thirty. So much for sleeping in on a Saturday morning.

Adam Jeffries met her on the court. For the next thirty minutes he alternately praised and offered suggestions on her serve and backhand as a machine punched out tennis balls in quick succession. Anne had to admit he was good at his job. She could see how her game would improve if she took his advice. Shame this was all for nothing.

"Good one," he said as she hammered what would have been a winner into the far corner of the court.

"Now if only I could translate that into a point in a real game. I wish I could play as well as Barb Lassiter. I had dinner the other night with Missy Warren and she said Barb was damn near professional level."

Jefferies snorted. "Not even close. Barbara Lassiter was an adequate player, although sometimes I wondered if she deliberately lost."

"Deliberately lost? To whom? And why?"

He shrugged. "Other men, mostly. I think it may have been all part of her…" he stopped abruptly.

"Her come on? I know. I've heard the rumors that she was—shall we say—on the prowl."

The pro served an ace into the empty opposing court. "Know what I've heard? I've heard that you seem to be asking a lot of questions about the Lassiters and that your fiancé is a cop."

Anne picked at a string in her racket. "That's right, he is. And I'm asking questions because I'm curious as to what kind of country club allows the behavior of its members to border on the obscene. If she was having affairs, I'd think that eventually the women members would lodge complaints. And what about her husband, Drew? If I were him, I'd be upset."

Jeffries turned to give her a frosty stare. "Let's just say Barbara was not my favorite person and leave it at that. Your lesson is over for today. In fact, I don't think you need any further instruction. Good luck, and have a nice day."

He walked off the court leaving Anne to suck in a deep breath. She'd almost had him when he suggested Barbara came on to members. And she had no idea her actions had become the object of discussion at the club. The thought was unsettling. No one would talk to her now about the Lassiters. She tossed a tennis ball into the air and hit it with all the strength she had sending it into the padding on the fence behind the court, then walked away.

Since she wasn't due to meet Jen on the terrace until two o'clock, Anne had the presence of mind to bring her workout clothes and swimsuit with her. Maybe taking out her frustration on the machines and in the pool would help her mood.

The gym was packed—mostly with men. Apparently, a lot of people showed up on the weekends instead of coming in before or after work. She spied Missy on the leg press apparatus. She glanced at Anne, and then looked away. Anne also ignored the other woman. Even with the crowd, she managed to get on the machines she wanted without too much of a wait. In an odd way, Anne would miss some of the activities when her trial membership was over. Exercise three days a week had its attraction. Oh well…

Her mind was still mulling over the possibilities of an escort service's effect on the club. Certainly the Lassiters had profited big time. And likely the golf and tennis pros had known about it. Even Missy had received a cut. But the biggest stumbling point was Jerry Bedford. What had he known and was it powerful enough to get him killed?

Anne had just finished her final grunt on the ab machine when Missy appeared next to her.

"Uh, look, I've been thinking about what you guys said the other night, and there's something I didn't tell you."

She noted the woman's wary expression. "What is it?"

"Well, Barbie and Drew had this condo over near the beach not far from the club, but Barbie told me she had another place closer on the other side of town. I'm not sure if it was a condo, an apartment, or a house."

"Another house? Do you know where?"

Missy shook her head. "No, but it wasn't for living. I think that's where the clients hooked up with the girls. Kinda like the parlor of a whorehouse or something you see in the movies."

"How do you know this?"

"Barbie let it slip the day she told me about the blackmail and her new business partner. At the time, I didn't think much about it. She was hammered and I wasn't sure if it was true. Looking back on it, I can see how that set-up would make sense. First introductions at the country club and if they want to connect, pick-ups at the condo."

Anne thought for a moment. "And that other place would most likely be leased. This is important, Missy. Thanks for telling me. Missed seeing you here yesterday."

"Yeah, well, I spent most of yesterday holed up in the hotel wondering if the killer was waiting in the lobby to get me. Finally decided being cooped up in a suite was worse than death. Besides, the only person who'd want to kill me is Candace Warren and she sure as shit won't be here. You guys scared the hell out of me."

Anne didn't have the heart to tell Missy Candace was back at the San Sebastian Inn.

"Didn't mean to do that. Just wanted to make you aware of the situation."

"Bullshit. I suppose you'll pass this information on to your boyfriend. How much did you tell him from the other night?"

"Most of it."

"I was afraid of that."

"Missy, if Drew and Barbara were running an escort service out of the country club, then that opens the door to a whole lot of suspects. I had to tell him."

"He's not going to want to talk to me is he?"

"Oh yes, I'm sure he will. Kinda surprised he hasn't called you already."

"Oh God, what am I going to tell Eric?"

"Don't worry about that until the time comes."

"Yeah, easy for you to say." With those parting words, Missy whirled and stalked toward a treadmill.

Anne walked over to the free weights and hefted two five pounders in each hand. Her mind jumped from supposition to supposition as she curled her biceps.

So, Barbara and Drew had a second house or condo. Missy's right about it making sense. It would also stand to reason that any financial transactions would take place there, too. Would something like that be a cash-only affair or did they take plastic?

Paying for a prostitute with a Visa card sounded way too strange, but then strange was rapidly becoming the norm in this day and age.

She finished her curls and set the weights back on

the rack, then stopped to stare. The barbells were racked according to weight beginning with three pounds up to fifty.

Oh, my God! She lifted the five-pound weight again. *No, way too heavy, but I'll bet this three pounder would do a nice job on the back of a man's head. Put it in a couple of heavy socks and wham!*

Anne tested the lighter weight by taking a few test swings. *Not hard at all. It wouldn't even take much strength. Anyone could have done it.*

Then another thought occurred. *Why bother with a sock? Just wrap it in a towel, like the kind you'd take into a swimming pool—or a hot tub.*

It was the simplest solution to the whole thing.

****

"You could be right about Jerry's murder weapon," Jen said when Anne relayed her theory. "I mean, the killer is in the gym, maybe even talks to Jerry, Jerry leaves mentioning the hot tub, and then the perp grabs a small weight, hides it in a towel and bam!"

"It makes sense to me." She also passed on the information Missy had given her.

"I'm not so sure about your reasoning with the other apartment or whatever the Lassiters had," Jen said.

She and Jen sat drinking iced tea at an out of the way table on the terrace.

"Why not?"

"Well, for starters, I doubt the women would meet up there with the johns. Barbara would probably give the man a cell number, and then he and the escort would work out time and place. Or they'd make the arrangements in the country club bar. Payment would be made to the escort at the time of the services who in turn would hand it off to her boss if it was a cash transaction."

"I thought it was strictly a cash business."

"There's nothing illegal about an escort service—on the surface. Some of them are even legit, so plastic is taken. The guy would probably give his credit card to whoever was collecting the fee."

"Then why have another residence?" Anne asked.

Jen sipped her tea and wrinkled her forehead. "Maybe as a bolt hole. You know, some place rented under an assumed name, close to the interstate or the airport in case they had to make a run from the cops. My guess would be the airport. Their cars were probably leased, so they'd just leave them in the airport parking lot or garage. It'd take months before anyone noticed. And if what Candace said is true about them having more than one identity, then they could use whatever ID they wanted to book plane tickets and get through security."

Anne sat back and stared. Jen had just nailed it.

"That makes perfect sense. I never even thought along those lines."

"What you're trying to say politely is, how did ditzy Jen come up with this explanation. Well, I watch a lot of *Law and Order* reruns and true crime shows," her friend said with a grin.

"You are not ditzy—well, not always, but if that's how they worked then finding this apartment will be next to impossible."

"Oh, I don't know. The police have a lot of technology at their beck and call. Plus Barbara and Drew may have used the name Lassiter to rent the apartment. Same with the cars."

"They probably used Lassiter to lease the cars and the condo they lived in. But that second apartment or whatever is another story. And don't forget, Drew is still here."

"As far as we know."

Anne sipped her tea and thought. "Didn't he say something the other night about having an apartment in Port Rosa? A place he rented after the so-called divorce?"

"Yeah, I seem to remember that. I wonder if it's under the Lassiter name."

"Maybe that's the place Missy was referring to." She sighed. "Well, with people beginning to notice all the questions I'm asking, I doubt if we'll get much more information from anyone. How did your lunch go with the people we met the other day?"

"I met with Phyllis. Lars was on the golf course. She said Drew approached them a few days ago with an investment opportunity. Something to do with timeshares in the Caribbean and Costa Rica. He introduced them to this Howard Sturgis and called him his partner. The upshot was he wanted them to hand over fifty grand to spend a cool three weeks in a luxury condo on St. Martin. Costa Rica was only worth thirty thousand."

"Did they bite?"

Jen shook her head. "Phyllis didn't like the price tag. Said they could spend considerably less at a hotel on St. Martin for a three-week stay. So, Sturgis switched his tactics and suggested investing in some property that would soon be available for a new upscale mall in the Tampa area. Phyllis said they told him they'd think about it, but on the way home Lars said no way. He doesn't like Drew Lassiter one bit. According to Phyllis, Drew was being oh-so-charming and pushy all through lunch. Her husband doesn't like to be pressured and was not pleased. Phyllis said the whole thing just sent up financial red flags."

"Big red flags. Did you try to warn them about these schemes?" she asked when Jen paused for breath.

"Yes. I told her I'd heard that Howard Sturgis was involved with several questionable business ventures. She'll make sure that gets to Sam Nordstrom and the board. Phyllis also said several club members *have* taken the bait, but she didn't know who."

"Some people have more money than sense," Anne said. "Did you go to Jerry Bedford's funeral?"

"Yeah. It was a good turnout. The Nordstrums were there along with most of the board members, but it was who wasn't there that caught my attention."

"Like who?"

"The Canfields—I guess he was too busy putting the moves on you to bother—Drew Lassiter, the Warrens, a lot of people from the club didn't show. Most of the attendees were family, friends, neighbors, and business associates."

"What did Jerry do for a living?" Anne asked.

"Real estate developer, both residential and commercial. He did very well." Jen glanced at her phone on the table. "Oh crap, I've got to get out of here. Carl and I are having guests over for dinner tonight. Is there anything else we need to discuss?"

"Not that I know of. Have a good evening."

Anne sat back and finished her tea. None of the information either she or Jen had uncovered today amounted to much.

I think my time here at the good, old San Sebastian Country Club may be over.

Chapter Sixteen

"I'd have to say the analysis about your future effectiveness at the country club is right. Thank God," Gil said. "Maybe you can get a partial refund on the money you forked over for a trial membership."

Anne sighed and leaned back. They sat across from each other in their favorite Thai restaurant. She'd filled him in on her latest conversations with Missy and Jen.

"But you have to admit, I gave you some good information. The Lassiters had another residence, and I think Jen's suggestion that it was close to an escape route like the airport and under an assumed name is spot on. Have you talked to Missy yet?"

"This afternoon. She came down to the station with a lawyer in tow and scared to death. She told me the same thing she told you and begged me not to tell her husband."

"I can see how she'd want to keep Eric in the dark. What did the lawyer have to say?"

"Only that Mrs. Warren thought of it as a way to make extra money and just didn't consider the prostitution angle or its consequences."

"She's not the brightest bulb on the Christmas tree, that's for sure."

"In the end, I warned her about withholding information and if she could think of anything else to let me know immediately. The whole interview took less than ninety minutes. Guess I'll have to ask her more questions about this second apartment or house, which she withheld—again."

"She claims to have totally forgotten about it." Now seemed like a good time to change the subject. "What about Howard Sturgis?"

"Someone should call Sam Nordstrum and give him a heads-up that he may have a potential problem on his hands."

"Jen told a member who said she'd pass it on."

"I can't say too much because Sturgis doesn't have a criminal record. He's just slippery and shady. I'm also going to have another chat with the golf and tennis pros."

"And the bar manager. Someone in that lounge had to know what was going down. What about Bobby Lanier?"

"Not answering his phone and his apartment super says he hasn't been seen in over a week. We're checking phone records and credit card receipts. He's gotta be somewhere."

"And of course, Drew Lassiter."

"I left another message in his voice mail to contact me right away. Did that the minute Mrs. Warren left the station. Haven't heard back yet on either call."

Anne also told him of her theory of the weapon used to kill Jerry Bedford.

"I'll tell Frank Roberts to ask the club to provide a three- and a five-pound weight. After all, it is his case. Then the medical examiner can match them against the X-rays taken during the autopsy. That should give a pretty good idea."

The waiter brought their food and for the next few

minutes they concentrated on the spicy lemongrass chicken. Finally, Ann laid her chopsticks aside.

"You haven't told me what you found in Barbara's condo."

"I shouldn't be telling you anything about an ongoing investigation. I've said that before—a lot."

"Oh, come on, Gil, we both know I'm involved in this up to my eyebrows. And I've said that before, too—a lot. Did you find anything?"

He sighed and rolled his eyes. "It was pretty clean. We did discover a couple of driver's licenses in the bottom of a dresser drawer—one for Barbara Messick of St. Louis, Missouri, and another for Barbara Ross of Baltimore, Maryland—both expired. We're checking with St. Louis and Baltimore PDs now. Also found some credit cards under the same names and one issued to a Barbara Taylor. The last one is only two months old."

"Missy said she saw an envelope addressed to a Barbara Taylor at the condo one day. Did she use it?"

"Not that we know of. We're still checking. My guess is she took it out in preparation for a new name and location."

"But why? She was doing land office business here. She had a new partner and a blackmail scam." She leaned forward. "What aren't you telling me? What about her financials? What about phone records and credit card transactions under the name Lassiter?"

Gil laid down his chopsticks and scratched his nose. "Do not tell this to anyone, is that clear?"

Anne nodded and held her breath.

"Her financials show a checking account under the name Lassiter with the grand total of twelve hundred dollars in it."

"That's all?"

"That's it."

"Then she must have had another account at a different bank under a different name."

"Or she funneled it to Drew Lassiter. We're also checking his financials."

"Why would she funnel it to him? According to Missy, he was out and Barbara had a new business partner."

Gil smiled and picked up his chopsticks again. "Did she? Her Lassiter credit cards show only minimal use, but the phone records show she called the number of what turned out to be another disposable phone at least four times a week. I suspect it was either the new partner or Drew. And if you remember, he told us at dinner the other night that he hadn't been in touch with her since the divorce."

"And that he was on some fishing boat in the Keys." She also resumed eating.

"Uh-huh. And that same disposable cell showed someone called her at least five or six times in that time frame—the last one just two days before the murder. It bounced off a cell tower not far from Barbara's condo, which is why we want to talk to him again."

"So, he lied."

"He lied—*if* that particular disposable phone was his. Remember the last call she made was to a different disposable cell."

"You know, when we were investigating Isadora Powell's murder, we discovered she transferred a lot of money out of the country. Twelve hundred bucks is a pittance of what they should have had. Do you think…?"

"I do. I'll bet the Lassiters or whoever they are, spent two or three months on some Caribbean island after every scam or escort service went out of business. They let the trail grow cold, then showed up again in a new city with new names. And now, I'm tired of talking about the Lassiters and discussing things I shouldn't with you. Let's talk about weddings. I've had a whole slew of people viewing the house in the last couple of days. I think I'll get an offer soon."

"Great. Let's finish here, go back to my place, and make a few plans."

"Do you think we'll actually get around to talking?"

She shot him a sexy look and winked. "Eventually."

****

Anne forked a chunk of waffle into her mouth and let the flavors of cinnamon, vanilla, and berry compote mingle.

"You know, we need to get married soon. You make a hell of a good brunch."

Gil laughed as he ate a piece of bacon. "I knew we wouldn't get around to talking about anything last night."

She giggled with him. "So, let's do it now, starting with a date."

"Well, it's almost the end of May. How about the end of June? I'm sure the house will sell by then."

"That's awfully soon and a popular month for weddings. Getting a place to hold it might be a problem, plus some people on the guest list may have already made vacation plans for June. I'd love to hold the ceremony at the Botanical Gardens, but the weather will be hot and June is the wettest month of the year. I think we should look more toward late August or early September."

Gil nodded. "That's fine, but if I sell the house in the next couple of weeks, I'm homeless."

"Nonsense. You'd move in here."

"I was hoping you'd say that." He paused. "We could get married in a church."

"I suppose, but we'd likely have the same problem with availability if we shoot for June or even August or September. I guess before discussing venue and time we need to figure out how many people we're going to invite. I was thinking just family and close friends."

"Same here."

"I seem to recall there's a small chapel on the Botanical Gardens property. Probably built for inclement weather conditions."

Gil smiled. "Great idea. So time of year might not be as important. And the reception can be held at any one of our favorite restaurants. I imagine they could all handle a wedding party of say forty or so, if that many. And if we select early September, the chances of them having an opening is greater, too."

"I think we're on to something here. I can begin calling for availability tomorrow. I'm not sure if it's considered good taste to invite your ex-spouse. Ken's engaged to Paula or so the kids say. What about your exes?"

Gil's eyebrows rose. "Somehow, I don't think that's a good idea."

"Not inviting them seems rude. I should check with a couple of women I know who…"

The doorbell rang. “Who could that be at ten o’clock on a Sunday morning?”

She rose. “Only way to find out is to open the door.”

Anne tightened the belt of her robe as she hurried through the foyer. Her jaw dropped when she peered through the peephole and jerked the door open.

“Nancy! Brad! What on earth? Come in, come in. Gil! Look who’s here.”

She grabbed Nancy’s arm, hauled her inside, and gave her a huge hug.

“Brad!” Gil exclaimed as he joined them. “When did you guys get back?”

“Here in San Sebastian—last night. In the States—a little over a week ago.”

“A week? Where have you been for a week?” Anne asked. “Come on into the kitchen. We were just having brunch. Gil made plenty if you want some.”

Brad grinned. “Brunch sounds great and we landed in L.A. a week ago last Thursday. Then we took a little side trip to Vegas.”

“Vegas? What on earth were you doing there?” Gil asked.

Brad’s grin widened. “Oh, nothing much. Just getting married.”

Nancy chuckled and held up her left hand to display a diamond studded white gold wedding band.

Anne gasped in surprise while Gil gaped.

“Married? Nancy, I’m so happy for you. You, too, Brad,” she said embracing them again.

“I don’t believe it,” Gil declared also giving the happy couple hugs. “You? Mr. I-Don’t-Have-The-Time-or-Inclination-To-Tie-The-Knot has tied the knot?"

"Details. I want details," Anne insisted.

"And I want brunch," Brad said.

"Same here. The time change has screwed with my internal eating clock," Nancy added.

They all trouped back to the kitchen and filled plates, then sat at the kitchen table.

"Now about those details," Anne reminded them. "The last I heard, you were on some island in the South Pacific."

"We were in Vanuatu. A volcano got rambunctious on one of the islands, so we hopped over there from New Britain," Nancy explained.

"It rumbled right up to a stage four, which meant mandatory evacuation of all residents and non-essential scientific personnel," Brad told them as he wolfed down waffles and bacon.

"I was non-essential, so they shipped me to Fiji," Nancy added.

"It finally settled down and the authorities allowed residents back on the island," Gil's brother continued. "But I was sent to do some tests on an island formed a few years ago in Tonga. Most of those eruption islets don't last long. The ocean waves erode them. At any rate, this one was hanging on, so I was sent to do my thing, which I did. Once I was finished, I joined Nancy in Fiji. My boss decided I needed to come back to the states to write reports and analyze data."

"He proposed on the flight to L.A. and we decided why wait? Let's just stop off in Las Vegas, get married, and honeymoon there. So, we did, and here we are. We'll live at my place while Brad makes his reports and such, and then who knows where we'll end up," Nancy said.

"Well, you've certainly knocked my socks off," Anne stated. "This calls for a celebration. You men head to the store and get some really good steaks, baking potatoes, salad makings, and a fancy dessert. Oh! And champagne. Expensive champagne."

Nancy eyed their clothing and chuckled. Anne noticed. Her cheeks burned. Gil also noticed.

"Yes, I spent the night. And your problem with that is?" he demanded.

"Not a damned thing," Nancy replied her eyes twinkling. "You're now my brother-in-law. Anne will soon be my sister-in-law, and isn't that a kick in the ass? Wait until the rest of the group hears about this."

Brad chuckled. "Hope third time is the charm for you, bro."

Anne had to laugh. *Life has a way of making you sit up and take notice.*

Gil tugged at her arm. "Come on, let's go get dressed so Brad and I can do your bidding."

Upstairs, Anne grabbed a pair of jeans.

"I don't suppose there's any sense in me warning you not to talk to Nancy about the murders, is there?" he said as he tugged on a T-shirt.

"None at all." She slid the jeans over her hips. "Besides, I gave her the basics in emails, so she's not exactly in the dark."

"I thought so."

Ten minutes later they were back downstairs where they found the newlyweds putting dirty dishes into the dishwasher.

"Okay, give the details on these murders," Nancy said when the task was finished and the men had left.

Anne filled her in on most of what had happened, and then paused as Nancy frowned, her brow wrinkling.

"What's wrong?" she asked when her friend made no comment.

"I'm just trying to figure out why you and the others believe Melissa Warren about her relationship with the Lassiter woman. I mean, I know I've never met her—Missy, I mean, but from what Candace told us, she strikes me as a chronic and habitual liar."

"No, I think she was being honest. Trust me, when Missy realized she could be on the hit list, she was scared. Too scared to lie."

"The new Mrs. Warren would lie anytime, anyplace if it benefited her. What if she is the new partner? What if she told you guys all about it just to throw suspicion off herself?"

"I guess that might be an explanation, but while Missy is cunning and knows how to spin a tale, she really isn't that smart, and I can't see Barbara Lassiter taking her on as anything more than a person who supplied the occasional girl for clients."

Nancy shrugged. "All right, let's look at this logically. Why would Barbara Lassiter get a new partner? She and her phony husband were doing good business. Don't fix what ain't broke. And who was doing the so-called blackmail. The Lassiter woman and her new partner or the Lassiter woman and the phony husband?"

"I'm not sure, but I had the impression it was the new partner," Anne replied. "Missy said Barbara let it slip when she was half-smashed one night."

Nancy shook her head. "That just doesn't sound right. This woman was sharp. Would she really get wasted and tell something like this to Missy—the woman who by all accounts, isn't too bright and whose husband she hit on?"

"Hmmm, you make a good point. Maybe the new partnership wasn't working out too well. Maybe Barbara wanted out. Maybe she was more into procuring than blackmailing."

"Were these old-fashioned video tapes or digital discs?"

"I have no idea."

"Were any of them found in her condo?"

"Not that I know of. Gil didn't say. I suppose they could be in the other place Missy mentioned."

"If they exist at all. After all, we only have Missy's word the blackmail even occurred. And I'm sure the guy you and Jen found in the hot tub knew about the escort service. Maybe *he* was the new partner and killed this Barbara if she wanted out."

"His name was Jerry Bedford. That's possible. He may have been at the Warrens' with Barbara near the time of her death. Witnesses saw a car similar to his in the driveway. But if that's the case, then who killed him?"

"A jealous wife?" Nancy suggested.

"Or a client of the service who was being blackmailed."

"Look at this from another angle. Suppose the Lassiters were the ones being blackmailed?"

Anne stared in surprise. "Someone who found out about the escort service and was willing to look the other way for a nice, hefty, regular income. Someone like Jerry Bedford? And did Barbara do it? That would work if Bedford was killed first. Doesn't make sense."

Nancy once again paused. "And rumor has it Bedford was sleeping with the Lassiter woman?"

"The worst kept secret at the San Sebastian Country Club."

"Was he married?"

"Wife's name is Darlene and before you ask, yes, I'm sure she knew about the affair. You think she may have killed both Barbara and Jerry?"

"Anything is possible. Maybe she'd had enough of public humiliation, killed Barbara and decided to off her cheating husband in the bargain."

"But how did she know Barbara would be at the Warrens'?" Anne asked.

"Maybe she was suspicious enough to follow her husband. He ended up at the house. Mrs. Bedford recognized the Lassiter car and did a slow burn. When hubby left, she popped the other woman. Later, perhaps hubby suspected she'd done it, so she killed him, too."

"There was a report from a neighbor of a dark-colored car at the house. I wonder what color car she drives."

"Ask Jen. She'll know. And Bedford was the former president of the club?"

"The new president came into office about six months ago. Name's Sam Nordstrum. He's a dick and his wife's a bitch."

"About the same time as the divorce that wasn't and the new partner coming on the scene." Nancy tapped her finger against her lips. "I wonder if the police could get a hold of the Lassiters' and the dead guy's tax returns. Probably doing that as we speak. It's harder to hide money than you think. There's always a paper trail somewhere. Look at Dorie and her

Caribbean accounts."

"True."

"And Mr. Lassiter's alibi is shaky. Even if there's no cell phone service on a boat in the Keys, there's always the radio. So, if this boat captain friend isn't available via cell phone, the Coast Guard can still get a hold of him on the radio and have him contact the police. It might take a while, but it can be done. They can broadcast on a specific channel and if he replies, can ask him to switch to another more private channel. There are no guarantees, especially if this guy doesn't want to be contacted—assuming he even exists," Nancy told her.

"Wow, I never thought of that. I'll have to tell Gil."

"My guess is he already has that figured out."

"If that's so, then maybe the boat and deep-sea fishing is all a lie."

"I'll bet Drew Lassiter was right here in San Sebastian on the day his faux-ex-wife was murdered."

Anne sat back and digested Nancy's theories.

Is Drew the killer? Could he have sneaked into the country club to nail Jerry Bedford? Or did it happen like Nancy says—Darlene did them both? And what was going on with this escort/blackmail business?

Both Darlene Bedford and Drew Lassiter were looking like more than persons-of-interest. But where was Drew?

The garage door opening caught her attention signaling her kids had come home from Orlando. Sure enough, a minute later, Ken and Lisa entered the kitchen.

"Mrs. Carlyle, you're back," Lisa said.

"Like crabgrass," Nancy replied.

"Nice to see you again, Mrs. Carlyle. I can't wait to hear all about the South Seas and volcanoes," Ken added.

"Be glad to tell you all about it, and it's no longer Mrs. Carlyle. I'm Mrs. Brad Collins now."

"Holy cow! You're going to be like, my aunt?" Lisa exclaimed.

Anne grabbed her phone and texted Gil to bring more food. "Sure looks that way. And why are you guys back so soon? It's not even two o'clock. I wasn't expecting you until after dinner."

Lisa wheeled her suitcase toward the foyer. "Oh, Dad and Paula had some kind of thing to go to tonight, plus I have some homework to finish."

"And storms were forecast for later this afternoon, so we just decided to leave early," Ken said, following his sister. "Congratulations, Mrs. Collins. I've always kind of thought of you as family anyway."

"Thanks, Ken," Nancy answered, blinking rapidly as if clearing tears from her eyes. She turned away from Anne. "Well, maybe we can set up the dining room table while we wait for the guys to get back."

"Good idea."

Anne hid a smile. A simple statement by her son almost had one of her best friends in tears. Yet in a way, he was dead on. Nancy, Rose, Jen, and even Candace were like family. They knew each other's trials and tribulations, the high spots and the low points in their lives. They'd helped each other through more than real family had over the years. As of now, it was too soon to know about Ellie, but she had a hunch things would work out fine with their newest critique partner.

She and Nancy chose the best linen to go with the crystal and china with Nancy keeping up a constant stream of dining experiences in the jungle—none of which Anne ever wanted to encounter.

"You ate a cockroach?"

"A sort of cockroach. It's considered a delicacy when roasted. Crunchy, kinda like potato chips. That's what I pretended it was when I popped it into my mouth. I should have pretended harder. The villagers, however, applauded my bravery. When in Rome…" Nancy said with a twinkle in her eye.

"And how many of them did you eat?"

"I didn't eat any villagers," she replied with a grin. "Sorry, had to critique your statement. I missed you all."

Anne laughed. "Okay, smart ass, how many cockroaches did you eat?"

"Just the one. My mama didn't raise no stupid kids."

Brad and Gil returned with filets and the rest of the main course. Dessert was carrot cake from Guilty Pleasures, the number one bakery in San Sebastian. The champagne was French and outrageously expensive.

Brad and the kids kept the dinner conversation centered on volcanoes. Anne didn't mind. It was a fascinating subject and she was still trying to wrap her mind around the fact that it was Nancy who'd participated.

"Wow," Ken said in an awed tone. "The ash billowed up?"

Brad nodded. "Like a bonfire complete with what looked like embers, but were really glowing volcanic rocks."

"Weren't you scared?"

"It's always a good idea to be a little scared, but I wanted to be closer to the action. Wasn't allowed to, though," he said with a shrug.

"Did you see any lava?" Lisa asked before idly forking a piece of very expensive steak into her mouth.

"Not on New Britain, but there was some on the other island," Brad admitted.

Ken transferred his gaze to Nancy. "And where were you during all of this?"

"Safely tucked away in Fiji," she replied. "Brad's boss insisted. Can't say I was unhappy about that. Those earthquakes were scary, not to mention the booming when the ash exploded out of the top of the mountain."

"Maybe I'll be a volcanologist," Ken mused. "Sounds exciting."

"You are going to be the coolest uncle ever," Lisa exclaimed. "This whole family will be the coolest. Imagine, a homicide detective for a dad and a volcanologist for an uncle. Wow, we'll corner the market on cool."

"And don't forget, your mother and Nancy are a couple of fine authors," Gil added.

Anne laughed along with the rest of them, but decided Lisa was right. Being a volcanologist or a homicide detective was certainly more exciting than being a writer.

After cleaning up, and then when everyone had left, Anne poured them each the last of the champagne. Nancy's analysis of the Lassiter and Bedford cases refused to leave her mind.

In the living room, she patted the seat cushion next

to her on the sofa. Gil joined her where she told him her and Nancy's conversation.

"So, I assume that after Missy's information you returned to the Lassiter condo and searched again."

"We did." A long pause ensued as he sipped his champagne.

Finally, she couldn't take the silence anymore.

"What did you find and why aren't you telling me?"

Chapter Seventeen

Gil sipped his champagne before answering. "I told you, there was very little to find."

"What about those blackmail tapes Missy said Barbara had?"

"Nothing."

"We have a whole lot of nothing going on here," Anne complained.

"Right now, we're waiting for phone records on those disposable cells. My guess is they're going to bounce off towers near the Lassiter condo, the country club, and hopefully from near the other place the couple rented."

"Did they own or rent the condo? If they owned it, then they must have had a mortgage."

"Not if they paid cash," he added. "However, they were renters."

"Where is the condo? I don't think I ever knew."

"Near the beach and not far from the country club. It's an upscale community, but not gated. The units sell in the three hundred-thousand-dollar range and rent for anywhere between two thousand and twenty-five hundred a month. The Lassiters paid the rent in cash on the first of the month like clockwork."

Anne sipped the champagne. "That's odd. Most people just write a check in case there's any disagreement on payment later. Did you find any receipts to show how much they, and later Barbara, paid?"

"Not a one."

"This is weird."

"Not if Drew Lassiter was doing the paying and kept the receipts," Gil said.

"Which means that he was in town after the so-called divorce or Barbara paid and sent the receipts to him."

"My money is on him being in town most of the time."

"So they communicated through disposable cells, probably met in out of the way places, and…what?"

"Made plans to leave town and start up again in another city under new names."

"But why? Why leave something so lucrative?" Anne wondered.

"Maybe it wasn't so lucrative anymore. The enterprise could have run its course. Or maybe the Lassiters didn't want to be part of a blackmail scheme and planned to ditch the new partner."

"And the new partner found out about it, killed Barbara and plans to continue the scheme with Drew? Or kill him, too?"

Gil sighed. "I can tell you that if I don't hear from Lassiter by tomorrow morning, an all-points is going out on him. I'm tired of his dodging me."

"Good. He's slippery and…"

Her comment was interrupted by his phone ringing. "Collins… Now? All right, I'll be there shortly." He hung up and put his almost full champagne glass on the coffee table. "Sorry, hon, but duty calls. We have an informant who wants to enlighten us on a series of burglaries this past week."

"You up for dinner here tomorrow night?" she asked as he rose.

"I'm always up for dinner if you're the cook."

She laughed and followed him to the foyer where he kissed her hard and long.

"What time tomorrow night?"

"Uh, six?" Anne replied slightly disoriented from the rush of his lips on hers.

"Six, it is. Have a good night."

She leaned against the door as he left and drew in a deep breath.

Whew! We gotta get married soon or I'm going to go nuts!

Returning to the living room, she drank the rest of the champagne in both glasses and headed upstairs. This Lassiter case was reaching a dead end as was the Bedford homicide. Too many suspects and not enough hard evidence to point a finger at the killer or killers.

Maybe a good night's sleep would help sharpen her investigative instincts.

****

The sound sleep Anne desired didn't happen. She spent most of the night tossing and turning, her mind whirling with motives, suspects, means, and opportunities.

She finally gave up at five-thirty, made a pot of coffee and organized notes for her next book—all about a series of murders at a country club. If nothing else, the Snoop Group gave her terrific plot ideas.

"Mom, you're up with the birds." Lisa entered the kitchen and poured a glass of orange juice.

"Couldn't sleep. Can I make you some breakfast?"

"No thanks. I want to get to school early so I can study in the library before class. This is finals week. Which reminds me, I forgot to mention last night that I won't be home for dinner. Lindy Meade is having a group of us over to study for the history exam. Her mother is a former teacher and has agreed to help and make dinner."

"Same goes for me, Mom." Ken came in on the tail-end of the conversation and headed for the laundry room. "Any clean shirts in here?"

"Probably. Are you going to Lindy's, too?"

"Uh-uh, I'll be at Jay Carson's, but the set-up is basically the same—a chemistry exam. Jay's folks are springing for pizza." He ambled back into the kitchen pulling a T-shirt over his head.

"How are you getting home, Lisa?" she asked eyeing the logo of a rock band she'd never heard of on her son's shirt. At least she hoped it was a rock band, although a brain eating zombie wasn't her idea of music.

"Not to worry. Mr. Meade has agreed to drive us all home. Guess you're on your own tonight."

"I won't be alone. Gil's dropping by for dinner. Just make sure you both are home before ten, okay?"

"No problem. Come on, sis, let's roll. I want to take advantage of the library, too."

She waved good-bye as the kids left. With nothing better to do, Anne took the time to make a small omelet and have another cup of coffee. Finished, she returned upstairs to shower and dress before calling Nancy.

"Good morning. How was your first night back in your own home?" she asked.

"Not bad. The water was hot, the A/C was

working, and the bed was just right. I can ask for no more. What's up?"

"Well, as I was getting dressed, I wondered if you'd like to see everyone at lunch today. I know the gang would love to see you."

"I'd love it! Brad has to work on his reports. He'll probably get a lot more done if I'm gone for a couple of hours. Where and when?"

"Rafferty's at eleven-thirty sound all right?"

"Sounds great, oh, and don't tell anyone I'm married. *I* want to spring that one on them."

Anne laughed. "The surprise is all yours. See you later."

She hung up and called the rest of the Snoop Group, including Candace and Ellie. All were happy to hear their friend was back and agreed to the time and place.

In a better frame of mind than earlier, she added another two scenes to her latest chapter of a work in progress. Today was shaping up to be fun after all. Lunch with her best friends and dinner with her fiancé.

****

Anne arrived at Rafferty's early to secure a table for six near the front windows. Nancy entered a few minutes later, closely followed by the rest of the group. Hugs and welcome-home kisses were distributed.

"So, do tell," Jen said in a rush as they took their seats. "How was the whole experience? Are you going to do it again? Are you and Brad still an item? How does it feel to be home again?"

Nancy laughed. "Whoa, slow down there, girl!"

"Well, you have to admit, it's been a long time," Rose declared with a grin.

"I can't wait to hear about the South Pacific," Ellie said. "I keep visualizing the movie. All that lush greenery and sunny skies day in, day out and, of course, Rossano Brazzi."

"Not quite true," Nancy replied. "It rains—a lot. And the humidity is enough to leave you dripping with sweat at six in the morning. And there was no Rossano Brazzi or songs about washing men right out of your hair."

"So, give us the details," Candace demanded. "What exactly did you do all this time?"

"Before we get into that, why don't we order?" Anne suggested. "That way we can eat and talk without indulging in a four-hour lunch."

They spent the next few minutes studying a menu they already knew by heart, so when a waiter appeared the women had their selections set.

"I'm curious, too. What did you do while out there?" Ellie asked.

"For the most part, I really did take notes for Brad. Sometimes, I had to use the old-fashioned method of actually using a pen and notepad. Internet service is often hit or miss in the jungle in spite of the uplinks we had at base camp."

Nancy went on to explain her role and her experiences with volcanoes and jungle living.

"Don't forget the part about the cockroach," Anne urged.

"Cockroach? What cockroach?" Rose asked.

Nancy laughed and related the joys of jungle dining.

"Oh, gross! How could you!" Jen stuck her tongue out in a gagging motion.

"Barf-o-rama as my eight-year-old would say," Rose added.

The waiter chose this inopportune time to serve lunch.

"I swear, if something on this plate moves, I'm gonna scream," Ellie said.

"Oh, the cockroach was quite dead and very crispy," Nancy said with a straight face, but a gleam in her eye.

"Terrific," Candace muttered as she stared at her club sandwich and chips. "So, it was kind of like a potato chip, huh? Anybody want my chips?"

Everyone laughed and dug into their food.

"So that's all you did, take notes?" Jen asked.

"Until the volcanoes became too active, then I had to evacuate to Fiji with the islanders. I spent a lot of time on the beach writing."

"How come you're home now?" Ellie wanted to know.

"Ran out of active volcanoes. Brad was ordered back home, so here we are."

"Now there's a subject I'd like to know more about," Rose stated. "Is Brad here in San Sebastian with you?"

Jen leaned forward. "Yes, are you and Brad still an item?"

Nancy wiped her lips with her napkin and smiled. "Brad is staying with me and yes, I guess you can say we're still an item since on the way home, we got married."

Conversation and eating ceased. Then Jen squealed and leaped from her chair to run around the table and embrace her friend. The others, with the exception of

Anne, followed babbling good wishes and surprise.

"We have to have a real celebration," Jen informed them when the hubbub had died down and they were all seated again. "A big blow-out at the club. And Candace, don't even think about not coming! I don't give a flip what other people think or say. You'll be my guest and that's the end of it."

Candace drew a deep breath and smiled. Anne had the feeling this time her friend would attend.

"How about next Wednesday night?" Jen rushed on. "I'll get a private room and all spouses or significant others are invited."

Everyone agreed and resumed eating.

"Now, I'd like to know more about what this latest Snoop Group endeavor is all about. Anne's told me most of it," Nancy said.

"Well, so far, this is mostly Anne and Jen taking the lead. They seem to be finding the most bodies," Candace replied. "And yes, I am kind of a suspect again, but I swear by all that's Holy, I didn't kill anyone this time."

Anne shot a quick glance at Ellie who picked at her seafood salad with downcast eyes. She licked her lips indicating she was still not comfortable in Candace's presence.

"Actually, there isn't much more to say. I told her just about all there is yesterday," Anne added.

Jen grinned. "Including good old Wes Canfield?"

"Who's Wes Canfield?" Nancy asked.

Anne giggled and related the clumsy pass the man made.

"Horny old goat," Rose replied.

"Actually, that doesn't surprise me," Ellie added.

"You know him?" Jen inquired.

"In a round about way. I play bridge with Bertie on occasion. A few months ago she hosted a three-table game. Her husband, Wes, was supposed to be relegated to the den, but he kept finding excuses to wander in to the living room, dining room, and kitchen to kibitz. Trust me; he was Mr. Touchy-Feely."

"Doesn't sound like you were an isolated incident, Anne," Candace said.

"And here I thought it was just my magnetic personality." She laughed lightly.

"How was he Mr. Touchy-Feely?" Rose wanted to know.

"Oh, you know, always resting his hand on someone's shoulder or leaning over to see if he could look down our blouses. I got up to go to the bathroom and when I came out, there he was. He smiled, winked, and tried to hug me. I pushed him away just as Bertie came down the hall. She told him to take a hike back to the den. He left, but not before winking again."

"What did Bertie say?" Jen asked.

"Nothing. She just turned and walked away, but I could tell she was damned mad. I had the feeling old Wes would get an earful later that night."

"Did she glare at you like it was your fault?" Anne wanted to know remembering her encounter of a few days ago.

"Yeah, she kind of did. Made me uncomfortable."

"It's funny, but I always thought of Wes Canfield as a dull, boring, slightly tiresome person. Any conversations I recall were mind-numbing," Candace commented.

"Add that to his sense of being a ladies' man and

you have a wife with a lot of patience," Anne said.

Rose chuckled. "Or eternally grateful he's not boring her to death in bed."

"At any rate, back to the Lassiters. Missy is afraid of both the killer and of her husband finding out about her little sideline enterprise," Anne said.

"Poor Eric. He chose poorly," Rose added.

Jen snorted. "Don't waste your pity on either of them. He was an idiot taken in by fake boobs. She's got the IQ of a gnat. They deserve each other."

Candace shook her head. "I don't know. He really does seem to love her and I think in her own way she loves him. I could spend hours delineating how I blame them for all that happened to me, but that's counterproductive. You can't erase the past. So I let it go and moved on."

"I guess that's something we should all do with things that adversely affect us," Ellie added.

"So, what's next on your agenda?" Rose asked Nancy. "Are you going to set up housekeeping here in San Sebastian?"

"For the moment. Brad has a condo in the DC area. It's close to his office, doesn't need much maintenance from him, which means he can pick up and go whenever he wants. On the other hand, he likes the idea of being close to family for a change and the Florida weather is seducing him more than I ever could. What's been happening to your writing careers? I've been a little lax in keeping up with that."

"I have a contract on the book about the conference last year. Just sent the first round of edits in a couple of weeks ago. My work in progress is about Fran and her death," Anne told her.

Jen sipped from her glass. “I sent *Love is All Around* in to the Charlotte contest for published authors at nationals last month. It’s my second book and got some really great reviews. I’m keeping my fingers crossed.”

Ellie shrugged. “I’m still plugging away, but did screw up the courage to enter a small contest for contemporary writers.”

“Good luck,” Rose said. “I have some hopeful news. I submitted *Too Hot to Handle* to Raging Hot Press. They contacted me a couple of weeks ago for a full manuscript, so maybe the third time is the charm.”

“I have the feeling you’re right,” Candace replied smiling. “You’re a good writer. It’ll happen.”

They finished lunch and left the restaurant with Jen promising to look into reserving a private room at the club to celebrate Nancy and Brad’s wedding.

On the drive home, Anne wished the best for all of her friends. Her happy mood, however, was dashed when she got home and checked her email.

We are sorry to inform you that your trial membership in the San Sebastian Country club has been rescinded. Your actions, along with those of Mrs. Swanson, are proving detrimental to other members’ and staff’s morale. They do not like being questioned about recent tragedies or the unfortunate people involved. Sincerely, Samuel Nordstrum, President.

“Of all the goddamned gall!” she fumed out loud. Anne immediately sent a reply.

I assume you will also be refunding the remainder of my trial membership fee. I believe I paid for a full month. I’ve only used two weeks of that time.

Then she reread the part concerning Jen. Uh-oh,

this could spell trouble. She called her friend.

"Yeah, I got a snotty email from him, too, saying I am to cease questioning members and staff regarding Barbara Lassiter and Jerry Bedford. I sent a reply telling him to go stuff himself. I'll ask anything I want."

"I don't want you to get in trouble."

"Phfffft. Like they can do anything. As of now, they don't know Jerry Bedford was murdered unless Darlene told them. Either way, I haven't done anything wrong. Wait'll Carl hears this. He doesn't like Nordstrum much. This could be the tipping point on us renewing our membership next year."

She told Jen about her response.

"You're damned right they owe you! And if they get pissy about it, tell 'em you'll sue."

Anne hung up not sure why she was so upset. *It's not like I planned on joining anyway. Maybe Sam and Lynne figured that out and decided to get rid of me sooner instead of later.* She was convinced the tennis pro, Adam Jefferies had complained. God knows, he didn't want to talk about Barbara and his relationship with her.

Oh well, at least Gil would be pleased. In his mind not going to the club equated with her personal safety.

An hour later, Sam replied to her email.

I'm sorry, but the fee is non-refundable.

She fired back. *Wanna bet? I either get a check for the remainder by the end of the week or you'll hear from my attorney.*

Anne heaved a huge breath. In a way it felt good to tell the pompous ass off. Given her encounters with Lynne Nordstrum, she itched for giving the same to her. She also had the feeling the check would be in the mail today. The San Sebastian Country Club didn't need any more bad publicity.

She sat at her desk with her chin in her hand remembering all she could about the Nordstrums, especially Lynne. That first meeting in the lobby when the woman had chastised Jen for inviting Candace set the tone. Every encounter had been abrasive. Not even the locker room on the day they'd discovered Jerry Bedford's body had been exempt from the hostility Lynne exuded.

Anne recalled that day with clarity. Lynne staring at her with an unfriendly gaze, her large tote bag over her shoulder as she told them she'd been playing racquetball and was joining her husband for dinner. It had been shortly afterward when she and Jen had entered the hot tub and found Bedford.

Her mind fumbled for a vision of Lynne. The tote bag had been green, her skirt blue, and her blouse white. What else should she remember? She wasn't sure if there was anything. She sighed, pushed her chair away from the desk, and stood. Then it hit her.

There was no racket in the tote bag.

Chapter Eighteen

Anne slowly walked from the room. *Okay, maybe Lynne just shoved the racket into a locker so she wouldn't have to deal with it during dinner. I suppose that could have happened.*

But the whole idea once again sent her mind back to the question of was Lynne Nordstrum actually playing racquetball when Jerry Bedford was murdered? As Jen had pointed out, you don't need a partner to play. Anyone could keep in shape or sharpen their game by smacking the ball off the walls to themselves.

Surely, somewhere there's someone who saw her on the court or at least close by with a racket in her hand.

Unfortunately, now that Anne had been kicked out of the country club, she had no way of asking questions to find out. And did it matter? Why would Lynne Nordstrum want to kill Jerry Bedford?

Jen could always ask around, but her friend had also been reprimanded by the club president. Anne didn't want her to get into more trouble.

Downstairs, Anne pulled the dinner makings out of the fridge. As she chopped onions and garlic for spaghetti sauce, she tried to put what she knew into perspective and prioritize her suspects.

Number one on the list of who offed Barbara Lassiter was the new partner, whoever he or she might be. Some gut instinct told her Drew was still in the picture, which meant the new partnership might be in trouble.

Number two, Darlene Bedford. What if she knew about her husband's affair with the woman, wasn't happy, and finally had had enough. Since it appeared Jerry had been to the Warren house that afternoon, his wife could easily have followed and taken care of the situation. The big question was did she also take care of her husband by whacking him in the head?

Possibly.

She added the golf and tennis pros to her list along with Bobby Lanier, wherever he was now.

Also on the horizon was the phony husband, Drew Lassiter. Maybe he didn't like being pushed out of a lucrative sideline. Maybe he killed Barbara and was now setting up business with the new partner. *He's dodging Gil and perhaps using yet another fake name all the while steering clear of the country club.*

And then there was the Howard Sturgis angle. With Barbara dead, was Lassiter setting up an investment scam with him? If so, then avoiding the country club made no sense. That's where the marks spent most of their time.

And the list of blackmail victims and their spouses added to the dilemma.

Anne's mind whirled as she browned the ground beef, onions and garlic in a pan.

Maybe I'm making this too complicated. The answer could be that we have two killers and the motives are totally unrelated.

Her train of thought was interrupted when she heard her kids come home from school.

"Ooo, smells good in here," Lisa said entering the kitchen. "Shame I'm going to miss it."

"I'm making a lot, so there'll be plenty for leftovers one night."

"Good."

"Where's your brother?"

"Waiting in the car for me to get some books. He's going to drop me at Lindy's for the study group, and then go to his own. We should be home by ten."

Anne waved goodbye a few minutes later and resumed her musings. No matter how she looked at the murders, there were too many suspects and too many motives.

With the sauce simmering and the salads made, she wandered upstairs to try and concentrate on her work in progress. An hour later, she gave up.

Honestly, if the Snoop Group and Gil don't find the killer soon I may never get another word written.

Oh, well, Gil was due for dinner in a short while. Maybe he'd have some more information. Enough to take her mind off real murder so she could focus on the fictional kind.

A quick shower and donning a new outfit put her in a better frame of mind.

Nothing like pretty clothes, good food, and a fabulous man to make the day. And with the kids gone…

She smiled in anticipation.

****

Anne stirred the sauce and added water yet again. Gil was half an hour late. It was unlike him to not call and give her a heads up. *I hope he's all right.*

She tried not to let the fact he was a cop prey on her mind too often, but sometimes the fear that he'd come up against some desperado with a gun sneaked in. It was something she'd have to learn to live with when they got married.

Finally, the doorbell rang. She hurried to answer.

Gil entered with a bottle of wine, a smile, and a hard kiss on the lips. Anne accepted all.

"Hmmm, good to see you. I was beginning to think you'd forgotten the way," she said leading him back toward the kitchen.

"I have been one busy police detective the last few days. Today was no exception. Sorry I didn't call, but was following up on some information." He set the wine on the breakfast bar and rummaged in a drawer until finding the corkscrew. "What smells so good?"

"Spaghetti and meat sauce. Simple to make and clean up. What's happening in the investigations? Did Missy's latest news bear any fruit?"

"Some very interesting fruit," he replied as he pulled the cork from the bottle and poured them each a glass of cabernet. "It seems Mr. Drew Lassiter is gone with the wind."

"What?"

"As you know, the second after you told me about the escort service I tried calling him. No answer. I left a message in his voice mail. No reply. So I went to the condo. Not there. A neighbor said he packed up a few things weeks ago and hasn't been around since."

"Packed up a few things? Like what? He didn't live there."

"Which leads me to believe he packed up something else."

"Like blackmail tapes? And weeks ago?"

"Uh-huh. My thoughts are right *before* Barbara

Lassiter was murdered. We got to the condo within a couple of hours of her death. Otherwise, we would have found those tapes along with any financial records, a list of clients, and the names of the women who worked for them. I'm sure Barbara used the condo, while he lived in either the Port Rosa apartment, which is rented to a Drew Lassiter, or he's hiding out at the place Mrs. Warren told us about, *or* he's rented yet another apartment no ones knows about. Plus, he could have simply scrammed. We've put out a BOLO and have our eyes open for him."

"Weeks ago. Wouldn't his so-called wife have noticed some things were missing?"

"Not if she approved and they planned on pulling up stakes."

"Didn't you tell him not to leave town?"

"Yep, but I have to say he didn't listen. And we have his phone records. Seems he and the late Mrs. Lassiter were in contact every other day or so after the divorce."

"That could be excused as discussing property or money settlements."

"Could be. It wasn't until a couple of months prior to her murder that the one disposable phone number began popping up on a regular basis. Nor can we find anyone by the name he gave us for his friend with the fishing charter business in Castaway Beach—or anywhere else in the Keys."

"So he did lie. Do you think he may have killed his phony ex?"

"I'm not sure unless he was going to blackmail Barbara and the new partner with whatever it was he took from the condo. And the new Mrs. Warren *has* enlightened us to their activities. The fact we can't find him simply makes me certain he's involved with more than an escort service."

"What are you going to do?" Anne asked as she stirred the meat sauce and added a touch more oregano before sliding the garlic bread into the oven, then lighting the burner under the pasta pot.

"I'm already doing it. Since I suspected he lied through his teeth when I talked to him the other day at the station, I contacted the morgue to see if he'd made any funeral arrangements."

"That's right. I don't recall anything being said about a funeral. There was nothing?"

"No funeral arrangements, but he did have the body shipped to a Mr. and Mrs. Thomas Richards in Waverly Crossing, Indiana."

"Who are they?" Anne joined him at the breakfast bar and sipped her wine.

"I called. Seems Mr. and Mrs. Richards are Barbara's parents. I found that interesting since when I talked to him he told me her parents were dead."

"Whoa! That kind of suggests he planned on disappearing." She paused and thought. "Yet he showed up at the country club to meet with Howard Sturgis and the Allens after he talked to you."

"Maybe trying to get in one more score before bugging out."

"Or to warn Sturgis of his plans. Bet old Howard isn't seen around the club again."

"I'd say that's a good bet. Anyway, after expressing my condolences to her parents, I asked them a few questions. They hadn't seen Barbara in over six years and couldn't tell me much other than to confirm their wayward daughter had a boyfriend she met while in college. A man they didn't approve of named—get this—Andrew Bateman."

"Andrew? Drew?"

"Makes sense to me.

"Why wayward?"

"I asked the same question. It seems Barbara and Drew were arrested and expelled from a university a few miles away in their sophomore year for pandering."

Anne almost choked on her wine. "Pandering? Isn't that like prostitution?"

"Technically, pandering is supplying the need for prostitutes to clients or convincing people to perform sex acts for money."

"So they were pimps then, too?"

"Pimping is slightly different. A pimp takes most of the prostitutes' money earned. It's a fine line between the two."

"Well, I guess Missy was telling the truth. So they both had records?"

"Nope. I called the university to confirm the information. At first they refused to discuss the matter, but when I told them this was an official homicide investigation and if they didn't cooperate I'd have to get subpoenas, they opened up."

He paused to sip more wine.

"And?"

"The campus cops got a call one night about a raucous fraternity party. When they arrived, they found a lot of women who were not students in various stages of undress. One of the frat brothers finally talked and admitted they had hired the women through a third party—an escort service. Eventually, the police found

Barbara and Drew."

"So, were they arrested?" she asked.

"They were arrested, but the charges were dropped."

"Why, for Pete's sake? What they were doing was illegal."

"According to the files, both Barbara and Drew claimed they had no idea sex was involved and that they were simply supplying some attractive women to a fraternity with a reputation for being dorks so they could attract less dorky pledges."

"You've got to be kidding!"

"On the whole, it wasn't a bad defense. If it had gone to trial, the fraternity would have looked bad, not to mention the university, so a deal was struck. The fraternity was put on three-year probation. And if Barbara and Drew did community service, the charges would be dismissed. They were also expelled and, as soon as they finished washing dishes at the homeless shelter, disappeared off the radar screen under their own names."

"They've obviously had a lot of aliases since then. How long ago did this occur?"

"About eight years."

"And Missy said she thought they'd come here from Baltimore. They got around." Anne dropped the spaghetti into the boiling water. "So what do you do now?"

"I wait. Sooner or later, he'll resurface. Now that I have their real names, I can ask for financial records, credit card receipts, and such. Not to mention passport activity. When's dinner? I'm starving."

"Just about ready. Why don't you take the salad

into the dining room? We can fill our plates right from the stove."

As Gil helped, Anne mused over this new information. She had the feeling the new Mrs. Warren knew a lot more than she had told. Which meant she needed to talk to Missy again. The only problem was Anne no longer had access to the gym at the club. Nor did she have Missy's phone number. *If she'd even bother to answer my call. For all I know, the woman is hiding out somewhere again, scared to death.*

During dinner she told Gil about being bounced from the country club.

"Can't say I'm either sorry or surprised. You were asking a lot of questions. Just make sure you get your money back."

"I am, believe me. Jen's madder than hell about it all."

"It's for the best. Sooner or later someone would try to brain you with a golf club."

Anne decided Gil didn't need to know about the steam room incident.

"It's time the Snoop Group pulled out of this one. We've got a lot of leads," he continued.

"What kind of leads?"

"Just leads. Now, let's finish this delicious food, clean up, and then discuss our after-dinner options."

She gave him a slow, sexy smile. "I've got my own ideas about after dinner options."

"So do I."

Anne let the subject of leads drop, but was determined to find out what he had learned and wasn't sharing.

While cleaning up, she discovered Gil's idea of

after dinner options coincided with hers. Unfortunately, his phone rang.

"Collins here… All right. Give me fifteen minutes. Is she sure she wants to press charges this time… Yeah, well family members can make a difference. Do we still have the boyfriend in custody… I didn't think so. Be there shortly."

He hung up and shook his head. "Damn."

"What is it?"

"Had a call last week. A woman came home from work and claimed an intruder beat her to a pulp. While we were there the boyfriend shows up drunk as all get out. I suspected he was the 'intruder,' but she denied it. Arrested him for drunk driving, but he made bail. Now that the woman is out of the hospital, her mother insisted she come in, tell the truth, and press charges. Kicker is she'll only talk to me."

He headed for the front door. "Sorry, honey, but it looks like the after-dinner options are on hold."

"Again." She stood on tiptoe to kiss him. "Take care."

"I will. I'll talk to you tomorrow."

Anne leaned against the door after he'd left.

When we get married, I'm going to canvass other police wives and find out if their sex lives are often put on hold, too.

****

"There! Done!" Anne crowed out loud. "Another chapter finished. I love it when I achieve my goals before lunch."

She rose from her chair and stretched. *Now what I need is a good meal.*

The problem was she didn't want to eat alone. Gil

had not called since he'd left last night. She didn't bother to phone him figuring he was busy and would get around to contacting her when he had the chance.

I wonder what Candace is doing.

Snatching up her phone, she dialed.

"Hi, Anne."

"Hey, girl, have you had lunch yet?"

"Was just thinking about it. You?"

"Same here. Want to meet at Rafferty's in say an hour?"

"Absolutely."

She hung up, changed out of her jammies, and did a few kitchen chores before grabbing her car keys.

"You're chipper this morning," Candace remarked when they met near the hostess desk.

"Yep. Got a chapter done that I thought was never going to come together. I deserve a hearty lunch and some good conversation."

Her friend chuckled. "Well, I don't know how good it'll be, but I can certainly talk."

They were shown to a booth near the front windows.

"I've got some news," Candace said. "As of this morning, Eric and Missy moved back into the house. I guess the stench has finally gone. In a way, I'm kind of sorry to see them leave the hotel. I got a kick out of watching them get indigestion from seeing me in the restaurant every night."

"Maybe I'll drop by soon. I need to talk to her again."

Anne related Gil's news from the night before about Barbara and Drew.

"I doubt if Missy will talk to you or anyone else

about Barbara or Drew Lassiter again. We managed to plant the seeds of fear in her the other night."

"Well, I can't accost her at the country club anymore. I got bounced." She told Candace about the email.

"That's outrageous! And you can bet it wasn't Sam Nordstrum who thought it up. It was Lynne. You and Jen must have struck a chord asking her the wrong questions. Mark my words, at this moment she's trying to get Jen and Carl out of the way, too."

"Jen and Carl have been members for years. They know too many people for her to be successful. But she can be a pain in the ass. I'm sorry for Jen. I never meant for her to get in trouble."

"Jen's never backed down from trouble. Neither has Carl. Don't worry, they'll be fine." She glanced over Anne's shoulder. "The waitress is hovering. Shall we order?"

The server quickly took their orders and left.

"You know, the Lassiters can call it an escort service, but in reality they've been running call girls for years," Candace said. "There has to be information on them from other cities, maybe even other countries."

"Countries?"

"Why not? Some of those third world countries aren't too fussy about business operations. Grease a few palms, pay off the right people and voila, you're good to go."

"I never thought of that angle before," Anne murmured. "Just pick a tourist friendly island in the Caribbean or in Central America. It could be a gold mine. So why mess around with an escort service here?"

"Simple. They were greedy."

Anne sat back and stared out the window. Swell, now an international complication had arisen. And how did Jerry Bedford tie into all of it?

****

It was long after dinner before Gil called.

"Hi, hon, how was your day?"

"Okay. I finished a chapter, had lunch with Candace, and then came home to read a bit. You sound tired. Bad day?"

"And night."

"I'm sorry. Did the woman press charges?"

"Woman? Oh, you mean last night. Yeah, she finally did. We found the boyfriend at the house and arrested him for assault, battery, and a few other things. He was not happy and threatened to kill her."

"Slug. Why was your day so awful?"

"I want you to do me a favor. Stay close to home for a while, okay? And if you have to go out, try to be with other people in a public place."

"Why? What's going on?"

"Just be careful. I don't want anything to happen to you."

"Why should anything happen to me? According to you, the country club was a dangerous place. What's going on?" she repeated.

He didn't answer her question and his sense of urgency sent chills up and down her arms. Something bad had happened. She knew it.

"Gil Collins, if you don't tell me exactly what's going on, I swear, I'll..." she left the sentence unfinished.

Gil sighed. "We got a call early this morning about

a body found in a parking lot behind a bar. Guy had been there for several hours. The bartender said the victim took a phone call and left immediately sometime around midnight."

"And? What has this got to do with me? Unless…who's body was it?" The name Drew Lassiter leaped into her mind.

Silence screamed in her ear for a moment before he answered.

"It was Howard Sturgis."

Chapter Nineteen

Anne's breath stopped somewhere between her chest and her throat. A surge of heat gushed through her body and for a moment she felt lightheaded.

"Wha…what? How was he killed?"

"Up close and personal. Shot in the chest at close range. Less than ten feet."

"Oh, my God, was it the same gun that killed Barbara Lassiter?"

"No. This one was a .32 caliber. Found the shell casing near the body."

"And no one heard the shot?"

"The noise level in the bar was high and the rest of the businesses surrounding it are either retail or office space. No one around."

"And no one found him until morning? It was a parking lot."

"His body was between two cars, one of which was his and the other of a patron who took a cab home."

"But what has this got to do with me? I never so much as met the man. I saw him at the club, but that's it."

"It all comes back to the San Sebastian Country Club. You asked a lot of questions. Now, do you see why I'm so concerned?"

"I know. I understand, but I won't be there anymore."

"Doesn't matter. I'm still worried."

It was nice to have someone care like that. "Are you sure Sturgis's death has anything to do with the club?"

"I didn't really connect it at first either. Sturgis has a long list of enemies. He sucked more money out of people than the IRS. Bound to be someone pissed enough to kill him."

"I can't believe the police hadn't nailed him yet."

"Sturgis wasn't a dummy. He paid a huge retainer to a very smart lawyer, and employed an even smarter accountant. Between them they managed to get him off the hook for most of his misdeeds."

Her mind was back to thinking again. "But I repeat—this has nothing to do with me. I saw him the other day when Jen and I met for lunch at the club. He was there with Drew Lassiter and another couple Jen knew. In fact, it was Jen who talked to him."

"What did she talk to him about?"

"She asked Sturgis if he was a new member and what he did for a living. He told her, and she made some comment about Carl being a commodities dealer and how they'd have to get together. Just prattle. You know Jen. When she prattles people tend to tune her out. Actually, it was Drew she spoke with first, inquiring about funeral arrangements for Barbara. He dodged the question. I guess now we know why. Drew and Sturgis looked irritated we even stopped by their table. I just stood there and kept my mouth shut."

"Maybe someone should tell Mrs. Swanson to keep her eyes open, too."

"Look, Gil, why do you say you suspected someone Sturgis gypped as the killer *at first*?"

"Because we looked at that last call he received. It was from one of the same disposable phones we found in Barbara Lassiter's records. I'm thinking Drew Lassiter."

"How on earth was Howard Sturgis connected to her? Oh, my God! Do you suppose he was Barbara's new partner?"

"We're not sure yet, but that's an extreme long shot. That's why I want you to take care. We've got experts working on finding out who owns those untraceable cells, but it's not easy."

"What about the people at the bar? Did they know Sturgis? Was he a regular?"

"Bartender says he came in occasionally. Last night he got there around ten, sat at a table with a man, and had a couple of drinks. The other guy left and Sturgis moved to the bar. He watched a baseball game on the TV, took the call, and left."

"Any idea who the man was?"

"Description was pretty generic at first, but then the waitress who served them remembered the other guy had a fabulous smile and flirted with her."

Anne gasped. "A fabulous smile? As in Drew Lassiter?"

"Possibly. Showed her a photo. She said it might have been him, but it was a busy night and she's used to getting hit on by customers. She's learned to ignore the attention. So Lassiter could still be in town—somewhere. I've got to go. Do me that favor and watch your back. Okay?"

"Yeah, sure. Take care."

She hung up and stared at the wall.

We know Lassiter and Sturgis were in some kind of

scheme using the country club. And neither has been seen there for several days. Someone must have alerted them a complaint had been lodged. And by now Lassiter knows Gil is looking for him. Did he come out of hiding long enough to meet his partner in crime, perhaps to back off from the scam, and then later lure Sturgis out of the bar with a phone call and kill him? And could he have also killed Barbara?

She wasn't sure her analysis was right. Why kill either of them? He and Sturgis could simply shift operations to another set of wealthy suckers. And even though Barbara may have had a new partner in the escort service, that didn't mean Drew was finished with the business. Both had potential for making money, especially since blackmail may have entered the picture.

And then there was the issue of the gun. Barbara was shot with a .22, Sturgis with a .32. Of course, there was nothing to say someone, Lassiter perhaps, didn't have more than one gun, possibly registered under different names in different states.

And through it all, Jerry Bedford's role in all of this was murky. *He must have known about the escort service, possibly even the blackmail angle, but what was his connection to Howard Sturgis—if there was one.*

Sighing, Anne leaned her head back against the sofa cushion and closed her eyes. Her mind whirled with all the possibilities. So much so, she couldn't concentrate on anything. Nothing made sense. And at the same time if she thought about everything on its own merit, it all made sense.

"I *am* a candidate for the looney bin," she said out

loud.

Her thoughts were interrupted by her phone ringing. It was Jen.

"You are simply not going to believe this," her friend gushed in her ear.

"Jen, there's something you should know. Howard…"

Jen trampled over Anne's words. "Carl came home early tonight and went absolutely ballistic when I showed him the email from Sam. And I mean ballistic. And when Carl gets mad, he doesn't believe in emails or phones. He wants it one-on-one. So, he stormed out and went to the club. I went along to make sure he didn't hurt the SOB."

"What happened?" She'd tell her about Sturgis when Jen ran out of steam. Right now, Jen was on a roll.

"Well, we got there and Carl barged right into Sam's office. Reamed him a new one. Said everyone should be asking questions about two deaths involving members, especially since both were murders. Then told Sam if he didn't apologize, he'd—meaning Carl—would tell everyone in the club about the email. Then I chimed in and said he—meaning Sam—was showing bad judgment by letting a member bring a man with a shady financial past into the club to drum up business."

"How did Carl know Jerry Bedford was murdered?"

"Everybody at the club knows it. Guess Darlene told someone who told someone who told someone else. The old jungle telegraph."

"What happened then?" Anne asked when Jen paused for breath.

"Sam said he'd spoken with both Drew and the other guy and told them to cease using the club as a trolling ground."

"He spoke with them? When? And was it face-to-face?"

"He didn't say. At any rate, I finally got an apology. I tried to get him to reinstate your trial membership, but he refused. Claimed you were disruptive. I told him he was full of shit. I wanted to say more, but Carl got what he came for and dragged me out. Too bad. I was just getting warmed up. We then went out to dinner to calm down. Got home about half an hour ago."

"Jen, there's something you need to know."

"What's that?"

"Howard Sturgis was murdered last night." She gave Jen the details as she knew them.

"Oh, my God. Gil must have more suspects than he knows what to do with. I mean, Sturgis sounds like he left a lot of disgruntled clients."

"I know, and some of them could have come from the club. If I were you, I'd keep a low profile for a while. You've been asking just as many questions as I have."

"True, but no one tried to lock me in a steam room. I'll be fine. I'm the one who just talks and talks. The airhead. Someone not to be taken seriously."

"Just do me a favor and keep your eyes open."

She hung up and hoped her friend took the advice.

She turned on the TV to catch the news. Maybe they'd say something about Sturgis.

It was the lead off story, but the reporter had nothing new to add. As the broadcast continued, her mind wandered.

She'd give her next royalty check to know where Drew Lassiter was now and what he was doing. While it was obvious Sturgis had stayed in town, what about Drew? Was he holed up in the "safe" apartment or had he already split for parts unknown? Or maybe he rented yet another place on a month-to-month basis until he could get out of town. Even now, he could be on a Caribbean island sipping a tropical drink and planning his next move.

One thing's for sure. He's going to need a new partner.

****

The following morning, Anne was savoring her third cup of coffee and contemplating the day's agenda when her phone rang. Caller ID showed it was Candace.

"Hi Candace, what's up?"

"Are you free for a while this morning?"

"I guess so. Nothing's pressing. Why?"

"Well, I was thinking maybe we could get started on that manuscript—the one Dorie stole."

"That's not a bad idea. I guess you're pretty close to moving."

"I closed on the St. Pete condo this morning. I'll give the police, my parole officer, and my attorney the address, then ask the cops to let me leave town. I won't be hard to find. The sooner I do this, the better for everyone involved."

"I suppose you're right, but I'm going to miss you."

Candace sighed. "I'll miss you, too, but you're only a phone call or an email away. I may even indulge in some social media from time to time assuming anyone cares that I walked on the beach and found a shell or two."

Anne laughed. "I care and would like or comment for sure."

"If you're ready to start the revisions on this book, then so am I. Is now a good time?"

"Now is fine. See you a few minutes."

She hung up, made a new pot of coffee, and hurried upstairs to gather notebooks and pens. Call it old-fashioned, but she preferred doing prelim work off the computer. Fifteen minutes later, her friend arrived.

"Which do you want to do first," Candace asked. "The original story or what happened afterwards?"

"Seems to me the original will only need more editing and revision. Since you're likely to be leaving soon, why don't we make an outline of the aftermath?"

"Okay." Candace poured a cup of coffee and sat at the kitchen table, then selected a notebook and a pen. "Going to seem strange to make an outline after all this time."

Her heavy sigh had Anne scrutinizing her friend. "Are you sure you're comfortable with this?"

"I'll never be comfortable with what I did, but maybe writing about it from my point of view—even a drunken one—is something I need to do. Kinda like therapy."

"I wonder if we should write it in first person."

"Might be hard to conceal the ending that way. To me third person makes it easier. I thought we'd start when we entered Dorie's house that morning."

"Good point. We could also consider a prologue if needed."

"We need a title," Candace said. "I thought of this last night—*A Novel Death*."

"I like it."

For the next two hours the women jotted down the things they remembered from their separate points of view. At noon they took a break, ordered in a pizza, and discussed the situation at the country club.

"So this Howard Sturgis was killed and you think Drew Lassiter did it?" Candace asked.

"Well, the description fits him in a vague way. He and Lassiter were at the club a few days ago trying to score some deals, but like Gil said, Sturgis had more enemies than the IRS, so it could have been anyone."

After lunch, they compared notes.

"I like how you delineated what happened before you…that is, prior to Dorie's…" Anne hesitated to finish the stumbling comment.

"It's okay. You mean the events preceding her demise," Candace said in a dry tone.

"Sorry, I didn't want to sound insensitive."

"You aren't. It is what it is." She closed her notebook. "Look, it's after two. Why don't we call it a day? If you need any more information, you can always call or email me."

"I will if I need more of the emotions running through you. And I think I'd like to expand on the drinking problem, too. Are you all right with that? I mean this whole project is going to lay your life out in print."

"Absolutely. I guess I should get used to the possibility of my past acts coming home to roost even though we'll be using fictional names in the book. Anne, I want to thank you for all you've done for me the last couple of years."

"I was glad to do it."

"I just hope this business at the country club is solved soon."

They went into the living room and spent the next half hour discussing theories as to the murders and how effective the Snoop Group had been.

"I think you've been more than effective. I'm totally useless at something like that. I may have tried to write about it, but there's no way in hell I could actually do it. Rose is a bit like me and I don't think Ellie likes it at all. You, Nancy, and Jen have all the guts."

"I'm not so sure if it's guts or just plain stupidity. Look at the scrapes I get into," Anne replied with a laugh.

"Yes, but you always get out of them and…"

The doorbell pealed and pealed, as though someone leaned on the damned thing. Anne hurried to the front door and opened it. Missy rushed in, her eyes wide and her lips trembling.

"Oh, Jesus, you gotta help me!"

"Missy, what on earth are you doing here?"

"Damn, you guys were right. He's gonna kill me."

"Come into the living room. Get a grip on yourself. Who's going to kill you and why?"

She steered the half-hysterical woman through the archway. Missy stopped dead when she saw Candace sitting in a chair.

"You!"

"Yes, me. I do have friends, you know," Candace replied in a no-nonsense tone.

Anne pushed her further into the room. "Sit down

and try to make sense. Who's going to kill you?"

Missy sat on the edge of the sofa. "The killer, of course."

"And the killer is…?"

"How the hell should I know? I just know he's gonna kill me."

"What makes you think that?"

"You got anything to drink?"

"Iced tea?"

"I was thinking more along the lines of scotch—neat."

Anne looked at Candace who shrugged before bringing the distraught woman a short glass of scotch. Missy downed it in one swift swallow and coughed.

"Now, why do you think the killer is after you now?"

"Because he's dead!"

"Oh, for God's sake, Missy. Will you make sense?" Candace snapped.

"Look, I sorta lied to you the other day at the gym."

"Why is it that doesn't surprise me?" Candace murmured. "I imagine you lie on a daily basis, especially to Eric."

Missy glared at her. "Look, I may lie about little things, but not the big ones. I was telling the truth when I told you I never cheated on him. The only things I lie about are how much I spend on clothes, shoes, and my age."

"Your age? How old are you?"

"Eric thinks I'm twenty-five. I'm really thirty-two. Why do you think I work out like a fiend?"

Anne waved a hand. "Never mind about that! What

did you lie to me about at the gym?"

"I do know where the second apartment is. When Barbie and I were still good friends, she asked me to go there once. Said she had a couple of friends coming in on an afternoon flight. She had an appointment or something and couldn't make it. All I had to do was open the door for them, give them each a key, and leave. When I asked who lived there, she said she had rented it when they first moved to town. She claimed she kept the lease to use it for storage and out of town guests."

"Guests? As in call girls?" Candace drawled.

Missy shrugged. "I guess. She brought them to the club later."

"When was this? Before or after the escort service started business?" Anne asked.

"Shortly after."

Candace shook her head. "You're as sleazy as Barbara Lassiter. No wonder someone wants you dead."

"You hate me, don't you? You'd love to see me laid out in the morgue. Then you might get Eric back."

"If its one thing I learned in prison, it's that hate is a useless emotion. It eats you up, and kills your soul. I hated you three years ago. Now, all I feel is a sense of pity. I feel sorry for you."

Missy's eyes widened and her jaw went slack. "Sorry for me? Why?"

"Because you're a thirty-two-year-old woman whose husband thinks she's twenty-five. Because one day you're going to wake up, look in the mirror, and see a fifty-year-old woman who has no real friends—just acquaintances. Eric is twenty-plus years your senior. He will either have divorced you, be in a nursing home, or dead. Missy, nobody will give a damn about you."

The new Mrs. Warren swallowed, and then wiped the tears welling in her eyes. "That's cruel."

"But true. Now, who's dead and why does the killer suddenly have you in his sights?" Candace asked again.

"Bobby's dead. Bobby Lanier."

"What?" Anne said with a gasp. "How do you know?"

"It was on the news at noon. The newscaster just said that a man identified as Robert Lanier, a former professional trainer, was found dead in a ditch along the interstate. A mowing crew discovered him early this morning."

"He was supposed to be in Tallahassee."

"Well, he obviously wasn't."

Candace looked at Anne. "Would Gil know?"

"Probably, but he's not letting me in the loop on everything. He thinks the Snoop Group should dissolve. Says I'm setting myself up for an attempted murder. Or worse yet a successful one."

Anne rose, snatched up her cell, and called Gil.

"How did Bobby Lanier die?" she asked when he answered.

"How did you find out?" His voice sounded testy.

"It's all over the noon news."

"And obviously the name has been released. Damn. I wanted more time before they did that."

"How did he die?" she repeated.

"He was shot in the head. Looked like he'd been worked over pretty good, too. He'd been in that ditch a while. Body was badly decomposed. IDed him from the driver's license in his wallet."

"Is it related to the other murders?"

"I don't know yet. This is the third person connected with that damned country club to be murdered. Four if you count Sturgis. Thank goodness, they rescinded your membership. I've got to go. Stay at home and try not to get into trouble. All right?"

"All right," she retorted in a clipped tone. She hung up. "Gil is not pleased with me."

"Don't you see? Bobby was one of Barbie's conquests. And he steered members her way to set up dates. I talked to him on Monday morning after Barbie's murder. He was scared. He said he'd been approached by Barbie the week before about paying a fee for not letting the club know what he'd done."

"Blackmail," Candace murmured.

Missy nodded. "Said Barbie told him her new partner was in charge now. Bobby was on tape not only doing Barbie, but making a list of men she wanted to set up for blackmail. And now they're both dead. I could be next. Like you guys said the other night. I'm scared, too."

Candace waved a hand in the air. "We only said that so you'd tell us what you knew."

"Did Bobby say who the new partner was?" Anne asked.

"No. And I didn't ask. As far as I was concerned, it was all over. I had nothing more to do with the operation." She hesitated as she wiped her eyes again. "Which is why I'm here. I need help."

"What kind of help?" Anne asked.

"Eric went out of town this morning. Now, with

Bobby dead, I'm scared to be in the house alone. I thought I'd go to the apartment and stay there. I mean, if the killer is after me, that would be the last place they'd look. Only, I don't want to do that alone either. I was kinda hoping you'd come with me. Just to make sure I was safe. You don't have to stay with me once I'm inside. I'll order in and hunker down."

"Why on earth ask us?" Candace demanded.

"I wasn't counting on you being here, but what does it matter? I'm *scared*." A tear slid down her cheek.

"But why *us*? Why not one of your friends? I don't think Anne and I qualify as that. We don't like you that much."

Missy sniffed. "Because you two won't ask questions. You already know the details. My other friends don't and I sure as hell don't want to explain. I…I guess you're the only ones I trust not to say anything."

"How do you plan on getting in?" Anne asked.

"The day I went to the apartment, she…she gave me a couple of keys for her guests. On the way over, I made a duplicate—just in case I should ever need it. I still have it."

"This is the most bizarre situation I've ever heard of," Candace muttered.

"Bizarre or not, please, please, help me. Eric will be home in a couple of days. Then I'll be safe at home again."

Anne thought fast. What Missy suggested was odd; however, the temptation to investigate the elusive apartment was strong. They'd drop Missy off, maybe get a quick look around, and then she'd call Gil with the address. *And when they show up, let her explain why she had withheld information—again. Would serve Missy right.*

“What’s the address?”

“Fifteen-oh-seven Grant Street, apartment A on the ground floor. It’s less than a mile from the airport.”

Anne bit her lip. “Look, this isn’t a good idea. Drew Lassiter is missing, too. The police are looking for him. Could be he’s holed up at this apartment. Just because Barbara rented it doesn’t mean Drew doesn’t know where it is.”

Missy shook her head. “Naw, he’s gone.”

“How do you know?”

“Eric and I had dinner at the club last night. While we had cocktails in the lounge, I overheard a couple of guys asking about Drew. Said they were supposed to meet him and some other guy—an investment dude or something—but that Drew had called them and cancelled. Something about an out-of-town emergency. Someone else also told him Drew had called to say goodbye. He was leaving San Sebastian. He’s gone for good.”

“Still doesn’t mean he isn’t there,” Anne insisted. “Do you know a man named Howard Sturgis?”

“Never heard of him.”

“Short, kind of tubby, weasel face.”

“Still haven’t heard of him. Look, are you going to help me or not? I’m telling you, Drew Lassiter is long gone, flown the coop, on the lam, whatever term you want to use. Why would he stay this long? I’d clean out bank accounts and scram.”

Near the airport? A bolt-hole like Jen suggested. Anne sighed. If Drew Lassiter had skipped town, that would have been where he’d stay overnight before grabbing a plane to who-knew-where.

Anne sighed. Temptation or common sense? Temptation won. “Okay, let’s go even though this is against my better judgment. We’ll follow you, see that you’re safely inside and no bogeyman is hiding under the bed, then leave. Is that clear? You coming, Candace?”

“I guess so.”

They gathered up their purses and headed out the door.

Chapter Twenty

Anne and Candace walked out to the driveway as Missy hurried to her car.

"I'll drive since I'm parked behind you," Candace said, sliding behind the wheel. "What's that address again? I'll program it into the GPS."

"Fifteen-oh-seven Grant Street, apartment A. You think we're crazy for doing this?"

"Certifiable."

"But it does give us a chance to just take a peek at the apartment."

"I can't imagine why we believe her. She's an accomplished liar. She could always hole up at a hotel and order room service," Candace grumbled.

Fifteen minutes later they pulled into the parking lot and stopped in a slot under a tree. Few other cars were around.

"Place looks deserted," Candace said.

"It's a working-class neighborhood. I imagine most people are at work."

Missy had parked in a slot near the front door and already approached the place.

Anne noted a white SUV, a red pick-up, a flashy silver convertible, and a dark sedan farther down the lot. All seemed quiet. Maybe too quiet. Was some curious unemployed neighbor peeking through the curtains at them? In spite of what Missy had said, her biggest fear was that they'd open the door and find Drew Lassiter in residence. She pulled out her phone to call Gil, then decided to wait until they left. No sense in giving Missy a heads up.

I am in such trouble. He's going to want to know who told me. And I have no intention of covering Missy's ass on this one.

"Come on. Let's get this over with."

They exited the car and walked quickly down the sidewalk to the door. Missy inserted the key.

"Maybe we should knock first—in case *anyone's* in there," Anne said.

Missy shot her an incredulous look. "Are you kidding? Who the hell's going to be here?"

Anne ignored her and knocked. No one answered. She repeated the action with still no response.

"Happy now?"

"You know, you're remarkably calm considering half an hour ago you were babbling incoherently with fear," Candace said in a dry tone.

Anne gave the younger woman a hard stare. "I noticed that, too. What gives?"

"Simple," Candace drawled. "We agreed to come help her."

Missy stamped her foot and shot her a look that clearly said, *Bitch.* "Can you two just get off the dead horse? We're here so we might as well go inside."

She twisted the key in the lock, pushed the door open and entered.

Anne held Candace back and whispered, "Don't touch anything. Fingerprints. And as soon as I tell you, we skedaddle."

Why are we doing this? If I had any brains, we'd

turn around and get the hell out of here. Damn me and my desire to solve who killed who and why.

They followed Missy inside. To the left was a living room, its only furnishings two lawn chairs. A glimpse through an archway showed an equally empty dining area.

"Missy, you can't stay here. There's no furniture. I bet there's not even a bed, and don't tell me you're going to sleep on the floor," Anne said in a cross tone.

"I have no intention of staying here. I just needed someone to come with me and help me look for something."

"Look for what?" Candace demanded.

"Tapes."

"What kind of tapes?"

"That condo had more cameras than a prison yard." She shot a nasty glance at her husband's ex-wife. "You should be familiar with that. At any rate, Barbie taped everyone who came in. Maybe not all video either. Now come on."

"Let me guess, maybe she recorded conversations for later blackmail purposes? Maybe even yours?" Candace suggested her voice rising.

Missy inhaled deeply. "Maybe. I got to thinking about it the other day. If she did, and the cops find the apartment, then I'm in a lot of trouble. I told them I didn't know about a lot of stuff Barbie did."

"When in reality, you knew damned near all. Right?" Anne shook her head remembering the information about Drew moving things from the condo weeks earlier. "And since the police didn't find a lot of anything at Barbara's condo, it could be stashed in this place. Is that what you're thinking?"

The younger woman shrugged. "Maybe she moved stuff here for safe-keeping."

As Missy marched through the foyer, Candace strode forward and grabbed the woman's arm.

"Do you seriously expect us to help you search for and steal an incriminating tape, either audio or video? You must be nuts. That's just what I need. Get caught snooping in a murdered woman's apartment," Candace said. "This is bullshit. Just call the police and come clean."

"I can't! If Eric finds out…" She left the sentence unfinished. "Please, help me. It shouldn't take long.

Anne left the two of them arguing and retreated to the front door where she quickly called Gil. He answered on the second ring.

"I know where Barbara Lassiter's hideaway apartment is. I'm here now with Candace and Missy."

"What the hell are you doing there?" His voice thundered in her ear. "Get out now, do you hear me!"

"We will." She gave him the address. "Missy had a key…"

Before she could give him details, he cut her off.

"I don't care. Just go. Now! I'm on my way."

Anne turned back to Missy and Candace who still argued in loud voices.

"Fine, take off. I don't need you. I'll find what I'm looking for on my own." Missy pulled away from Candace and stalked down the hallway.

"I called Gil. He's on his way. Let's get out of here."

"I hope he arrests her for a change."

"That would be…"

Anne's reply was cut off by a scream from the

back of the apartment. They ran to see what the commotion was all about.

Missy stood just inside the doorway to a bedroom.

"What the hell is going on?" Anne demanded.

Missy whirled and shoved them aside, still screaming. Candace grabbed her shoulder and slammed her against the wall.

"Will you shut up? What's wrong?"

The distraught woman didn't answer, but merely pointed a violently shaking finger in the room's direction. They crept to the doorway.

"Oh, my God," Anne gasped.

A moment later, Candace did the same.

A man's body was lying face up on the floor, his eyes staring sightlessly at the ceiling. Blood drenched his chest and had seeped down into the carpet. Anne stood rooted to the floor and wondered how many times he'd been shot—or had he been stabbed—and what did it matter?

"Who is it?" Candace asked in a breathless tone.

Anne gulped air. "Drew Lassiter. Come on. We've got to get out of here."

Missy had stopped screaming, but now stood with her eyes closed and muttering, "Oh, shit," over and over.

"Grab her," Anne ordered. "This is recent. Whoever did it could still be around."

"And is," a voice said from a doorway across the hall.

They whirled to face Lynne Nordstrum holding a wicked-looking gun in her hand. It never wavered. She appeared calm and focused, not a hair out of place, her face a mask of anger touched with fear.

Missy screamed again.

The gun swung in her direction. "Shut up, you little slut or you'll be joining the late Mr. Lassiter."

Candace once again grabbed Missy's arm. "Do as she says."

Missy complied, but shook uncontrollably, her breaths ragged and loud.

Lynne motioned them to move with her gun. "All of you, into the living room and stand against the wall facing me. Now!"

The three women did as ordered. Anne assumed Lynne had not heard her phone call over the angry words exchanged by the other two.

Lynne turned the gun back on Anne. "You bitch, I knew you would be trouble the minute I learned your fiancé was the lead detective on Barbara's case. You and your friend Jennifer were asking way too many questions, and learning way too much. What a shame you got out of that steam room so fast."

"Why kill them?" Anne said in the calmest voice she could muster. *Come on, Gil.*

"Why do you care? You didn't know any of them."

"Well, I seem to be the one finding bodies. I'd like to know."

"And I'm the one they suspect, so I'd like to know, too," Candace added, her voice shaking.

Lynne snorted. "Let's just say that my stupid husband invested a lot of our retirement money with Drew Lassiter and a guy named Howard Sturgis. Some kind of real estate deal in the Tampa area that was supposed to pay off big time. It didn't. The whole thing went belly up. Then he invested more on another deal. It didn't go anywhere either. And all on the advice of

Jerry Bedford. Bastard. He was their silent partner."

"You killed Jerry," Anne said hoping her tone didn't show fear. Her heart pounded and her knees went weak. She had to keep Lynne talking and occupied until the police arrived.

"I met Bedford in the gym one day and demanded our money back. He spouted some kind of sanctimonious crap about how investing is always a gamble. Later, he passed me in the corridor as I headed for the locker room. He was wearing swim trunks and a self-satisfied smirk. I went back to the gym, grabbed a weight, wrapped it in my towel, and followed him to the hot tub. I sneaked up behind him and let him have it. He pitched face-first into the water. I pulled him back onto the bench, turned off the lights, and left."

Anne jumped when her phone rang. It had to be Gil calling to see if she had left as ordered.

Lynne pointed the gun at her. "Don't even think about it."

"I won't. I swear." She licked her lips. "You tracked down Howard Sturgis, too, didn't you?" Gil would be suspicious when she didn't answer. *Gil! Please hurry!*

"Damned straight I did. Never met the guy. Then we got a complaint from a member about him and Drew hustling investments out of the club. I looked up his address from the club visitor records. The other night while Sam had some kind of board meeting, I drove over to Sturgis's place and staked it out. I got lucky. He left and went to some bar over on Third Avenue. I parked near his car and waited. A couple of hours later, he came out. I asked if he was Howard Sturgis and when he said yes, I plugged the son-of-a-bitch."

"And Drew?"

Lynne smirked. "Yeah, good old Drew. I figured with Barbara dead, he could take her place in my scheme of things."

"You were the new partner?" Missy managed to croak out.

"I had their little enterprise nailed last fall. I told them that if they didn't cut me in on the take, I'd call the cops. When they decided to get a divorce, it seemed logical to move in further, especially since I had some wonderful new ideas on how to make money. I had to replace the dough my lame-brained husband lost."

Anne had a clear view of the half-open front door. No movement in the parking lot that she could see. "Why kill Drew?"

"The bastard was going to run out on me and take all those wonderful sex tapes with him. Then he'd have everything to himself. I suspected that was his and Barbara's plan all along. I didn't know about this place. I'd swing by his apartment in Port Rosa every once in a while, but he wasn't there. Then I got lucky again. He showed up this morning and left a few minutes later with a couple of suitcases. I followed him here, forced him inside, and when he begged for his life, shot him anyway."

"So why kill Barbara in my house?" Candace asked.

"*My* house," Missy interjected.

Lynne moved closer to the women. No more than fifteen feet separated them. Anne gripped her purse tighter. The strap slid down her shoulder.

I'm going to die. We all are. Oh, Gil, where are you?

Then through the partially open door, she spied movement. A police car, then another, and finally a third flashed by, lights and sirens off. Gil's car was close behind. *Thank you, God.*

The killer focused on Missy. "I am so sick of you. I know Barbara told you more than you should know about Reliable Escorts. We didn't need you, your big mouth, or your bubble brain in the operation. You were the first one I should have killed. So you can be the first now." She raised the gun.

"No!" Missy screamed.

Candace moved fast to shove the younger woman out of the way just as Lynne fired. The bullet caught Candace in the right side slamming her against the wall where she slid to the floor in wide-eyed shock.

At the same time, Anne swung her purse at the Nordstrum woman with all the strength she could muster. It hit her in the face. The gun fell with a thud on the carpet. She was conscious of Lynne crying out in fury as she scrambled to retrieve it, Missy screaming like a banshee, and Candace moaning. An instant later the police burst through the door with guns drawn.

"Hands up and everybody on the floor," Gil ordered.

Anne had no idea if Lynne or Missy complied. She rushed toward Candace who sat clasping her side.

"Candace!" she knelt beside her friend.

"Oh shit, this really fucking hurts."

"Why? Why did you do it?" Anne sobbed.

"Damned if I know." Then she collapsed onto her side and lay still.

"No! Candace!"

Strong hands pulled her away. Gil knelt and placed

his fingers on Candace's neck.

"She's alive. Just unconscious. Paramedics are on the way. Are you all right?"

Anne nodded. Dimly, she was aware Missy had finally ceased screeching.

"Honey, I love you, but at the moment I'm so mad I could shoot you myself." He turned to one of the officers. "Carter, take Ms. Jamieson and Mrs. Warren out to the cars."

"Drew…Drew Lassiter is in the back bedroom. Dead," she said in a barely audible voice.

The policeman holstered his gun and helped Anne to her feet. Missy had slithered as far away from Candace as possible.

"Come on, ladies."

He marched them past a snarling, sobbing Lynne Nordstrum. She was lying on her stomach with her hands trussed behind her.

Officer Carter put Missy in one car and her in another. Missy appeared to be jabbering away on her cell. Anne hoped she was talking to her attorney.

After what seemed like a lifetime, the paramedics and the ambulance arrived. After another eternity, they wheeled Candace out on a stretcher, loaded her in, and took off for the hospital with siren blazing. In the meantime, more police cruisers arrived. What few neighbors were home stood outside and gawked.

Finally, Gil emerged. He opened the door and glared at her. "The officer is going to take you to the station where you will make a formal statement. I haven't decided yet whether or not to file charges against the lot of you for hindering a police investigation. When you're done, go home. Stay there.

And tomorrow morning I want all of the Snoop Group to meet at your house at ten o'clock. Everyone! No exceptions. If someone doesn't show, I'll send a squad car for them. Let 'em explain *that* to their husbands and neighbors. Is that clear? We are all going to have a serious discussion."

Tears spilled from her eyes and ran down her cheeks. "Okay. Gil, how's Candace? Is she going to live?"

"Probably. The bullet appears to have gone straight through. In and out. Another inch to the left and it could have been a different story." He looked up at the policeman. "Get her out of here."

Gil slammed the door and stalked back toward the apartment.

Anne breathed a sigh of relief. Candace would make it, but she wasn't sure about herself. Never had she seen Gil so angry—or afraid. She realized now his gruff voice and glares were as much from fear as fury. She leaned her head back against the seat. She deserved every angry word and glare.

I'm surprised he didn't arrest me. He may still.

At the station, she gave her statement leaving out nothing. She didn't see Missy again and didn't want to. A cab deposited her at home where the kids met her at the door.

"Where have you been?" Ken asked.

"We were worried," Lisa asked.

"I'm fine. And I don't want to talk about it right now. Let's just say this hasn't been a good day."

She stumbled up the stairs to her office where she called the rest of the group to tell them what happened and of Gil's orders. For once, no one asked questions, just said they'd be there.

Anne crossed her arms on the desk and rested her head in them, then cried like a five-year-old. Not only had her sleuthing and lack of judgment once again gotten her in hot water, but Candace had damn near died.

She didn't even want to think about how she might have damaged her relationship with the man she loved.

****

Anne sat in a chair flanking the sofa. Jen sat opposite her. Nancy and Rose were seated on the sofa. Gil stood in front of them and glared at each until they all squirmed. It reminded her of the time they'd been caught breaking and entering at Isadora Powell's. Finally, he cleared his throat and centered his attention on her.

"Isn't there one of you missing?"

"Ellie Campion, but I didn't bother to call her. She didn't have very much to do with the sleuthing end of things. She didn't like it. I'm…I'm sure she'd come if you insist."

"Leave her alone. Sounds like she's the only one who has good sense. Ladies, as of now, the Snoop Group is no longer in business. What you did yesterday was inexcusable. I should have arrested Anne and both Mrs. Warrens for hindering an investigation. I did detain Melissa Warren for a few hours. Her one phone call was to her husband. He showed up with a lawyer. He was not a happy camper."

So, Eric wasn't out of town. Missy did spin us a tale. I should have known.

"In spite of all my warnings, you ignored everyone's safety by going to an apartment you suspected could have been occupied by a wanted man. And for what purpose? To look for evidence. *That* is the job of the police department."

"We didn't know Missy was looking for evidence. She told us she was…"

Gil waved his hand and cut her off. "Doesn't matter why you were there. What matters is you were. Candace Warren damn near got killed. Drew Lassiter was."

Anne blotted her tearing eyes with a tissue. "I'm sorry. I don't know what I was thinking. I guess the thought of taking a peek at the apartment overrode my good judgment. But I'd found two bodies and wanted answers."

"You all never seem to differentiate between reality and fiction. Reality is danger along with honest to God dead bodies—and they aren't pretty. Fiction is Nancy Drew and Jessica Fletcher. The heroines go places and do things they shouldn't and get away with it. And never get arrested for their actions. Doesn't happen in real life."

Rose sniffed. "Honestly, Gil, all I ever did was make a few phone calls and ask a few questions."

"And you have to admit that people did talk to us," Jen said. "We *did* help find the killers."

"I think the point Gil is trying to make is that yes we helped by passing along information, but stepped over the line by actually going places to investigate like Dorie's house on a couple of occasions, Fran's antique store, Jeffery Wainwright's apartment," Nancy added.

Anne wet her lips and looked him in the eye. "We never meant for anything bad to happen."

"But it did. You were dealing with killers—real

killers with nothing to lose. I don't want it happening again."

"Are you going to arrest me, Candace, and Missy?"

He drew in a deep breath. "Probably not since we caught the killer, but you deserve to be brought up in front of a judge."

"Then I guess the Snoop Group is a thing of the past." Anne gulped back a sob. All of the women nodded their heads, but said nothing.

"Okay. And if I catch even one of you snooping into anything along these lines again, I'll tell your husbands," Gil threatened.

Rose crossed her heart. "You have my promise. I'd be the next body you'd find because Jack would kill me if he found out."

"Carl wouldn't be too pleased either," Jen told them.

Nancy shrugged. "Brad already knows. I told him last night. He actually thought it sounded kind of cool."

Gil rolled his eyes. "He would."

Anne bit her lip. "What's happening to Lynne Nordstrum?"

"She's being charged with three counts of first-degree murder and at least one count of attempted murder, plus other related charges. I think she's due for arraignment later this afternoon."

"Will she get the death penalty?"

Gil shrugged. "Probably, unless she plea bargains and makes a full confession in exchange for consecutive life sentences. That's not up to me. The evidence is overwhelming. We matched the bullets from Sturgis, Lassiter, and out of the apartment wall as having come from the gun she had in her possession.

Plus, there's the confession she made to you about killing Jerry Bedford."

"She deserves all she gets and then some," Jen said.

"Have you heard anything more about Candace? How is she?" Rose asked.

"I called the hospital this morning," Anne said. "She's resting comfortably and will be allowed visitors tomorrow morning."

Gil waved the other ladies toward the door. "Now, all of you go home and stay out of trouble for a while."

After they had left, he pulled Anne into his arms and held her tightly.

"I really am sorry," she said in a soft voice.

"Do you know how scared I was when I saw that open door, and then heard that shot? When I got your call, I suspected there'd be trouble. And when you didn't answer your phone, I knew it."

"I know. If I'd had my heroine doing this, reviewers would have called her too stupid to live. Did you find out anything more from Lynne, I mean other than what she spouted off about while holding us at gunpoint?"

"Some, but nothing we weren't already investigating."

"Lynne Nordstrum, the leader of a prostitution ring." Anne shook her head. "I don't see how that would ever have been successful. The woman has the personality of a street dog."

"She viewed her actions as justified," Gil said. "Her husband lost a buttload of money investing in Howard Sturgis, Drew Lassiter, and Jerry Bedford's real estate schemes."

"And when Jerry and Drew told her the money was gone, she plotted to get as much back as possible."

"And to kill them in the process. She commented to you that she suspected Drew had no intention of sticking around to implement more of Lynne's blackmail plan. She was right. We found two tickets to George Town, Grand Cayman charged on the Barbara Taylor credit card the day of her murder. Departure was the day after her death."

"So they were going to bug out. But why kill Barbara? Lynne didn't know that then."

"She didn't," Gil informed her. "She had an alibi. She was playing racquetball with another lady at the club at the time of her murder."

"Then who did kill the Lassiter woman?"

"We aren't incompetent. We did some checking and discovered that Jerry Bedford wasn't the only person at the club to drive a white SUV. So do eight other men. Seven had corroborated alibis. Only one didn't."

Anne stared at him as the silence built. "Well! Who?"

"Wesley Canfield."

Anne gasped. "Wes Canfield killed Barbara?"

"Nope. The neighbor who heard the shot and had the television on confirmed the show she was watching was a popular old Western. It was on from three until three-thirty. She says she heard the shot about halfway through. She just assumed at the time that it came from the TV. At three-ten, Wes Canfield was getting a speeding ticket six miles away."

"I don't get it," Anne said with a frown. "If Wes didn't do it, who did?"

"Another neighbor reported a dark-colored car at the house around the same time. Believe it or not, it was something you said that had me investigating further."

"What was that?"

"Remember the day you told me Wes had hit on you and how you saw his wife shove him into her car?"

"Yes." The light bulb lit. "A dark blue Mercedes. Oh, my God! Bertie? Bertie killed Barbara?"

"Wes Canfield is the owner of a registered .22 caliber pistol. When we asked him about it, he claimed he hadn't seen it in months. Then when we asked him his whereabouts at the time of the murder, he hemmed and hawed before finally admitting to the ticket and that he had been with the Lassiter woman between roughly two-thirty and three. We obtained a search warrant for the house and the cars. Found the gun in Bertie's console. Ballistics matched it. We arrested her this morning. She called a lawyer and gave us a full statement."

"So it was Wes at the house and not Jerry Bedford? I can't believe this. Go on. I take it she followed Wes."

Gil nodded. "Said she overheard him on the phone talking sweet nothings—as she described it—to someone. So she told her husband she was going to the club, parked down the street, and followed him. When he left the Warren's, Bertie slipped in through the side gate. Apparently Mrs. Lassiter was standing there naked, on the phone, and never heard her approach. As soon as the woman hung up, Mrs. Canfield shot her, calmly walked back to her car, and drove away. Found the shell casing in the bushes near the pool deck."

Anne drew in a deep breath. "This is too wild not to be true. Bertie kills Barbara in a jealous fit, Lynne kills Jerry, Howard, and Drew for revenge and to further her new career as a madam, and…wait a minute, why did she kill Bobby Lanier?"

"She didn't. The late Mr. Lanier was into a drug dealer for some big bucks and way behind on his payments. That's why he was leaving town. It had nothing to do with the club or the escort service, although he helped the Lassiters procure clients off and on. With Barbara dead, he must have figured it was time to split. He wasn't fast enough. He bought two in the back of the head, execution style."

Gil pulled her back into his arms and kissed her hard. "I have a full plate most of the day. How about we meet for lunch tomorrow? We can discuss wedding plans."

A small chuckle emerged from her throat. "I'll spend the time between now and then plotting a new book."

"All about murders at a country club?"

"Of course."

He kissed her again, making her toes curl and reminding her how lucky she was to not only be alive, but to have such a wonderful man willing to put up with her.

Chapter Twenty-One

Anne and Gil lunched the next day at a cozy French bistro near the ocean where they discussed wedding plans.

"I called the San Sebastian Botanical Gardens yesterday and would you believe the indoor chapel wasn't available until the second weekend in September? I went ahead and booked it, but left in the possibility of having the ceremony in the gardens of the weather is decent. That gives us almost four months to get out invitations and arrange for catering," she said.

"And compile a guest list."

"I think we need to keep it short. Just family and close friends. I took a poll among the group and the consensus was under no circumstances invite ex-wives or former husbands."

"I agree. In the meantime, I can scout out honeymoon sites. Any place special you'd like to go?"

She squeezed his hand. "Anywhere with you would be perfect."

He lifted her hand to his lips. "I just hope you're as agreeable about other things."

A half-hour later, Anne was amazed as how quickly the plans fell into place. Even the wedding party made sense with Lisa as her maid of honor and Nancy a bridesmaid. Gil named Brad as his best man and Ken, Jr. a groomsman.

"Would you like to stop by the hospital and see Candace?" he asked after paying the bill. "I need to ask her a few follow-up questions."

"I was going to suggest the same thing."

Noontime traffic was snarled around the hospital, but eventually they knocked on Candace's door and opened it.

"Hi, do you feel like seeing a couple of visitors?" Anne said.

A pale, but composed Candace smiled from the bed. "Of course!"

"Hello, Candace," Gil greeted. "How are you feeling?"

She made a face. "I hurt like hell. They wanted to give me some painkillers, but I told them I'd make do with ibuprofen. No opioids for me given my addictive personality."

"Good call," Anne said pulling a chair to the side of the bed.

"Think you can answer a couple of questions?" Gil pulled a notebook and pen from his pocket. "Just follow up to your statement."

Candace winced as she pushed the button to raise the head of her bed. "I guess so. What do you need to know?"

"How well did you know Lynne Nordstrum?"

"Not all that well. We didn't run in the same country club circles. Plus she was not the most pleasant person to be around. Very opinionated and self-important. Sam always struck me as the kind who liked to pretend he was more knowledgeable about things than he really was, if you get my drift."

Gil asked a few more questions to clarify her

statement and then closed his notebook.

"Can you bring me up to date on what's happened since Lynne shot me?"

Gil told her about the arrest and the plea bargain Lynne had made to escape the death penalty after the arraignment along with the motives for it all. He also had other news.

"The apartment was chock-full of business records, banking transactions—mostly offshore—and names of not only clients, but the escorts as well. Once they decided to shut down operations in one location, I imagine the Lassiters would ship the stuff to another town where they'd store it until ready to set up shop again, and then take a long vacation before resuming their activities. All in all, their businesses spanned eight years and at least four cities. My guess is Drew Lassiter was likely there to pack up and move on. And we found the infamous tapes or rather digital discs—two small boxes in the back bedroom where Drew was killed, and two in the trunk of Lynne Nordstrum's car. You guys obviously interrupted her removing them."

"Sounds as if we'd been fifteen minutes later, she'd have been gone," Candace said.

Anne nodded. "That's about the size of it. I talked to Jen this morning. Sam Nordstrum resigned as president of the country club yesterday. She wasn't sorry to see him go. Also according to Jen, Ted Saunders, the golf pro, admitted to introducing several men to Drew Lassiter calling him an investment broker. Adam Jefferies also confessed to doing much the same and to helping with the escort service via the tennis courts. He was fired as was the bar manager who was getting a cut by allowing the lounge to be used as a procurement site or whatever. Apparently, Saunders still has his job, but for how long is anybody's guess. Doesn't look like he knew much about the escort service and steered clear of it."

Candace snorted. "And Bertie Canfield offing the Lassiter woman is one step short of bizarre. I mean, I never suspected Bertie at all, although I did have the thought that Lynne could have been involved. I just didn't know to what extent. Makes me glad I'm not a member anymore."

"And here's another piece of good news—Rose was offered a contract on *Too Hot to Handle* by Hot Press Publishing. She's so excited she's ready to burst!" Anne added.

A huge grin split Candace's face. "That's wonderful. She deserves it!"

"That she does! And the Snoop Group is officially out of business."

"My heart couldn't stand the things you guys did," Gil said with a groan.

Candace chuckled. "Just as well. I wasn't any good at it anyway."

"Amateurs have no business poking their noses into places only professionals should go." Gil gave Anne a sidelong glance.

"Are you finished? I think Candace needs to get some rest."

"There is one more question you can answer for me." Gil eyed the woman in the hospital bed.

"What's that?"

"The reason you were at the house in the first place the day Barbara Lassiter was killed."

"I told you, Eric called me about an odor and

demanded that I meet Missy there to discuss it. I didn't want to go. It was their house now, but he insisted."

"I seem to recall a foul smell when I walked in. I take it the smell is now gone," he said.

Candace shrugged. "I suppose so since they moved back in."

"What's so special about the smell?" Anne asked. "It was probably a dead roof rat up in the attic. Happens all the time in South Florida."

"I find it odd that the odor suddenly appeared just as the ex-husband and his new wife took up residence." He smiled. "How'd you do it, Candace?"

Her friend stared for a moment, and then chuckled again. Soon the chuckle grew into laughter. "Ouch, that hurts," she said placing her hand over her wounded side.

"Candace?" Anne questioned.

"Busted." She got the laugher under control.

"Did you put a dead rat in the attic?" he asked.

"Not on your life. I'd rather die than touch one."

"So, what did you do?" Gil pressed.

"I moved out on Monday and they moved in the following day, but before I left I gave them a little housewarming gift. That afternoon I went to the grocery store and bought a pound of shrimp. I then proceeded to shove as many as possible into the drapery rods. I pried off the finials on the ends and used a stick to ram the little buggers as far in as possible, then put the finials back on. I hit the den and the dining room, but saved most for the master bedroom."

Gil's mouth twitched, then he broke out into a laugh.

Anne joined him. "So you weren't surprised when

Eric called that day at my house."

"I figured Missy would pitch a fit and make Eric do something. Eric's idea of doing something is getting on the phone and demanding. I thought maybe he'd call exterminators who, of course, would find nothing in the attic. Eventually, the smell would go away, but it would stay in the drapes forever. So, when he called and insisted I meet with Missy at the house, I couldn't refuse. I had to see her expression."

"Patient revenge." Anne grinned and shook her head.

"It was a spur of the moment thing," Candace admitted. "I was cleaning out the fridge when some overripe fruit had me wrinkling my nose. Then, bam, the idea hit me."

"I think that's the kind of thing only a writer would do," Gil said. "If nothing else, you people are creative."

Anne rose, walked to the side of the bed and hugged her friend. "When are you going to be released?"

"The doctor said tomorrow or the next day. He wants me to take it easy for another week or so. I'll stay with my son, and then head for St. Pete."

"Let us know when you leave. We'll have a bang-up going away party."

"I'm sure Jen's already on it."

A tentative knock on the open door caught their attention. Missy stood in the threshold with an uncertain expression.

"May I come in?"

Anne and Gil looked at Candace who shrugged. "Sure, why not?"

"Have a seat," Anne said. "We were just leaving."

"No, thanks, what I have to say won't take but a minute. There's no need for you to go." She walked into the room, stood at the foot of the bed, and wet her lips. "I…I just dropped by to say thank you for doing what you did. If you hadn't shoved me out of the way, that crazy bitch would have killed me."

Candace fiddled with the edge of her blanket, her eyes downcast. "She planned on shooting all of us anyway. Guess it was just something to distract her."

"Well, I appreciate it. And I also wanted to tell you that I've come clean with Eric. I told him everything—the escort service, the blackmail, why I was at the apartment, I even told him my real age," Missy confessed with a smile.

"How did he take it all?" Anne asked.

"He said he knew my real age from the beginning. As for the rest, well, he was pretty upset. I don't know which scared me more—being in police custody or facing him with what I'd done. God, was he ever pissed. He's staying at the San Sebastian Inn again. Said he wanted to clear his mind. I just hope he comes back. I really do love him. I know you don't believe me, but it's true."

"On the contrary, I do," Candace replied in a soft tone.

"I've made a lot of silly mistakes in my time, but getting involved with Barbara Lassiter was the dumbest. If Eric returns home, I promise to change my attitude and try to be a better person."

"He will," Candace said. "Divorcing you would mean admitting he made a mistake. Eric doesn't make mistakes. He loves you, Missy. I guess you both have to adjust to the age difference and make compromises.

Life is all about compromises—and consequences. I, of all people, should know."

"I…I suppose you're right. Well, I'd better be going. Like I said, I just wanted you to know how grateful I am for what you did. Maybe…maybe we can do lunch sometime. At the club and really give them something to talk about." She gazed at all of them with a shaky smile.

Candace shrugged. "Maybe."

With a nod to everyone, Missy walked out the door.

"Well," Anne said in surprise. "That was unexpected. Nice, but unexpected. Maybe she's learned something from all of this."

"Perhaps. And she does seem to love Eric. She might not be so bad after all. I may take her up on that lunch deal," Candace said in a grudging voice as she cast her gaze on Gil. "You don't seem surprised by any of this. Did she confess to you, too?"

He nodded. "The other day at the police station. She's certain Lassiter recorded a conversation they had at the condo one day about how the escort service would work and her slice of the pie. It may or may not exist. We haven't found any audio tapes. The discs are dated and the earliest we've found so far is well after Reliable Escorts was formed."

"So that's it," Candace said with a sigh. "It's all over and I assume I can leave for St. Pete with no strings attached."

"You are free as a bird," Gil said with a smile. "Now, I suggest we go home. It looks like we'll be getting married the second Saturday in September at the San Sebastian Botanical Gardens. You're invited,

Candace, and hope to see you there. If not, I hope you get better soon."

"Thanks, and I'll be there rain or shine."

Anne and Gil left the room and walked toward the elevators.

"Amazing how things turn out, isn't it?" she said.

"I believe a lot of things in life happen for the best. The Snoop Group is a thing of the past, we're getting married, and another case is solved."

"And *I* have to say that Candace's revenge was brilliant. Rotting shrimp in drapery rods. It really is too funny."

"Like I said, writers are certainly creative. You know, I think Candace Warren will be all right," he said with a smile.

Anne nodded and smiled back. Yes, her friend of many years would start a new life with new friends in a new city and come out on top.

As for the Snoop Group, well, that remains to be seen. Who knows when I'll trip over the next body?

A word about the author...

I was born in Indianapolis, Indiana, but have been fortunate enough to live in several diverse cities—St. Louis, Missouri; Rockford, Illinois; Memphis, Tennessee; and Fort Lauderdale, Florida. I have two adult children and seven grandchildren. My husband and I recently moved back to Memphis to be nearer to family.

Much of my spare time is used to indulge in my guilty pleasures like floating around in my pool on a hot summer day. And if I happen to think up a good plot line while doing so, all the better. I also have little containers of ice cream stashed in out of the way places in my freezer.

I love writing and hope readers enjoy the journey of my stories along with me.

Thank you for purchasing
this publication of The Wild Rose Press, Inc.

For questions or more information
contact us at
info@thewildrosepress.com.

The Wild Rose Press, Inc.
www.thewildrosepress.com

www.ingramcontent.com/pod-product-compliance
Lightning Source LLC
Chambersburg PA
CBHW070047030726
47506CB00002B/385